C0-ALM-366

Marrying
Ameera

PLEASE RETURN TO
BRANSON RESOURCE CENTER
P.O. BOX 909
WHEATON IL 60187

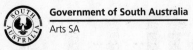 

Government of South Australia
Arts SA

Asialink
Leaders in Australia–Asia Engagement

The writing of *Marrying Ameera* has been assisted by the Government of South Australia through ARTS SA & Asialink, and completed under a Carclew Fellowship.
This is a work of fiction and, except in the case of historical fact, any resemblance to actual persons, living or dead, is purely coincidental.

Marrying Ameera

Rosanne Hawke

Best wishes

Rosanne Hawke

Angus&Robertson
An imprint of HarperCollins*Publishers*

PLEASE RETURN TO
FRANSON RESOURCE CENTER
P.O. BOX 969
WHEATON IL 60187

While efforts have been made to trace all copyright holders, in some cases this has been unsuccessful. These copyright holders are very welcome to contact the author care of HarperCollins*Publishers*.

Angus&Robertson

An imprint of HarperCollins*Publishers*, Australia

First published in Australia in 2010
by HarperCollins*Publishers* Australia Pty Limited
ABN 36 009 913 517
harpercollins.com.au

Copyright © Rosanne Hawke 2010

The right of Rosanne Hawke to be identified as the author of this work has been asserted by her under the *Copyright Amendment (Moral Rights) Act 2000*.

This work is copyright. Apart from any use as permitted under the *Copyright Act 1968*, no part may be reproduced, copied, scanned, stored in a retrieval system, recorded, or transmitted, in any form or by any means, without the prior written permission of the publisher.

HarperCollins*Publishers*
25 Ryde Road, Pymble, Sydney, NSW 2073, Australia
31 View Road, Glenfield, Auckland 0627, New Zealand
A 53, Sector 57, Noida, UP, India
77–85 Fulham Palace Road, London, W6 8JB, United Kingdom
2 Bloor Street East, 20th floor, Toronto, Ontario M4W 1A8, Canada
10 East 53rd Street, New York NY 10022, USA

National Library of Australia Cataloguing-in-Publication data:

Hawke, Rosanne.
Marrying Ameera / Rosanne Hawke.
ISBN: 9780732291440 (pbk.)
For secondary school age.
A823.3

Cover and internal design by Natalie Winter
Cover images: Woman wearing veil by Colin Anderson/Getty Images; woman running by Diana Healey/Getty Images; passage by Paul Miles/Getty Images; all other images by shutterstock.com
Typeset in 10.5/15pt Sabon by Kirby Jones
Printed and bound in Australia by Griffin Press
73gsm Bulky Book Ivory used by HarperCollins*Publishers* is a natural, recyclable product made from wood grown in sustainable forests. The manufacturing processes conform to the environmental regulations in the country of origin, Australia.

5 4 3 2 1   10 11 12 13

For Kathryn Hawke

The bards still sing the song of Hir and Ranjha. Hir was the beautiful daughter of a chieftain called Chochak Sial, and when she heard Ranjha's flute playing she was entranced. 'Stay and look after my father's cattle,' she said. Every day she slipped away to spend time with him. People gossiped, and her crippled uncle limped up the hill to complain to Chochak Sial. Hir was locked in her room and a marriage was quickly arranged with the son of the Khera clan. 'You are lucky,' her friends said. 'Saida Khera is handsome and a landowner.' Hir bore it in silence but at the wedding ceremony she refused her consent. It was as if the priest didn't hear her. She was bundled into the waiting doli and taken to the Kheras' home. 'No,' she screamed, 'I am not married,' but no one heard.

That evening when Saida sat on her bed, she told him, 'You are not my husband. I have been brought here against my will.' Saida stood. He knew there was plenty of time to woo her.

Hir lived in Saida's house until one day a beggar came to the door. When Hir saw him she fainted, for it was no

1

true beggar but Ranjha, looking for a glimpse of her. One night Ranjha helped her escape. They lived in the forest for a time until Saida tracked them down. The lovers fled across the desert and swam a river but the Kheras had horses and rode until they found them. They beat Ranjha and hauled Hir before the governor of the city. 'She's an adulteress,' they cried.

Hir told her story and the governor said to speak with her father and then marry who he chose. 'But he won't listen to me,' Hir said, so the governor accompanied her to advise her father.

Finally, Chochak Sial told Ranjha to prepare a wedding procession fit for the daughter of a chieftain. As Hir sat in her gold finery waiting for Ranjha she heard the happy sounds of wedding drums and horns. Her uncle's servant girl brought her a drink of buttermilk. Hir didn't notice the faintly bitter taste. Suddenly her breath failed and she slipped to the floor. When Ranjha entered the bridal room to see his bride, she lay still, poisoned by hate and prejudice.

Hir is buried near the town of Jhang on the Jhelum, the river of legend. As the tale goes, Hir's grave opened to allow Ranjha to enter, where he now lies beside his bride forever.

part 1
A Good Daughter

I

'Ameera!'

I heard my name and then the single toot; Riaz was in his car already. I didn't want to make him wait; it was becoming harder to persuade him to take me places even though Papa said it was his responsibility as a brother. I didn't want to be someone else's responsibility.

I slipped on my two gold bangles — a gift from Papa's last rug-buying trip to Azad Kashmir — grabbed my bag and raced down the stairs. I hurried across the rugs — the treasures we thoughtlessly walked on every day — and past the gilt photos of our family in Kashmir, my bracelets clinking. A voice from the lounge stopped me. 'Slow down, beti.' Papa. He hated to see me run. 'Let me look at you properly.'

I paused in the doorway, my long dupatta fluttering in the stream of the air conditioner. As I'd got older Papa didn't express his approval of me as much as he used to, but now an odd look crept into his eyes. 'Today, beti, you are looking as beautiful as my mother.'

I crossed the carpet and kissed his cheek. 'Thank you, Abu ji.'

He usually liked it when I used the Urdu endearment but today his thoughts were far away. I hurried to pull open the carved security door that he'd had installed. Sometimes I wondered if he thought he was still living in a fort like his Pushtun ancestors.

'C'mon, Ames. I haven't got all night,' Riaz called, and revved the engine of his Astra.

His iPod was playing his favourite rock band as I climbed into the back of the car that Papa had bought for him. I didn't hear any murmurs about a car being bought for me. I sighed inwardly. *When I'm older*, I thought, *I'll work on Papa for a driver's licence.*

'We have to pick up Raniya too,' I told Riaz.

He groaned, but made a U-turn and pulled up outside Raniya's house. He didn't dare toot for her, but she was watching for us and came through the garden as fast as decorum allowed. Raniya was the perfect Pakistani girl: demure, wore a scarf full-time and cleaned her brothers' rooms. She even took a prayer rug to school so she could pray in the storeroom at lunchtime. She'd invited me to join her but there were enough things at school to make me different without making it worse.

She climbed into the back with me. 'Ameera, what an amazing top.'

'Thanks.' I had made the outfit myself. Raniya appreciated it when I wore Pakistani clothes. We both liked wearing them: they were comfortable, with baggy trousers and a long shift top. Papa never skimped on these clothes. It was when I needed a new pair of jeans that his expression became as closed as his wallet.

'Your shalwar qameez is lovely too,' I said.

Riaz raised his eyebrows at me in the rear-vision mirror and grinned at our politeness, his annoyance gone.

'Aunty Rubina made it,' she said. It was royal-blue silk and it sparkled. Too gaudy for an Australian party but just right for Maryam's place. As I thought of Maryam and her family, my stomach tightened.

'So glad the exams are over at last.' Raniya tucked a stray curl of hair under her scarf. 'I hope we get into the same uni.'

'Me too.' We had both worked hard enough during Year 12.

Raniya glanced at me. 'Which one of your preferences did you finally apply for?'

'Teaching. Papa says it's a respected profession in Pakistan.' Then I grinned. 'After medicine, of course.'

Raniya laughed. Both our fathers had asked us to do medicine, but I didn't want to. It was the first thing, other than being able to wear jeans, that Papa had ever backed down on. Maybe my Bs in Maths helped. I hated Physics and Chemistry too, even though Papa had made me study them. I was thinking how much fun it would be choosing my own subjects at uni when Riaz stopped the Astra outside Maryam's gate. He couldn't wait to be rid of us and I knew he was itching to go to the mall. He had an Anglo girlfriend and later they would go to a nightclub.

'When will you pick me up?' I asked.

His jaw slackened; he hadn't remembered that part of his responsibility.

I pretended a stern frown. 'Papa said I have to be back by eleven.'

'Eleven!' Riaz's voice actually squeaked. 'What a baby you are.'

'Blame Papa, not me.'

'But nothing gets going until eleven.'

I made a show of shrugging.

'Look, if I can't get back in time, isn't there some other way? What about Maryam's brother. Can't he drive you?'

I paused, determined not to let the shock of his words show. He shouldn't be pushing me onto someone else's brother. Yet the fact that I didn't mind disturbed me even more.

'What if he's out like you?' I tried to say it casually.

'Message me if you get stuck but try and find another ride, right?'

I nodded and he drove off, then backed up beside me again. 'And don't tell Dad.' He roared off, leaving the smell of burnt rubber.

Raniya stared after him. 'My father would kill my brothers if they said that to me.'

I grinned. 'So will mine, if he finds out.'

Maryam had invited some of our other friends from school. Natasha jumped up from the couch as soon as she saw me and hugged me. 'You look ravishing, Amie.'

Natasha had on jeans and a T-shirt. She was Anglo and could wear whatever she liked. Some other girls, like Raniya, wore head scarves but Maryam didn't. 'Everyone thinks because I'm Pakistani I should wear a scarf but I only wear one in church,' she'd said once. Maryam's family were Christian Pakistanis. Raniya's parents didn't mind her going to the Yusufs, but if it wasn't for Mum I wouldn't have been allowed to. I think the closeness I felt to Maryam and to girls like Natasha was because my mother was Australian. Mum fell in love with Papa at uni. She said he was the most handsome and polite young man on campus. I doubt if they ever considered how their marriage would affect their children. Mum tried her best: she went to Eid celebrations at the mosque and wore a scarf out of respect, even though she didn't understand what was going on. The other women were polite to her, but when they got together they spoke Urdu, which Mum had never learnt. The only Pakistani woman Mum had anything to do with was Mrs Yusuf and she wasn't even Muslim.

Papa tried to make sure we had lots of Pakistani culture growing up, even though his family wasn't here. He went to see his relatives more often than we did. The last time I went to Azad Kashmir was when I was ten, for the funeral of Dada Zufar, Papa's father. Apparently he was like a king reigning over his family. There were so many relatives but the one I remembered the most was Meena. I thought she was like a Bollywood actress even though she was only fourteen. She took me to the bazaar in Muzaffarabad and bought me a lassi drink. It wasn't the rich taste of the yoghurt and mango, but the time she'd spent with me that made the memory linger.

Muzaffarabad was okay but I wouldn't want to live there; it was nothing like Australia. There were too many people, lots of them living in poverty; and since the earthquake in 2005 there would be even more families without houses. Our relatives' houses had been damaged during the earthquake too; Papa had gone over at the time to help out. I remembered him grumbling as he packed about how all of Kashmir should be Pakistani. 'That stupid maharaja they had in 1947 — most of his people were Muslim and just because he was Hindu he went over to India.' It didn't take much to turn Papa onto Kashmiri politics.

Mrs Yusuf and Maryam's younger sister came in with food — shami kebabs, pakoras, meatballs. All the things my mother had learnt to like but couldn't cook.

Ten thirty came and the other girls started to leave. Raniya's brothers picked her up at eleven.

'See you soon,' she said to me. 'I'll message and we'll go out for coffee.' She paused. 'I'm sorry, we'd take you home except ...'

We both knew Papa wouldn't like me riding home in a car full of young men, even if Raniya was with me.

'I'll be fine. Riaz will come soon.' I messaged him to pick me up but he didn't answer. I glared at the phone.

Before long I was the last girl still there. 'I'm sorry, Riaz must have forgotten,' I told Maryam. I couldn't blow his cover though she probably guessed where he was.

'Daddy's already gone to bed ...' She left the next part of her sentence unsaid but I knew what it would be: what about your father? But I couldn't ring Papa; Riaz would get in awful trouble. And there was no way I could stay over without Papa finding out about Riaz.

'I think my father will be in bed too,' I said. 'I'm really sorry.'

Maryam was staring at me. 'Tariq's awake in his room.'

'Your brother?'

Of course I knew Tariq was her brother, it was just a shock to hear her make such an offer. But Riaz had suggested it too. What if Papa saw Tariq drop me home? Did he wait at the window looking out for me?

Maryam saw my indecision. 'I'll come too.'

I wished I could drive myself, but I could just imagine Papa not letting me get a licence until I was married. And what if I married someone like Papa who wouldn't let me drive? Someone who said, 'Girls get into trouble when they have too much independence.' Those were Papa's words last time I asked about learning to drive. It wasn't fair; Mum drove but he had different rules for me. It was easier for Maryam: her parents weren't so strict. I wondered if they'd even mind if she had a boyfriend. Maybe she would be allowed to choose her own husband.

Riaz still hadn't replied to my text. There was no other option but to have Maryam's brother take me home. I forced a smile. 'Okay, thanks.'

I perched on the edge of the couch while Maryam went to get Tariq. I wished Tariq was short and pimply and the same age as us, but he wasn't. I had seen him before at Maryam's. If Raniya had a party her brothers were told to go out or keep to their rooms. But Tariq was still allowed the run of the house if Maryam had friends over. The last time I'd visited, he saw me in the kitchen and half-smiled. It seemed as if he'd stood there longer than necessary before he swiftly turned and headed for his room.

If Papa saw me in a car with Tariq he would think the worst, and would I be free of fault? Wasn't thinking something as bad as actually doing it?

'Hi, Ameera.' Tariq strolled into the lounge. His hair was messed up and he swallowed a yawn.

'I'm sorry for the trouble.'

'It's nothing,' he said. 'Don't worry about it.' He didn't mention Riaz and I appreciated that. He smiled at me and I saw how the right side of his mouth curved a second before the left.

Even from the back seat of his car, Tariq was interesting. I noticed that his hair curled onto his T-shirt. Maryam kept talking about what we'd do in the holidays but I barely heard her and too soon we were at my house. I glanced up at my parents' window: no light. That meant they were still in the lounge, which was good, or they were asleep already, even better. I got out and hurriedly said goodbye to Maryam and Tariq, keeping my voice low. I was glad Tariq didn't answer. I didn't want Papa to hear a male voice. I rushed up the front steps and looked back. *Leave*, I whispered to myself. I waved at them and Tariq turned the car back towards their home.

When I opened the front door I could hear my parents in the lounge. They were arguing.

'And how many boys do you think she sees at these parties she goes to?' my father said.

'They're girls' parties, Hassan. At good homes with the parents present.'

'But the brothers of these girls will pick them up — like Riaz.'

My mother made a sound with her tongue. 'You live in Australia now. You're overreacting.'

Papa's voice rose. 'Overreacting? When dreadful things happen here? Look at Abdul Haq's daughter — ran off with an Australian who doesn't even believe in God. She isn't Muslim any more and the whole family is dishonoured. The shame of it. No one respects him. They only think how could he let such a thing happen.'

Mum laughed. 'Honour. You're making too much of an old tradition.'

I heard a bang as though Papa had thumped the coffee table. 'This is no laughing matter, Marelle. Honour is everything. Look at Abdul — none of his relatives will face him. He may as well be dead. Now the whole family is tainted. No one will give their daughter to marry his son.' His voice lowered but I could still hear every word. 'Nothing like that will happen in this family, you hear? Ameera will obey and make an honourable marriage.'

Mum was conciliatory. 'There's no need to worry, Hassan. Ameera's a good girl. She understands your wishes about an arranged marriage and no dating.' She paused and a different note entered her voice. 'But I want her to have a choice.'

'Choice? What is choice? My sister didn't have a choice, nor did she think she should. She was a good daughter bringing honour to the family, happy to marry who my parents chose.'

There was another pause before Mum said, 'You had a choice.'

'That's different —' He stopped. I bet Mum was giving him one of her stares. I hated it when they fought.

I let the front door bang as if Riaz had just dropped me off. 'I'm home,' I called and raced up to my room. I didn't want to answer questions about Riaz. Let him do his own dirty work at breakfast.

2

Papa smiled at me as I entered the kitchen in the morning. 'Piari beti, darling daughter.'

I leaned over him and kissed his cheek. I loved the feel of Papa's beard; it was starting to show wiry grey hairs amongst the black.

'Did you have a good time at the Yusufs' home?' he asked, as if he thought it would be a difficult feat to manage. Anglo-Australians could be friends with anyone but Papa had certain ideals. Even though Mr Yusuf was a top orthodontist, they were Christian Pakistanis and I was sure Papa still thought in terms of caste. I always trod a careful path when I spoke of the Yusufs.

'Yes,' I said. 'There were lots of girls from my class there.'

Bad move. Papa's hand paused over the butter. 'What were they wearing?'

Mum made a noise with her tongue. She was doing that a lot lately.

'Covering shirts, Papa. Only girls were there.'

I caught a glance pass between Mum and Papa. She was warning him but he didn't take any notice.

He buttered his toast, his knife scraping on the plate. 'Did their brothers pick them up?'

'I didn't see who picked them up. They didn't come in.'

The right response and Papa relaxed. 'So where is your brother?'

'He must be still asleep.' *Don't ask me about last night, please.*

It was Mum who saved me. 'Hassan, can you pick up some things from the market?' She put a list in front of him.

Papa seemed to relish doing things like this for Mum. He'd told me that in some areas of Pakistan, the women never go outside the house. The men bring everything from the bazaar for them, even bolts of cloth and shoes to match. How awful would that be? I like choosing my own clothes. Poor Papa, if that was the way he'd grown up, he'd had a lot to get used to in Australia with Mum working three days a week teaching English.

Just then my phone rang. It was Raniya. 'Just checking you got home okay,' she said.

I left the table. I couldn't tell her what had happened with Papa's ears flapping. 'Maryam and Tariq brought me home in the end.'

There was a silence, then, 'Her brother?'

'Yes, it was fine.'

'You want to be careful there. He's not Muslim.'

'Why should that matter?' I felt like saying that Mum wasn't Muslim either.

She must have caught my tone. 'All I meant was he mightn't have the same code of behaviour as our boys.'

'He was no different at all.'

Was I telling the truth? Actually he was better than 'our boys'. Look how my own brother had left me to find my way home alone.

Raniya didn't linger. We made arrangements for coffee the next day in the mall. 'Let's shop for shoes after, okay, Ameera?'

'Sure.' I made an effort at enthusiasm and her 'bye' sounded relieved.

When I returned to the kitchen, Papa was at me again. 'What will you do today, beti?'

I stared at him. Would I have to account for every minute now that school had finished? 'I'm not sure yet. Tomorrow I'm meeting Raniya.'

I expected him to object but he didn't. I shouldn't have been surprised. He respected Raniya's family: her father was friendly with the imam at the mosque.

'You can come with me to the shop today and be useful,' he said.

'The shop?'

Why not Riaz? But then Riaz didn't share Papa's passion for carpets, not like I did. What would I do though? Roll up the carpets after a customer had viewed them? Papa pulled out dozens at once and spent most of his day rolling them back up. His shop looked like an art gallery, with special pieces hanging on the wall and from the ceiling. Papa sat on carpet cushions while he talked to the customers, and he always rang for coffee and cake from the deli next door. It surprised people but he was just fulfilling his Pushtun duty of hospitality. One customer had said the shop looked like a harem. Papa laughed about that when he came home, but I guessed it would look exotic to someone who had never travelled.

'It's about time I showed you how to do the books,' he told me. 'You can help me right through your holidays.' He paused and glanced at me. 'Then I may have a surprise for you.'

I looked at Mum. I could tell she didn't know what he was referring to either. He didn't enlighten us, just rubbed his hands together as he went out of the room.

'Mum, do I have to go? I could make up that green silk Aunty Khushida sent from Kashmir.'

'Just humour him today, love.'

I took a novel with me because I knew that Papa's idea of me helping wouldn't entail me speaking to customers or doing anything interesting. He would closet me in his stuffy little office fixing up his invoices on his business software.

I wasn't wrong about the office work but Papa did surprise me at lunchtime. 'Come,' he said. 'We'll shut the shop and eat at the café.'

He took me to an Italian café, one of my favourite foods. I was so touched. It had felt lately as if he'd forgotten who I was and what I liked, but that lunch was special. He spoke a lot about his family in Azad Kashmir and how they were getting their business back in order after the earthquake. I knew he telephoned them often at night.

'They asked after you,' he said.

I smiled. 'That's nice. Did Meena too?'

'Yes, yes, Meena too.' Then he put his hand on mine. 'Ameera, you are my only daughter and I want the best for you.'

I blinked at him. He sounded so serious.

'Parents make decisions for their children because they love them. You understand this?'

I nodded slowly, even though I had no idea what he had in mind.

The next day I managed to slip out to the mall without any questions from Papa. I met Raniya and we went to a café.

Raniya was wearing a short Indonesian scarf covering her hair. I'd noticed she was wearing short scarves more lately. I still just wore my long Pakistani dupatta around my neck. Papa hadn't insisted I cover my head though he'd be proud of me if I did. Mum felt that covering your head in a non-Muslim country defeated the purpose. 'Isn't it so as not to draw attention to yourself?' she'd said one day. It was true that Raniya got more attention than I did when we were out together.

'Papa took me out yesterday,' I told her. 'It was nice but it wasn't the same as when I was young. He and I used to get on so well. Now, it's like he's noticed that I'm growing up and he's keeping his distance but still has to protect me. We're in Australia — there are no terrorists, no war, and who's going to kidnap me? He's overprotective — it's annoying.'

'All Muslim fathers are the same. Even Natasha says her father's paranoid about her and they're Australian.'

'What's their problem?' I didn't mean to sound so grouchy.

Raniya gave me a measured glance. 'You were brought up Muslim — you understand.'

'Morality,' I said with a sigh. 'We have to be good, be hospitable, pray. I agree with those ideals, but why does it have to be so difficult? Papa's stricter than your father. Why can't he trust me? That old movie we saw recently, *The Go-Between*, remember? The fiancé said that nothing is a lady's fault. Well, my father thinks the opposite. I bet if he'd caught Tariq bringing me home, he would have blamed me, not Riaz. It's not fair.'

Raniya stirred another sugar into her cappuccino. 'We gain favour in God's eyes if we submit. It's more important to impress God than to please ourselves.' She kept her head down as she spoke.

I was speechless. I was just letting off steam; I didn't need a sermon.

Then Raniya dropped another bomb. 'Maybe it's because of your mother.'

'What do you mean?'

'Maybe your father's stricter because he thinks you'll be influenced by your mother's faith.'

Any mention of my mother like this made the blood rush to my head. I bet they all thought Mum was a bad influence on us. 'But Riaz and I have been brought up Muslim. Mum agreed.' It was hard to keep my tone even.

'I didn't mean to upset you, Amie. It's just a possible explanation.' Then she smiled. 'How about we check out the shoes in David Jones?'

I nodded and finished my coffee. Maybe Raniya was right about Mum. It was easier for her as both her parents thought the same about everything. Mum had tried not to let her world-view influence Riaz and me, but it was impossible not to see the flickers of disbelief that crossed her face at times. It had been much easier when I was younger, when life simply involved following Papa's rules. It was Mum's Christianity that had seemed harder then. 'All you have to do is believe,' she'd tried to explain to me one day — one of the few times she'd ever discussed her faith. 'Even the believing is a gift. Just be yourself — the special person God made you to be.' Papa said it was important to follow the rules, then we'd have a chance of paradise. Mum acted as though she already knew that was where she was going.

Shoes were usually my passion, but it was difficult to find the enthusiasm today. Raniya was deciding between a pair of black or red high heels when I heard a squeal. 'Amie!' It was Maryam. With her were Seema and Natasha. I looked behind them to see if anyone else was there and realised Papa may have a point. If I wasn't allowed out at night I would never have met Maryam's brother.

'Let's have coffee,' Maryam said.

Raniya and I looked at each other and shrugged. We could have said we'd just had one but that would have disappointed Maryam.

Off to Billy Baxter's we went. Natasha was telling us about her latest trip to the beach with her boyfriend when I saw Tariq in the café too. He sat apart from us but had the air of an older brother told to keep an eye on his sister and her friends. When I looked at him again I found his gaze on me. He smiled gently. I glanced at Raniya; she was listening to Natasha's story. When I looked up again Tariq was walking away. This time Raniya caught me staring. She followed my gaze, then raised her eyebrows at me. I could imagine what she was thinking: Muslim girls don't acknowledge a guy's attention. My problem was that I wanted to acknowledge Tariq. I wanted to speak to him, to find out what he was like, to talk about normal things as I had done with boys when I was younger. Would Tariq want to talk to me though? He must have been twenty-two at least, even older than Riaz. He was doing his Masters at uni, Maryam had said, in social work. At least at uni, people of any age could meet as equals, I thought. My stomach did a flip at the idea of sitting in the café with Tariq and discussing our studies. I had the feeling Tariq would be a free spirit. One of Raniya's brothers would never have smiled at me, they were much too predictable.

'What do you think, Ameera?'

'Pardon?' I missed what Maryam was asking me. Raniya was still watching me.

'Let's go to the movies,' Maryam said. 'Tariq can come back with us on the train to keep us safe.' She laughed and I thought how life seemed so simple for her.

'I'm in,' Natasha said.

'Cool, me too,' said Seema, who always managed to do whatever Natasha did. She even bleached her hair and wore blue contacts. Probably the kids at school had no idea her parents were Pakistani.

'I'm not sure,' I murmured.

I glanced at Raniya; she too was weighing up the pros and cons. Then suddenly I knew I wanted to go. Why shouldn't I see a movie with my friends? No point asking Papa. In Pakistan, good girls didn't go to movie theatres. I rang Mum instead.

Mum was hesitant. Years of asking Papa everything had taken its toll. 'I wonder what your father would say.'

I knew what he would say. 'What about you, Mum?'

She sighed. 'What movie is it?'

Papa only liked me watching old movies on DVD or ones from Bollywood. He didn't realise there was a sex scene in *The Go-Between*.

'Which movie?' I asked Maryam.

She shrugged. 'The cleanest and most classic.'

Finally Mum agreed. I bet she'd gone to the movies whenever she felt like it when she was my age. Still, I could imagine the tug of war going on inside her before she gave me permission.

'Okay.' Maryam and I gave each other a high five. That meant Raniya had to come whether she liked it or not as she wasn't supposed to walk home by herself.

'Are you okay with this?' I asked her.

She nodded. 'I'll come. Besides, someone has to look after you.'

I hoped she was joking.

3

The movie was fun: a romantic comedy. Most Bollywood movies were romantic comedies too, though some, like *Veer-Zaara*, portrayed years of sacrifice and much crying (Shahrukh Khan was the best crier, Papa said) before their love was finally realised. Others had tragic endings if a girl fell in love with a man she shouldn't marry. Then the lovers had to die, like in the romantic folk tales Papa told me. The story about Hir and Ranjha was his favourite. It had been written as a poem by the famous Waris Shah and sung for centuries. But living in Australia had lulled me into the Hollywood fantasy that everything would turn out fine and the lovers would have a happy ending. I forgot that the entertainment industry doesn't tell the truth.

Tariq turned up at the railway station. Maryam had lost her mobile so she must have messaged him on Natasha's but he didn't seem annoyed to be summoned like a genie. He had been shopping — I noted the Officeworks bag. He looked at us amiably, maybe counting how many girls he was responsible for. This time he didn't smile at me and I was glad; it would have been too obvious.

The train ride was uneventful, but the walk back to Maryam's house wasn't. Tariq was ahead and turned to check on us once or twice. It would have been hard to lose us: Seema and Natasha were giggling about scenes in the movie. 'Wasn't it cool when he first saw her tattoo?' Seema said, then swore and laughed. She was so different from Raniya. I wondered if she was trying too hard to fit in, but who was I to talk? Sometimes I felt my life was in fragments that were too hard to fit together.

I didn't notice the two guys until they were in front of us. They deliberately didn't make way and pushed through our group.

'Hey,' Natasha shouted.

One was wearing baggy jeans that exposed his underpants. He said to Maryam, 'Dirty wog, where's your scarf?' The other one ripped my dupatta from my neck. I thought he'd give it to Maryam, but he stuffed it in his jeans pocket. Gross. I watched in horror. Maryam cried out, but Tariq was already there.

'Give back the scarf,' he said.

Tariq was older and bigger than the other guys. The one with my scarf said, 'Keep your shirt on, mate, we're just teasing.' He handed my dupatta to Tariq and he and his friend crossed the road, giving each other high fives.

'Are you all right?' Tariq didn't seem to know whether to comfort Maryam or me.

Maryam nodded but then Tariq touched my cheek with his finger. When he brought it away there was blood on it. The guy who'd ripped off my dupatta must have caught a ring on my skin.

'Oh, you're hurt.' Maryam pulled out a tissue and dabbed at me.

'I'm fine.'

I was watching Tariq. He hadn't wiped his finger yet. Then Maryam turned to him with the tissue and she wiped it clean. For an instant I wished he was my brother and I could touch him like that. He held out my dupatta. I watched it fluttering between his fingers and hoped I didn't take too long to retrieve it.

At Maryam's house I rang Mum to get me, but it was Papa who arrived. He noticed my scratch since Mrs Yusuf had put a bandaid on it. Tariq spoke to him about what had happened. Tariq probably thought he was doing the right thing; and, truly, he was looking after us all — I wasn't alone with him. But I could tell from Papa's frosty stance that he wasn't happy. He thanked Tariq curtly and motioned for me to go.

Papa was quiet on the way home but as soon as we walked in he had a go at Mum. 'Look what happened. She goes to the movie theatre and is accosted on the way home.' He turned to me. 'Why didn't you ring Riaz? Isn't that why I gave you the mobile phone? He could have brought you home and you wouldn't have been with the Yusuf boy.'

'But, Papa, Tariq helped us.'

That was a mistake. Papa's eyes narrowed, impaling me. 'You know this boy's name?'

'He's Maryam's brother. Everyone knows his name.'

Papa sighed noisily.

'Papa, I've done nothing wrong. Just some guys were rude to us, that's all.'

'Things are not what they should be. In Pakistan, girls do not know boys' names. It is a morally deficient country we live in.'

'Hassan —' my mother began.

'And you, Marelle, did you give permission?'

I cut in. 'Papa, we only went to the movies, just us girls.'

'You go to your room. I will discuss this with your mother.'

I could hear Mum remonstrating with him as I skulked up the stairs. I phoned Maryam from my room.

'Amie? You okay?'

'Yes, but Papa's being difficult. He's acting like it was my fault.' I didn't mention that he thought it was Tariq's fault too.

'That's too bad. Tariq feels responsible. He's sorry it happened.'

'It wasn't his fault either.'

'I know but he likes you. He wouldn't let anything happen to you.'

My next sentence died in my throat.

'Amie? Are you still there?'

'What was that you said?'

'Tariq wouldn't let anything bad happen to you.'

Maybe she meant as a sister, yes, that was it. She meant that Tariq would protect me just as he would protect Maryam.

'That's nice,' was all I could manage in reply.

'Let's do something tomorrow.'

'Okay, I'll ring.'

That night by some miracle Riaz was home. He gave a rhythmic knock on my door — our private code — and strode in. 'Heard some guys roughed you up.'

'Not really.' I told him what had happened.

'So what's Dad in a storm for?'

'I don't know.'

'He had a go at me for not bringing you home, but I didn't know about it this time, Ames.'

I didn't point out that he might not have come even if I had rung. 'Maryam said her brother would escort us home on the train. He didn't seem to mind.'

Riaz nodded. 'Tariq's a good mate.'

I stared at Riaz and tried to stay with the subject I had in mind. 'Something's bothering Papa and it's not just this. Do you have any idea what it is?'

Riaz shrugged.

'He's not the same,' I went on. 'He used to play with us and laugh, tell jokes and stories. You must remember all those stories at bedtime. Those awful videos he took everywhere we went.'

Riaz hugged me. 'Hey, Ames. We're not little kids any more.'

Was that all it was? Papa was uptight because we were older and getting harder to bring up?

Riaz pulled back to look at me. 'Thanks for not blowing my cover.'

When Riaz was like this I could forgive him anything. 'You owe me one.' I smiled at him. 'Honestly, it's okay, but I hope you'd come if I was in real trouble.'

'You better believe it. I would have smashed those guys' faces if I was there today.'

'Imagine the headlines: "Muslim gang beats up Christian boys in street".'

We both laughed, although we knew how quickly anti-Muslim feeling could rise, like it did after the Bali bombing. Riaz's laugh came from deep inside him, warm and infectious, like Papa's used to be when we were kids. I wondered how far his good mood would stretch.

'Riaz, I want to invite Maryam over tomorrow night. Why don't you ask Tariq so he can drive her?'

Riaz's eyes flickered slightly. 'Hmm. What're you up to?'

'It's difficult for me, Riaz. You can go out to see whoever you please. If Tariq came here with Maryam, Mum could meet him. I know they'd have a lot in common. Then she could talk to Papa. You know Papa won't let me have any friends at all lately unless he's met them first.'

Riaz pursed his lips. Would he be like Raniya's brothers after all, determined to uphold my honour and that of the family at any cost? I prayed enough of Mum had rubbed off on him. Finally he smiled. 'I'll only do this because Tariq's my mate. But be careful: Big Brother will be watching.'

'He won't speak to me. I just want Mum to meet him. Can you manage that?'

'Sure thing.' Riaz winked at me as he left.

How easy was that? I punched Maryam's home number into my phone.

4

Maryam bounded up the stairs to my room. It was obvious her parents didn't care if she met Riaz in our house. 'Shall we watch a DVD on your computer?' she said.

'Okay,' but I was half-hearted. I paused in my doorway. I could hear Riaz and Tariq in the kitchen. Cupboard doors banged. Good. That would bring Mum in.

'How about *Pride and Prejudice*?'

'Sure.' Most of me was in the kitchen. Mum's voice said, 'Nice to meet you.' There was Tariq's deeper one in reply. Then Riaz making espresso coffee, the murmur of voices. It was working. I grinned broadly at Maryam. '*Pride and Prejudice* it is.'

'Are you okay?'

'Yes.' And I led her into my room and into nineteenth-century Britain, the era Papa wanted to keep me in. At least in Jane Austen's world, some girls had a choice or could refuse a suitor. I sighed as Darcy proposed to Elizabeth. Tariq would never propose to me. He would have to ask his parents to visit mine to make a match.

But Papa would never agree. He wanted me to marry a Muslim. All I could hope for from Tariq was friendship. In Australia people of opposite sexes and different ages were friends all the time. But for me, a Muslim Pakistani girl, even securing a friendship was a problem.

The movie finished and so had our drinks and chips. 'Would you like coffee?' I asked.

Maryam nodded. She and I had dispensed with a lot of the Pakistani ways of doing things. It was polite there to refuse twice and accept the third time, but Anglo–Australians didn't ask you a third time. 'I'll come down with you,' she said.

We passed the lounge where the guys were watching soccer with Papa. That was good: sport seemed to be a leveller. At least Papa wasn't interrogating Tariq.

Mum was putting Anzac biscuits in the oven. 'Hi, Mum.' I took mugs out of the cupboard. 'Can we try those when they're cooked?'

'Not too many. They're for my class tomorrow.' She smiled at Maryam. 'I'm glad you brought your brother tonight. He's a treat.'

'We think so too,' Maryam said.

Mum glanced at me and I froze. What if she caught on that I had engineered Tariq's visit? But her gaze was thoughtful and soon passed over me. 'Ten minutes for those biscuits and only take a few,' she said. 'Tell that to your brother too if he comes in.'

I lingered as long as possible making the coffee, listening to Maryam chat on about a movie she'd seen. Finally, the tray of coffee and biscuits was ready and we had to go back to my room. It was disappointing, but what had I expected? How could Tariq come into the kitchen to see me with Papa home? One step at a time, I reminded myself.

When it was time for Maryam and Tariq to leave, Maryam hugged me on the front step. 'Thanks for inviting me, it was fun. Just think, we have three months off. Let's go to the beach soon.'

'Okay.' I smiled and forced myself not to look at Tariq. Still, I was as aware of him as if he was standing directly in front of me.

I heard Papa say to Riaz as he shut the door, 'Your friend seems a nice enough boy.' My heart soared. Maybe Papa thought Tariq would be a steadying influence on Riaz. I made sure I didn't hang around to listen, but soon enough Riaz knocked our secret code on my door.

'So, Ames, that went okay.' He dropped onto my bed.

I pulled my pillow out from under his head. 'Maryam enjoyed herself.'

'That's not what I meant and you know it. Tariq charmed Mum, and even Dad's surprised he's not as bad as he thought.'

'Truly?' I was sure my eyes were shining.

He leaned on his elbow. 'But don't get any ideas. Tariq's Christian and you know what Dad's like lately. Tariq's okay to be my mate but not for you.'

'But I just want to be friends.' At that moment I truly believed it. 'He'd think I'm too young for anything else.'

Riaz regarded me for a while. Then he handed over a piece of paper. 'I know you'll be sensible with this. It's Tariq's mobile number.'

I snatched it out of his hand.

'It's only because Maryam doesn't have a new mobile yet,' he said. 'If you get stuck and can't catch a ride or you can't find me, I trust Tariq to bring you home.'

I almost stroked the paper but managed to drum up some self-control. Riaz had a stern look on his face but I caught the twinkle in his eyes. If it wasn't for wanting to spend time alone with his girlfriend, I was sure he would never have given me Tariq's number. But the arrangement suited him well, and he didn't need to remind me to keep it a secret.

It took me two days to find the courage to call Tariq. Even then I hit the stop button twice. When I finally rang and Tariq answered, I almost hung up.

'Hello. Hello?'

If I left it any longer, he'd end the call. 'T-Tariq, is that you?'

'Ameera.' It was a whisper, like soft wings brushing against my face.

'Y-yes. It's me.' How did he know? 'Riaz gave me your number in case I was in trouble.'

His voice was instantly louder, as if he had stood up. 'Is there a problem?'

'No. I'm fine. I just wanted to check the number was right.'

'Oh.' I heard the smile in his voice; imagined it breaking across his face.

There was nothing more I could or should say. I'd heard Natasha say things to her boyfriend like 'See you around' or 'Let's catch a movie'. What simple words when she flung them out, but not simple for me.

'Okay, I'll go now.'

I heard Tariq's 'bye' but I didn't want to hang up. The urge to keep him on the phone was so strong. My breath came faster. *Say something, say something. Stupid girl, say something.*

'Bye,' I said.

I pressed the end button and burst into tears.

It was that time in the early morning when hope is just a dream. I lay on my bed covered by a sheet, wondering if I'd lost my senses. Six months before I would never have dreamed of contacting a boy. Could such a friendship ever work? Was I wrong to try?

I thought of a story Papa had told me. A boy called Adam and a girl called Durkhane loved each other, but her marriage to another had already been arranged. After the wedding Adam tried to rescue Durkhane by hiring a war chief to abduct her for him. But it didn't work out as her husband paid a higher price. Adam was betrayed and he lost Durkhane forever. He went to play his stringed rabaab up on the hills, and was so grief-stricken he fell to his death. When Durkhane heard of the accident, she became ill and never recovered. Even though Adam's friend played his rabaab to her it didn't help. Papa said she died of a broken heart. She was buried with Adam.

Why was I thinking about that story now? Because deep down I knew it was impossible to be friends with Tariq? Papa had never told me a story where the lovers simply got married. Were there such stories?

Just then my phone vibrated. I leaned over to answer it.

'Good morning, Ameera.'

'Tariq.' Waves rippled in my stomach.

'Did you sleep well?'

I hesitated. 'Yes.'

'Are your parents well?'

'Yes.' I smiled. He sounded as if he was visiting or writing a letter. That was the way we wrote to Papa's family in Azad Kashmir: we would ask after everyone's health and then send them our love. Our love. My smile faded.

'Tariq, how is your family?'

'Fine, thank you.'

'And Maryam?'

'She's fine too.'

We wouldn't get anywhere at this rate.

'Ameera?'

'Yes?'

'I don't want to cause you trouble.' He used the Urdu word: 'tuklief'.

I sat up and felt the prickling behind my eyes. 'I understand.' I held my breath. *Too soon*, my heart shrieked, *too soon for the end*.

'But may I ring you sometimes?'

I blew out my breath; saw a stranger in the mirror. This was it: the crossroad. *I could say no, should say no. This number is only for emergencies.*

Papa would think Tariq was immoral to ask me such a question. Maybe Riaz had never meant us to ring each other, but he'd given me the number. In doing so he'd given me a choice. I would treasure that even if nothing came of it. Now Tariq also held out a choice. The power to choose was not something that a girl like Natasha would think remarkable, but for me it was a heady feeling.

I tried to keep my voice steady as I answered. 'Yes, that's fine.'

The next time Tariq rang he spoke of his studies and asked me about my uni choices.

'I applied for Adelaide uni, the same one as you,' I told him.

'Then we will meet and talk over coffee.'

His words were warm, flowing over me, caressing me. If we had been able to meet openly would it have been the same?

Besides his studies, Tariq had a part-time job with a government agency and on weekends he worked in a music shop. He sent songs to my phone. We both liked Junoon and the way their rock blended with traditional Sufi music. They had been banned in Pakistan until recently, their songs deemed too political for their outlining of social injustices. Tariq called them the U2 of South-East Asia.

The calls became longer. I messaged him when I was alone and he'd ring. Tariq could recite poetry: Hafez, Rumi, also the Psalms from the Bible. I told him stories.

36

'The Ruby Prince' was the only story I knew that ended happily. The Ruby Prince was a pari, and his human wife risked her life to dance before the Fairy King to win him back. Tariq mentioned 'Hir and Ranjha' and the tragedy of it.

'In most folk tales the lovers can only be together once they're dead. It's a spiritual joining,' I said, remembering how Papa had explained it to me. Then I added hopefully, 'But they're just stories, like *Romeo and Juliet*.'

Tariq chuckled. 'They're stories with a purpose. How else do you think they get generations of people to marry who their parents want them to marry?'

'But it's our belief.'

'Is it?'

I was silent, thinking about the seventy-five per cent of the world that practised arranged marriages.

'I bet you won't find in the Koran that you can't marry for love,' Tariq added.

'But Papa says Muslim girls should marry Muslim boys —' I stopped, mortified. This was me I was talking about now. If friendship was the only thing I could ever have with Tariq then surely he would say so? Instead he carried on with his argument.

'That's a cultural thing. All the Koran specifies about marriage is that two people willingly enter into it.'

I'd never heard it described like that before.

Tariq's voice became softer. 'That means, Ameera, if anyone like us wished to be married, they could.'

I held my breath. What was he saying? That he wanted me?

5

It was Tariq who first mentioned meeting. 'My friend Samuel is having a party at his house,' he told me. 'His sister is inviting her friends to come too.'

I was silent. A mixed party. I knew what Papa would think of that.

'What's his sister's name?'

'Natasha.'

My heart jumped. 'Natasha Collins?'

'Yes. You could tell Maryam you heard about the party and you can go with her. The Collinses won't mind. Riaz could bring you to our house.'

At least Tariq understood the difficulties. Imagine trying to explain to an Anglo–Australian boy that I couldn't be seen alone with him.

'Thank you. I'll ask Mum.'

It was as if a weight had been lifted from Tariq when I agreed. He started telling me a story from the Bible. 'There's a whole book about a king and the girl he loves. The king even wishes he was the girl's brother so that at least he could see her and talk to her.'

Hadn't I also felt like that? Tariq must have too. I hesitated: I knew it wasn't wise for me to go to Natasha's. But I told myself this wasn't dating, not by Natasha's standards. This was just meeting a friend. Wise or not, I did it: I asked Mum to explain to Papa that I needed to see my girlfriends. I omitted to tell her that boys would be present. I felt guilty but I didn't want to put Mum in a situation where she'd have to keep a secret from Papa.

Mum dropped me at Maryam's on the night of the party. I knew she wanted me to see there wasn't just one way to live. And why couldn't that include a few boys, I told myself. It was as if Papa thought boys only had one thing on their minds. I wished he could cut me some slack and trust me, but it all came back to that honour thing he was so concerned about. 'The best way to keep the family honour intact is to look after your daughters in the first place,' he always said. It was such a burden being responsible for the family honour.

The Collinses house was bigger than ours. Lights flashed and there was a Christmas tree set up. Mum celebrated Christmas with Riaz and me, but Papa wouldn't let her put up a tree. 'What a pagan practice that is, worshipping a tree,' he said. Mum had tried explaining how it reminded her of Christ's eternal life, but that set Papa off again. 'Blasphemy! Don't say such things. Do you want the imam coming to put us right?' My father was so concerned about doing the right thing; it would have killed him to be embarrassed in front of the imam or his friends.

Natasha looked stunning in tight pants and a halterneck top. I had on a kurta over jeans and a dupatta slung around my neck. It was hard finding clothes to suit both Papa's dress code and fashion — a long covering top like a kurta was the best compromise.

Natasha took Maryam and me to the backyard where everything happens in Anglo–Australian homes. I could feel the thump of the music in my chest. 'I'm glad you came.' Natasha was looking me in the eyes and I smiled brightly. 'Help yourself to a drink. There's everything …' Her glance flickered as she paused slightly. 'Everything from Coke to juice.'

I knew from Riaz that there would be beer and cask wine as well, but I didn't have any interest in alcohol. It was daring enough just to be there.

'There's a karaoke machine,' Maryam said.

We watched a girl sing a song following the words flashing across the screen. She even danced. Then Samuel, Natasha's brother, started singing with her. It looked like fun.

'Imagine being able to do that,' I said in Maryam's ear.

She nodded, then she turned to me and her eyes shone. 'We could try.'

The thought of putting myself on public display like that terrified me. 'No, I couldn't.'

Then I spotted Tariq. He was watching Samuel sing and had a faint smile on his face. In that instant, his head turned and he looked directly at me. He knew I was there. My breath caught in my throat. How were we going to do this? How could we talk and make it seem normal?

The song finished and Natasha rushed up to the girl. 'That was great, Allie.'

A boy approached Natasha and put his hands on her shoulders. She turned and laughed at him. 'Want to try, Brian?' The boy said nothing, but his hand caressed Natasha's arm. 'I'll sing too.' She slipped her arm through his as their heads bent over the list of songs. It looked so simple and natural for them — but not for me.

I glanced back at Tariq but he was gone. I looked around and there he was, making his way towards us. I tried not to stare at him as he stood next to Maryam. He said something to her that I couldn't hear, then he turned to me. 'Hello, Ameera.' The words were bland, but when I looked up to answer him, his eyes were bright. His smile washed over me like a wave in a sun-warmed rockpool.

'Hi,' I managed.

'It's good to see you. How is Riaz?'

I grinned at the Pakistani politeness. He would ask about my parents next. 'Okay. He's working at the Tandoor Kitchen tonight.'

Maryam was watching Natasha and Brian, who'd started their song. The music was loud but my ears were tuned in only to Tariq.

'And your parents? I enjoyed visiting last week.'

I relaxed. This was what I was used to. 'They're fine. Papa's got a secret.'

Tariq's eyebrows rose. 'What sort of secret?'

'A surprise, he says.'

'For you?' Tariq was next to me now. Maryam was slightly in front of us with her eyes glued to the singers. I hoped it looked as if Tariq and I were discussing the song.

'Papa won't say.'

'A Christmas present?'

'He doesn't celebrate Christmas.' Then I grew daring. 'Maybe when you're over next time you can find out.'

Listen to me; was I flirting? I didn't know what had come over me. The words 'next time' echoed in my head and were reflected in Tariq's smile.

Natasha's brother joined us and rested his arm across Tariq's shoulders. 'Hi, Rick, how ya doing?'

'Fine, and you?'

Samuel smirked at Tariq's manners. 'You playing soccer with us next season, mate?'

'Sure thing.'

Samuel glanced at me but Tariq didn't introduce me. 'You holding out on me, mate? Who's your girlfriend?'

I nearly choked. There was an awkward pause while Tariq worked out what to say. In Pakistan, no one would ever ask a man the name of the woman with him. It's such bad manners; and in tribal areas a man could be killed for it. But Samuel had no idea.

'This is Ameera,' Tariq said grudgingly.

Samuel winked at me.

I glanced away and caught sight of a guy near the karaoke machine. He looked like Ibram, one of Raniya's brothers, though I couldn't be sure as I hadn't seen him since I started Year 11. He was looking at me with scorn and all of a sudden I felt naked. I had my dupatta around my neck, the way it was worn in Pakistani cities, rather than over my hair. The guy glanced from Tariq to me and then to Samuel and my shame turned to dread. The

42

tumbling feeling in my stomach wouldn't subside, even when Samuel sauntered off.

I said I wanted a drink and dragged Maryam with us to the veranda. Fortunately she understood. She knew Papa would not like me walking alone with Tariq.

I was too shocked to tell Maryam about Raniya's brother. Nor did I want to draw her attention to the fact that Tariq had been talking to me. I simply stayed close to her, marking time until we could leave.

Brian and Natasha joined us and Brian handed Tariq a beer. He drank a mouthful, then caught me staring at him and put the beer down. Why did that disturb me? Riaz drank; and Maryam had told me that her family could drink in moderation if they didn't offend anybody. I turned my attention to Brian instead. He was discussing a movie he'd seen about terrorism in Africa and wanted to know our views on it. Maryam and I rolled our eyes at each other. We'd got those comments at school too. Just because our parents were Pakistani we were supposed to know everything about terrorism.

Tariq said, 'Some terrorists may be fighting for political reasons and think of themselves as militants or freedom fighters. Governments need to find out why they're doing it.'

'But you do think terrorism is bad?' Brian said. 'I mean, violence doesn't help.' He said it as though we needed to be convinced.

We all stared at him, and Natasha belted him on the arm.

'It depends which side you're on as to who the terrorists are,' I said.

Brian frowned at that and Tariq cut in. 'In the movie, the guy wasn't a terrorist at first. He became one because of how he was treated.'

'Is that any excuse?' Brian asked. 'If I get caught speeding and get roughed up by the police, I'm not going to blow up the police station.'

'No,' Tariq said. 'But you haven't had hundreds of years of dispossession and persecution either.'

That comment was a little too pointed and Brian didn't answer. The conversation changed to discussion of another movie. When I looked back to the drinks table, I saw Ibram pulling the ring off a can. He was glaring at me.

6

Tariq rang as soon as I reached my room. 'I'm sorry about Samuel's comment and telling your name,' he said. 'I could see it upset you.'

I should have told him that seeing Ibram had upset me more, but what good would it have done? It would have created bad blood between Tariq and Raniya's brothers, and caused more trouble than it was worth.

'I should have ignored him,' Tariq went on, 'or explained.'

'No, it's okay, Tariq. There are enough differences without outlining more. I can cope with being introduced. My Uncle Richard does it all the time.'

'I'm glad you're not upset with me.' There was a different tone in his voice; I let it wash over me like water from a healing spring.

'Ameera?'

'Yes?'

'I have another idea.'

I felt a quiver of excitement but it was coupled with dread.

'Maryam will ask you to go to the movies. Make sure you sit on the end of the row but leave the aisle seat free. I'll pretend there are no other seats. I have to be nearby in the dark to watch Maryam doesn't come to harm.'

I laughed. Natasha would have called Tariq's protection stifling, but I was Pakistani enough to feel the care and honour given when we girls were 'looked after'. But Papa would think it should be Riaz looking after me, not his friend.

I was a mess at the cinema, worrying about how to stay at the back of the line of girls walking down the aisle so I'd be the one sitting at the end of the row. What if one of the girls decided to sit on the other side of me to chat? Then Tariq's plan would be stuffed.

Besides Maryam and me, there was Natasha, her Anglo friend Luanne, Raniya and Seema. They all filed in licking ice-creams. My stomach was in too much of a knot to eat one. I managed to sit down last but there were two seats vacant beside me. *Uh-oh.* Tariq would have to sit in the furthest seat. I couldn't ask everyone to shift up one: it would only draw their attention to him. But he didn't come.

The ads began; still no Tariq.

'I thought your brother was coming,' Natasha said to Maryam.

Maryam crunched on the cone. 'He'll be around somewhere.' She didn't sound concerned. Luanne was leaning over, listening. 'Is Maryam's brother your boyfriend?' she asked Raniya. 'He's so hot.'

Natasha understood our customs and began to explain, but Raniya cut in. 'We don't date, Luanne.'

Luanne's mouth fell open. 'You're kidding? What if you like someone? How do you get married?' She giggled uncertainly. 'You can't all be nuns.'

Raniya frowned. 'Our parents arrange our marriages. We have input, of course,' she added. 'I'll go on dates with my fiancé when we're engaged.'

'Is that the first time you get to kiss him?' Luanne asked.

Raniya kept her face calm but I knew how scandalised she was. 'We will be chaperoned.' It came out of her mouth as a tight hiss.

Luanne didn't know what that meant and Natasha had to explain. Luanne looked even more horrified.

Seema stared at her lap; she hated it when our customs were criticised, especially since each family had variations on the theme. Mum had told me some Pakistani families were allowing love marriages now, but I knew Papa would never agree to that. I'd asked Maryam recently about marriage in her family. 'I'm allowed to choose,' she'd said, 'but Mummy and Daddy want me to choose a Christian. They say it will be easier to marry someone with the same world-view.'

Raniya began explaining our customs to Luanne but I had the odd impression her words were directed at me. Perhaps it was my own guilt or the way she looked at me once or twice. Still, I couldn't stop myself from continually glancing to the empty aisle seat.

Then the lights dimmed and I felt the seat next to me move, heard the faint squish of flattened leather, smelled cologne, subtle and fresh like a beach breeze. Tariq. I could just see his smile, the left side of his mouth following the right as always. He'd left the aisle seat vacant and was sitting right next to me. He bent close and said in my ear, 'Good to see you, Ameera.' My ear burned with his breath.

I couldn't say a word about the movie later; throughout, I was only aware of Tariq's presence. At one point we both fumbled with the armrest and our hands brushed. For a second too long he left his hand on mine and I felt as though the movie theatre had faded away and we were alone. In that moment I knew this wasn't simple friendship. I felt his care like a fierce physical embrace. If I'd been asked to explain why I cared for him in return, I wouldn't have been able to. I just knew I did.

Papa had told me folk tales from Pakistan about lovers who fell in love at first sight. I used to think that was unrealistic and romantic, but Mum said it was like that with her and Papa. And now I felt it too. I guess when you don't meet many boys socially, things can happen quicker.

Papa would say that love should come after marriage but I knew now that wasn't true. He probably thought you could only love someone after you'd slept with them. How unfair of him not to allow his children to marry for love when that was what he'd done.

At the swell of the closing music, Tariq shifted to the aisle seat. When the lights came on, the girls began to chat about the movie. I glanced at Tariq. He half-smiled and his gaze lingered on my face. I turned back to my friends and caught Raniya watching me. Her glance flickered to Tariq. Did she guess he'd been sitting close beside me, a place reserved only for a brother, father or husband?

7

It was the week before Christmas when my world fell apart. I had been at Maryam's house, and yes, I saw Tariq there, but mainly we girls watched music DVDs and made gulab jarmins for dessert. It was daytime so I took the chance to walk back by myself, and as I approached our house I saw an unfamiliar car take off. When I let myself in, Papa was stalking up and down the lounge room. I remember noticing the rug: an antique faded red Bukhara, one of Papa's favourites. Mum was watching him from the couch. I hadn't seen her look like that before, as though something terrible would happen if she left the room. She saw me first and motioned quickly for me to go upstairs. She looked frantic, which had the opposite effect of what she wanted: I was rooted to the spot with apprehension.

'What's wrong?' I said.

Papa turned on me. 'You!' he said. Gone was his usual loving greeting of 'beti ji'. He was a stranger.

Mum stood up. 'Hassan.' But her warning was tentative. Neither of us had ever seen him like this.

He jabbed the air in front of me. 'You have been seen. Acting dishonourably with boys.'

I was too shocked to defend myself.

Mum cut in. 'I'm sure it's a misunderstanding, Hassan. Ask her.'

'How will we hold up our heads in the community?' Papa raged. 'What will the family say in Kashmir?'

I wanted to say he'd got it all wrong, but would he believe me?

'The imam has visited — he said I should know so I can deal with it. You have been seen at a mixed party. You, Ameera. How could you do this to us?'

I licked my lips. His anger was spilling into sorrow; the combination wasn't good to see. 'Papa, I've done nothing immoral.'

Mum smiled at me, a little too brightly. 'See, Hassan, it's all a mistake.'

He shouted, 'Were you at a mixed party? Was the Yusuf boy there and others?'

I couldn't lie so I said nothing. Papa would say even the phone calls were immoral. He must never know about them; that would get Riaz into trouble as well.

Mum was looking more concerned now. 'Ameera?'

'I was there, but it was innocent. I went with Maryam.'

'It was a boy's party. You cannot go to boys' parties. It is not seemly. Everyone will think you have a relationship.' Papa said 'relationship' as if it was a swearword.

'Hassan, stop. Ameera is a good girl.'

He swung around on me then, so close I thought he'd hit me. I flinched, but his next words hurt more than his hand would have. 'You are not a good girl.' He spaced the words so I wouldn't miss any. 'You have brought dishonour to this family. Where there is smoke there is fire. Chello, go to your room. I will decide what is to be done.'

What did he mean? I understood the dishonour part — though I disagreed — but what had to be done?

Mum was the one who voiced it. 'Hassan? What do you mean? What are you going to do?'

I didn't get to hear an answer, for Papa shouted, 'Go!'

I ran to my room like a disgraced little girl.

I didn't know if it was Raniya who had told her parents about the party — for my own good, no doubt — or her brother. Someone had said it and that was enough. I'd never seen Papa so angry and I felt sick with fear. What was he thinking of doing? Two months in my room with only bread and water? Would he do that? No computer or phone for a month?

My phone. I began erasing Tariq's messages. I could hear the warmth of his voice even in the texts. His beautiful words. I was crying as I read each one before I hit the delete button. Then the music. It was like cutting my heart out. But Papa must never know I spoke to Tariq late at night.

No one came near me that first night, not even Mum. Fortunately, I had my own bathroom and toilet. It wasn't until Papa went to work in the morning that she brought me breakfast. I fell into her arms and sobbed. She cried too.

'I'm so sorry,' she said. 'I never thought it would come to this.'

'You don't think I'm bad, do you, Mum?'

She stroked the hair away from my face. 'Course not. But you do need to tell me what's happened so I know what I'm dealing with.' She raised her eyebrows.

I knew Mum would still love me even if I'd slept with Tariq, but I'd be too ashamed to ever tell her something like that. With relief I said, 'I haven't done anything wrong. I haven't even kissed anyone.'

Mum looked sideways at me as she pulled me to sit next to her on the bed. 'What about the party?'

I bit my lip; I knew what she'd say next.

'You didn't tell us it was Natasha's brother's party. You led us to believe it was hers.'

'I'm sorry, Mum. I just wanted to go. Maryam went.'

'She's not Muslim, love.' Mum sighed.

Nor did Maryam have a father like mine. Mum wasn't about to say that to me, but I could sense her disapproval wasn't all directed at me.

'What's Papa going to do?'

She frowned. 'I don't know. He did have a surprise for you, but I don't know if he'll follow through on that now.'

'What sort of surprise?' I could tell by Mum's tone she didn't think I'd like it. What if he stopped me from going to uni and I had to join the carpet business? I didn't want to do that any more than Riaz did.

'You'll have to wait and see. Ameera, I need to know.' She put her hands on my shoulders. 'Do you feel something for Tariq?'

'Will you tell Papa?'

'Not necessarily, but I need to know how serious it is.'

'We just talk. He's nice, Mum.'

'I already know how nice he is. I presume it was you who arranged his visit to Riaz that night?'

I nodded slowly.

'What if your father arranged a marriage with him?'

I tried to appear deadpan but my eyes betrayed me. Mum dropped her hands from my shoulders and rubbed her forehead. She looked at me and I saw that she was almost crying.

'So you love him,' she said.

'What can be done?' There was hope in my voice, but Mum didn't share my tone.

'If it's a question of honour —'

'But I haven't done anything.'

'I believe you, but in your father's eyes you've dishonoured him. Dishonour sticks like slander. He says it stains like dye, you can never erase it.' She thought for a second. 'Sometimes dishonour can be fixed with a marriage.'

'But Tariq's Christian — that's why I kept my interest secret.'

Mum nodded slowly. 'I know — it's a problem. I just needed to know what you felt in case your father thinks of it as an option. Though the way he talks about the Yusufs, I doubt it.'

Mum gave me another long hug then got up to leave. 'This will calm down, Ameera. I'll talk to him. But please don't do anything rash, like going to Maryam's house. It would increase the shame your father already feels, maybe force him to act more strictly than he normally would. I'm sorry.'

At the door; she turned and rushed back to hug me again. 'Oh, Ameera, God loves you so much. He is your true father — He will look after you.'

She kissed me and left. I sat there after she'd gone, astonished. Mum rarely spoke to us about what she thought of God. I knew Papa wouldn't agree that God was my father. But what if He were? Could I dare to ask Him to look after me better than my own father?

8

That night Riaz came to my room with chicken korma. Mum had made it using curry paste from a jar but he'd gone to the Tandoor Kitchen to buy me a garlic naan. He knew how much I loved naan.

'Riaz, you're an angel. I'm so hungry.'

He watched me while I fell on the food. 'Ameera, I'm sorry if giving you Tariq's phone number caused all this.'

I swallowed down a mouthful. 'I could have refused the number or not used it. Besides, it was worth it.' I looked up at him. He seemed truly concerned. 'Tariq was never my boyfriend — we only ever talked.'

'I believe you, Ames.'

That was when it hit me: my 'friendship' with Tariq would have to end. Papa would watch me like a falcon forever now.

'I suppose I'll be lucky if I get to go to uni after this,' I said.

Then I saw the look on Riaz's face. The concern had morphed into sorrow and pity; it made him look older.

'Riaz?'

He moved to the bed and put an arm around me. 'Ames, I want you to know how sorry I am.'

Not sorry enough, I thought. If he was, wouldn't he have stood with me, taken half the blame? But maybe he didn't see how having a girlfriend had led him to give me Tariq's number. Still, it was my choice to use it, and I was proud of that. I couldn't blame Riaz. Though a little voice whispered that Papa probably wouldn't be as angry about Riaz having a girlfriend.

Riaz hadn't finished. 'I love you, Ames. And I mean this — if something happens that you don't like, you call me and I'll come.'

I gaped at him, amazed. What did he mean? He couldn't leave a nightclub on time to drive me home, so why promise something like this? But he was serious. There was a concern in his eyes that I'd rarely seen.

'Is something wrong?' I asked.

'I hope not. I hope this gets sorted okay.'

He'd overheard something, I could tell, but he wouldn't let on. He just held me for an age then left the room, taking my plate with him.

I didn't dare ask Papa what was going on. I used to be able to talk to Papa, but he was a different person now. I yearned for the days when we had been close. He'd taught me Urdu and it had transported me into his world. He told me stories, and those stories had taught me everything I needed to know: how to behave, how to treat others, how to obey, and how I would have an arranged marriage. Papa said I was the princess in the stories, that I was as beautiful as the moon.

I remembered the story of Punnu and Sassi. Sassi was beautiful and the astrologer said at her birth that she would marry a man from another faith. To save the community from such bad karma, her Brahman parents put her on the Indus river in a basket, and a Muslim washerman found her and adopted her. She married Punnu, a chieftain's son from a faraway place. His family weren't happy and his brothers abducted him after the marriage. Sassi wandered into the desert to find him. One night each could hear the other calling above the wind, but each believed it to be an hallucination produced by the desert. They didn't know they were only a few yards apart, unable to see one another because of the driving wind and sand. And so Sassi and Punnu each died alone.

My eyes always teared up when I remembered that story but it had become even more poignant now. Would Tariq have changed his life for me, like Punnu? Become a Muslim? But I wouldn't expect that of anyone. I loved the movie *My Big Fat Greek Wedding* — guess that's because I could relate to it — but Toula's boyfriend converted because he didn't believe in anything. Tariq did, and he wouldn't be who he was if he couldn't practise his faith. Even if he changed, Papa had a thing about new converts. 'It's the family you marry, not the boy,' he always said.

It hurt not speaking to Tariq. He rang many times and left messages, but I didn't dare ring him back and his calls gradually stopped. Maryam called to make a time to hang out but I said I didn't feel like it. I felt awful. When she asked how I was I knew she was fishing but I couldn't tell her about Tariq. I think she thought I was having a bad period and didn't press for details.

When Papa was at work, Mum allowed me to leave my room. I read books I didn't have time for during the term and watched BBC DVDs Mum borrowed from the library. Papa still didn't want to see me and it had been days. I knew that he believed his decisions concerning me were based on good parenting: 'in your best interests' and 'because I love you' were phrases he often used. I believed him, and no one could fault his concern for my welfare. But my personal wishes? They were never considered. When I was ten Maryam had given me a kitten. Papa had told me to give it back. 'What a gift,' he fumed. 'I'm the one to pay for it.' I was too young to point out that Maryam knew I wanted the kitten. If I'd said that, though, I would have been frivolous at best, disobedient at worst. Papa hadn't spoken to me until the kitten was returned. I didn't like remembering that; it made me feel disloyal and I prayed for forgiveness.

On the fifth day Papa relented. I was asked to come down to breakfast. I checked his face as I tiptoed in. It was an awful feeling to be nervous of my own father. He seemed at peace; the anger was gone. If I had known why, I wouldn't have relaxed.

'I'm sorry, Abu ji, for causing you pain,' I said.

He looked gratified. Mum seemed surprised. It was a good sign, I thought, and hoped this would be the end of it. Christmas was in a few days; Mum would be glad to have this over before she celebrated with her family. But would I be allowed to go?

I remember exactly what I was doing when Papa told me his 'surprise'. I was pouring milk into my muesli. I missed the bowl, but was too shocked to get the dishcloth to wipe it up. Mum took the carton from me. Papa had to say it all again.

'Your Uncle Rasheed said you can stay with them for a while. Your cousin Jamila is getting married. You can be involved in the wedding.'

'But, Papa, they live in Azad Kashmir.'

'Ji.' Papa gave a half-smile. 'It is a surprise I've been working on for some time. I know we've had this ... little problem, but there is no reason why you still can't go.'

I looked at Mum. She didn't seem very happy about the idea.

'What about uni?' I said. 'Will I be back in time? Weddings can take ages.'

Papa frowned. 'It is just for some weeks. I've organised it all.' He said this last bit as though he'd bought me a new car.

Mum was studying him, trying to read between his words. Why the turnaround, I wondered. Why give me a surprise when I had disappointed him so badly? It didn't make sense and I could tell Mum thought so too. Riaz's face rose in my mind: how he had looked so sad for me and held me close. Then I realised: it wasn't a surprise overseas trip; I was being sent away. How long for? As long as it took for the gossip in the community to die down? How many people knew I had 'gone off the rails'?

Papa's smile was almost his old one. He looked at me as if he was about to deliver the best news in the world. 'Your flight leaves tomorrow.'

I stared at him in horror. 'Tomorrow!'

'Hassan, you never said so soon. She'll miss Christmas.' Mum's voice squeezed to a squeak and then she burst into tears. 'She's my daughter too. How can you do this without any discussion?' Then she stopped. 'The elections. Have you thought, Hassan? She won't be safe.'

But Papa wasn't listening to her pain, only the words. 'Of course she'll be safe — she'll be with the family. This is for the best, the best for Ameera. She'll have a nice holiday in Kashmir and see how to live properly the Muslim life. She'll come back a true Muslim.' He looked so pleased with himself.

'Papa, I'm Muslim already.'

'I mean, to follow God's path. You only follow your own.'

That was when I cried. The tears slid silently down my face. How could he say something like that to me?

Mum pulled herself together enough to stick up for me. 'Hassan, that's too harsh. You know she tries hard for you.'

'Then she won't mind going to the family for a few weeks. Stop those tears, both of you. Anyone would think something terrible is happening.' Papa passed me the ticket. 'See? A holiday in Kashmir. Any Australian girl would jump at the chance.'

I checked the ticket before passing it to Mum. The return date was in a month. I breathed out slowly. A month wasn't so bad; I'd be back in plenty of time before uni started. I gave Mum a tentative smile. I would miss her and my friends. All those things we were going to do: movies, shopping, the beach. And Tariq ... but I closed my mind to him.

9

Papa said he wouldn't take me to Kashmir himself. 'You will get to know your relatives better on your own. It will be good for you. Your uncle will meet you at Islamabad airport. You'll go through Singapore — it's the safest and shortest way. Just wait in the airport and wear your dupatta — no one will bother you.' He had thought of everything.

'Will Uncle Rasheed know me?' I asked.

Papa smiled. 'I have sent last year's school picture. He will see the family resemblance.'

Only a day to pack. I went through my wardrobe. It was winter there; I had a thicker shalwar qameez I could take. Mum came and helped me.

'Your father will pay for clothes when you arrive so you won't need to pack much,' she told me.

She looked so sad that I stopped what I was doing and hugged her.

'Are you okay with this, Ameera?' she said suddenly. 'You don't have to go. We could get around it somehow. Leave the house or something.'

I wondered why she was talking like that. How could we go against what Papa wanted? I would be worse than ungrateful. Maybe this trip would help everything get back to normal when I returned. I didn't want anything to interfere with going to uni. *I may even enjoy myself*, I thought. I would see Meena again, though she'd married since I saw her last. And I could brush up on my Urdu, even though Uncle's family were educated and also spoke English.

I pulled away from Mum. 'Why would we leave? Because he made a decision without you?'

Mum faltered. 'It could lead to other things ...'

I knew Mum would never leave. She might argue with Papa but in the end she did what he wanted. I understood, for I was the same.

'I'll go,' I said. 'Papa wants me to. It's just been so long since I was there.' Then I smiled at her. 'I wish you were coming too.'

'I suggested that, but your father says you need to spend time with the family by yourself. If I went, we'd do things together, speak English.' She frowned. 'I guess it is only a month. If that wasn't a return ticket ...'

Since I was leaving the next day I risked a message to Tariq. Leaving 4 pakistan in morning, was all I wrote.

He rang immediately. There were none of his usual preliminaries. 'What's going on?'

'Papa's little surprise — a trip to Azad Kashmir for a month.'

There was a short silence, then, 'Pakistan.'

'Yes.'

'And you want to go?'

I heard the hurt tone in his voice and hesitated. If I hadn't met Tariq I would love to go to Kashmir for a holiday. 'Papa really wants me to go. He's been planning it for ages.'

'I haven't heard from you. You blocked my calls.'

'I'm sorry.' What could I say? I decided to tell him the truth. 'Someone saw me at Samuel Collinses party.'

'I can come and explain.'

He made it sound easy, but he didn't understand what a traditionalist Papa had become.

'No. That's kind, Tariq, but Papa knows you were there too. Best you stay clear of him for a while.'

There was a longer silence. I almost asked if he was still there. Then he said slowly, 'So he's still sending you on a trip. Is it a reward for finishing school?'

'I don't know.'

Again I felt the unease that had come when Papa first told me about his surprise. Why was he rewarding me when I'd disappointed him so badly? I pushed away the feeling of being sent away in disgrace. Maybe he was sorry for what he'd said to me.

'I don't think Azad Kashmir will be the same since the earthquake,' Tariq said. 'Where does your family live?'

'Muzaffarabad.'

'Take your mobile. You can buy a prepaid phone card, and ringing from there is cheap.' He paused. 'I won't ring you in case it makes trouble for you.' There was another silence before he spoke again. 'I'm glad for you. I hope you have a good time.' I felt his words wash over me, warm and cleansing. 'But,' his voice quietened and I had to strain to hear, 'I will miss you, Ameera.'

His voice caught on my name and I knew he still cared. What had I been thinking of, not ringing him when I needed him the most?

I echoed his words: 'I'll miss you too.'

I should have said that I wouldn't ring him again; that if Papa knew about this call I wouldn't be getting a trip. But I couldn't say it. He hung up while I sat with the phone warm in my hands.

Mum came in when I was transferring my shampoo and conditioner into travel bottles. I'd already packed sanitary items that I mightn't find in Muzaffarabad.

'You can't take any liquids into the cabin with you,' she said. 'Terrorism restrictions.' She slipped me some money. 'Your father said he's sent money to your uncle for your keep, but you might not see it. This is in case you need anything personal.'

'Mum, you're a treasure.'

We stood leaning against each other. 'What are they like?' I asked. 'I can't remember them much, except Meena.'

Mum thought for a minute. 'Your uncle's an older version of your father. Your Aunt Khushida's quite a bit younger than Rasheed — you'll be able to talk to her. Then there's your Aunt Bibi, your father's big sister. He is very fond of her — she should be kind to you.'

'I don't know what I'd do without you,' I said, giving her a hug. 'What if Papa had married someone like Raniya's mother? I'd have no one to talk to.'

Mum's tone was dry as she answered. 'If he had married someone like her, he might not be acting like this now.' She frowned and looked out the window.

Raniya had said that too; was it true? Raniya's parents were both practising Muslims but Raniya was allowed to make her own decisions. She just happened to make the right ones. Perhaps that was the result of growing up with two parents with the same faith and ideals.

'Mum, you love Papa, don't you?'

She didn't hesitate. 'Yes. I always have.'

'But you think he's changed?'

Mum sat heavily on the bed. 'I don't know what's happened. When I met him he was so easy-going. He said he'd respect my faith, though our children must be brought up Muslim. I accepted that. It didn't seem so different at the time. We both believed in one God, we had the same kind of morality and ideas about the world. He kept his word, but I didn't realise how traditional he was underneath. His father had traditional ideals and wanted the women in his family to keep purdah.' She sighed. 'This last year Hassan's not been himself at all. He'd hate to think he's growing like his father. Many men change with added responsibility, go through some sort of mid-life crisis, but it seems more than that.' She paused. 'Sameena Yusuf told me that it can be difficult for traditional men in a Western culture. It gets to them after a while.'

'Can you talk to him about it?'

Mum shook her head. 'He won't talk, and won't go to a counsellor. He doesn't think he has a problem. Still, I feel he's under some sort of stress. It's not the business — he says that's going well. I don't know what it is.' She turned to me. 'Even though he's difficult at times, he does love you and wants what's best for you.' She frowned again. 'It's just that we think so differently now about what's best for you children.'

I sat quietly. I thought I knew the reason for my father's stress. It was me. He'd changed when I went into Year 11, as if he'd just realised he had to bring me up properly and how hard it was to do that in Australia. Maybe if I went away for a while, to Kashmir, where I'd be amongst his family, he could relax. Though I didn't think he would totally relax until I was safely married. And that wouldn't happen for years. First there was university.

PART 2
The Girl in the Mirror

10

Maryam came with us to the airport. After I hugged her, she gave me a small package to open on the plane. Her eyes were curious as I took it. Perhaps she was wondering why Papa had decided to send me overseas so suddenly. I smiled as I accepted the package, thinking how Mum would find a framed picture of me under her pillow later.

'Have some puri halva for me in Muzaffarabad,' Maryam said. 'And jellabies.'

'I will.'

We were saying silly things. I couldn't believe how nervous I was. It was the first time I had gone anywhere alone. My whole life I had been almost cloistered, except for school, and here I was being shipped ten thousand kilometres by myself.

When we checked in, Papa ordered halal food for me on the plane and even asked for the stewards to be told I was travelling unaccompanied.

'I'm seventeen,' I hissed at him as the check-in attendant tied a label to my handbag.

Papa seemed happy, almost his old self as he hugged me. 'You will have a nice time, beti. You will thank me for this trip — it will be the making of you, the trip of a lifetime.'

Mum and I stared at him. How could a trip to an earthquake-ravaged area be the trip of a lifetime? Maybe he meant that in Azad Kashmir I would get to see life in all its rawness and suffering. No doubt that would be maturing. He often said life was too easy in Australia.

Riaz hugged me goodbye and whispered in my ear, 'Remember: if a month is too long let us know. You don't have to put up with something you don't want.'

I stood back and nodded at him, amazed at how he had changed so much in the last week.

I hugged Mum the longest. People were filing through the gate when I finally let go. 'Keep in contact,' she said quickly when Papa pulled me away from her. For a moment she looked frightened.

'I'll be okay, Mum.' I waved, but then the line pushed me forward and I couldn't see her any more.

I found my seat inside the plane; it was near the stewards' station with all the unaccompanied kids. A Chinese girl said, 'Are you helping to look after us?'

I let her think that, and all the way to Singapore I took kids to the toilet and the cockpit, and ripped open their refresher towels. Good thing Papa had pre-ordered my meal, for all the kids had hamburgers with bacon. I would have gone hungry.

Maryam's package made a bump in my handbag and I took out and unwrapped it. How nice of her to give

72

me a gift when I was only going on a holiday. Then my hands stilled. It wasn't from Maryam. There was a note:

Piari Ameera, you are the moon and I am but an unworthy star daring to shine in your glory. I made this for you to wear, and one day I hope to exchange it for gold. Tariq

It was a necklace of wooden and ceramic beads, blue and purple. How sweet was that? I tied it around my neck. His reference to gold thrilled me. I knew his intentions now: he wanted to marry me. I would persuade Papa to accept Tariq when I was older. Papa loved me; surely he would want the best for me and what made me happiest? I sat staring out the window. Tariq and I were kindred spirits; it was as if we experienced the world with the same soul. I didn't have to touch him to know he felt the same.

Singapore airport was clean and ordered. I had five hours to wait there before my flight to Islamabad. Papa had booked my backpack straight through. I sat near a Pakistani family and hoped people would think I was with them. It didn't stop a young man, about Tariq's age, from approaching me. He took a seat nearby.

'Where are you going?' he asked.

'Azad Kashmir.' I wasn't sure if I should be talking to him. He looked Pakistani and should have known better.

'Would you like coffee?' he said.

I repeated Papa's instructions: 'You need to ask my father.'

The young man realised his mistake. 'I'm sorry, I include your father as well. It's just that you look so like a Bollywood actress, I didn't think. Please excuse me.' And he abruptly left.

I sat bemused. A Bollywood actress? That was a modern metaphor for a beautiful girl. Wouldn't Riaz laugh? I was fairer than most Pakistanis because of Mum. Papa's skin wasn't very dark either: something to do with being a Kashmiri with Pushtun ancestors. And my hair was dark brown, not almost-black like Maryam's and Tariq's. Fair skin and brown hair adds up to beauty in Pakistan.

Eventually, I was back on a plane and drawing closer to Pakistan by the hour. I was also becoming more nervous. What if I didn't recognise Uncle Rasheed and he missed me? What would I do alone in a strange country? And my backpack: what if it didn't arrive? *Stop worrying*, I told myself. Pakistan was the land of my father's ancestors. At least I'd look like I belonged.

I had dual citizenship and two passports, so when I arrived in Islamabad I joined the Pakistani line. The man behind the counter appeared bored but as he checked me through his camera lens, he said, 'Khushumderd, welcome home,' and smiled politely.

'Shukriya, thank you.' He unsettled me for I hadn't come home.

I followed a line to pick up my bag, and then went to an exit. I held my breath, waited for a family to walk through and tagged along with them. 'Don't advertise you are travelling alone,' Papa had said. His instructions were seared into my brain.

Outside I was met by the noise of traffic and the cool, sharp smell of spices and drains. Even though it was late at night, there were so many people — mainly men — waiting to claim their relatives. How would I find Uncle? Instantly my excitement dissipated; here I was visiting the land of my ancestors and all I felt was fear. I followed the line of travellers, trying not to look any men in the eyes yet searching for Uncle. I saw a man holding up a card with something written in Urdu. Perhaps Uncle would do that too, but I couldn't read Urdu. Some cards were in English and I scanned as many as I could as I walked. Then I noticed a man who looked like Papa. He had a grey beard and his card was held high. 'Welcome Ameera Hassan' was written in English capitals. I was so relieved I could have hugged him.

'Uncle Rasheed?'

His eyes widened. 'Ameera? But you've grown so ... so ...' Then he remembered his manners and smiled. 'Photos never tell the full story, beti.' He called me 'daughter', as Papa did, and I felt a calmness steal over me.

He took my backpack, slung it over his shoulder and led me to his car. Porters asked to help and beggars thrust their hands in my face, but Uncle waved them away.

When we got to the car, it looked like a wreck; the Australian police would have ordered it off the road. I wasn't sure whether it was safe to get in, and hovered by the front door, but an old beggar kept pestering me for money. 'Muaf karo, forgive me,' I said. What was I supposed to do? I didn't have any local currency yet.

Uncle Rasheed slipped the beggar some money. The man called down Allah's blessings on us and melted into the night.

'Get into the back, beti,' Uncle said, and opened the door for me. Just as well, for it stuck and he had to thump it to release the catch. Just as I slipped into the lumpy back seat, a young man hurried over, yanked open the front door, jumped in and slammed it shut. The little car rocked. My uncle stared at him as if he was counting to ten. I thought he'd tell him off, but all he said was, 'Haider, this is your cousin. Say hello.'

Haider barely turned his head, only enough for me to see his beardless features, a hooked nose like Papa's, and his skin just a shade darker than mine. I heard a grunt.

I hoped my other cousins were friendlier.

II

When we arrived at my uncle's house, Haider slunk away. I was tired but Aunty Khushida had stayed awake to welcome me. I had to drink chai and eat cake that she'd bought especially. I don't like cakes, even though I make them, but politeness decreed I had to eat it. She looked gratified at my every bite. Then she brought out a jumper and a shawl.

'I made this sweater for you, Ameera. It is very cold here this time of year.'

The jumper was lilac and tight-fitting, not unlike what was available at home in winter.

'Thank you, Aunty ji.'

'The shawl comes from our shop in the bazaar. You will never find such a warm one in Australia.'

I fingered the wool. Papa had told me he'd sent gifts already to Uncle and Aunty for having me but I still wished I'd had time to buy something for them from Australia.

It was 3 a.m. before I crawled into bed in the same room as my cousin Jamila, but the Azan, the call to prayer, woke me early. Allahu Akbar, God is Great. That was my cue to get up and pray but I was never good at the pre-dawn prayer. The voice droned on and I must have dozed off, for the next sound I heard was the thump of spices being pounded. The aroma of freshly ground coriander and cumin wafted into my room.

There were other sounds too: a giggling voice outside my door, an annoyed whisper, a knock, more giggling, more telling off. It was so warm under the heavy cotton quilt but I thought it was time I got up and put my younger cousins out of their misery. There was a door from my bedroom into the bathroom. There was a second door inside the bathroom and I guessed it was between the bedrooms. I negotiated the squat toilet, quickly washed and dressed, put on my new jumper and shawl, and braved the cold outside. A veranda with blinds opened into a courtyard and a high wall enclosed the whole area. No one was there. I hugged the shawl around me. There had been damage to the cement work of the house: huge cracks snaked across the tops of the walls.

Then I heard a squeal, which was abruptly cut off, and I saw a girl of about nine peeking at me, her hand over the bottom part of her face. 'Hello,' I said, and smiled. She ran back into a room. A boy came out immediately and grinned at me. If I could have squeezed Riaz into a thirteen-year-old's body he would have looked like this.

'What's your name?' I asked, though I knew.

'Asher.' He stood up straighter. 'Are you our Cousin Ameera?'

'Yes.'

He came closer and shook my hand. This wasn't something many men did in Pakistan so I knew he was trying to make me feel at home.

'Do you see many kangaroos?' he asked, showing off his clipped English.

'Not really. They're in the wild.'

'If you went driving in the countryside you would see one?'

I nodded. 'Once we saw one jumping across the road at night.'

'How high do they jump?'

'High enough to clear a car or a fence.'

He was impressed. 'Please come. Eat some breakfast. I have been helping. Zeba too.'

I smiled at him. 'Your sister?'

'My youngest sister. Then there is Jamila — she is nineteen and has finished college — and Meena, but she's old and married. She even has a baby now. It cries all the time.'

'I hope I meet them all soon.'

'Yes, but Jamila is unhappy. It is to do with the wedding.' He used the Urdu word: 'shadi'.

'Asher!' My aunt rushed out of a room. 'There you are and you have found Ameera.'

'Yes, Ummie ji, and she has seen a kangaroo.'

'Of course she has, silly boy — she lives in Australia.'

Asher turned and winked at me. He was certainly the opposite of Haider.

'You look like Meena,' Asher informed me on the way into a family room furnished with lots of couches.

'Do I? That sounds like a compliment, thank you.'

Asher gave me a conspiring smile.

'Ameera, sit here. You are our guest,' Aunty Khushida said.

She fluttered around me with a pot of chai. Asher had obviously been given the job of being nice to me; he sat by me. Zeba stood apart with her head half-lowered but I knew she was aware of my every move. I smiled in her direction but it did no good. Now that I was awake it seemed her giggles had dried up.

I tried to tell Aunty I could get my own breakfast. 'Papa said I should think of your family as my own.'

For a moment she frowned. 'Hahn ji. You are our daughter while you are here, but you must settle first. You can help later on, Inshallah.'

An older girl walked in with a basket of chapattis and a plate of fried eggs. I looked with interest at her — she must be Jamila. The glance she flashed at me and then her mother was one of pure annoyance. My smile faded.

'This is Ameera,' Aunty Khushida said unnecessarily.

'Go and get the plate,' Jamila said crossly to Zeba.

Zeba ran into the kitchen and returned with a warm plate held in a tea towel. She set it on the table and regarded me openly for the first time. Then she came and sat on the other side of me. I smiled at both of them: Zeba and Asher, the perfect hospitable pair. Pity Jamila and Haider had grown out of being polite.

I ate under the watchful gaze of my two youngest cousins while Aunty and Jamila worked in the kitchen. I scooped up the runny egg with pieces of the flatbread. Asher offered me salt and pepper, but I refused the pepper; there was enough chilli on the eggs already.

Afterwards they took me on a tour of the house.

'This is the mejalis,' Asher said. 'It has a door to the lane and is where Abu meets with his friends. He sleeps here with Haider and me, but sometimes Zeba can sleep with Haider and me too.'

'Where do you sleep usually?' I asked Zeba.

She spoke to me for the first time, in Urdu. 'With Ummie ji. She has a big soft bed.'

'When Meena was home, she and Jamila slept in the room you are in. If we have many guests Jamila sleeps in the lounge room,' Asher explained. He took me further around the courtyard and pushed open a door. 'We had this room but the earthquake made it dangerous. We lost another room too.'

There were blocks of cement jutting out into the space where the 'lost' room had been. With the sunken cement, plaster falling off the walls and huge cracks, it looked like a demolition site.

'We are not allowed to go inside,' Zeba added when she saw Asher's foot on the threshold.

'Is this the only damage you had?' I asked. 'You were lucky. You still have a nice house.'

Papa had said his brother was well-off and had a good carpet business in Muzaffarabad, yet their house wasn't as big as ours in Adelaide.

Asher and Zeba took me into the garden. On that side of the house, the garden wall had fallen away and the earth had slid down an embankment. Yet I heard the sound of running water. We walked through an archway and into a miniature Persian garden, secluded on two sides by walls and a row of cedar trees on the third side.

A water channel ran east to west, and a shorter one from north to south. A fountain circulated the water. Blue tiles at the bottom of the pool around it made the water appear deeper. At one end of the longest channel was a bench with a pavilion over it. I gazed around in awe: somebody was a creative gardener.

'Ummie lost her roses,' Zeba said. 'They just disappeared, goom gea. Along with the wall.' She flung her hands up in the air as if a bird had flown from her wrist.

'Truly?'

'Mmm.' She nodded solemnly. 'Now the garden is ruined.'

'Baba's hut was destroyed too,' Asher added. 'He is the chowkidar. He has to sleep in a tent now, but he gets a good view of any robbers from up there.'

I followed his gaze to the roof and saw a tent near a satellite dish.

'Doesn't he get cold?' I asked.

'He lights a fire on the roof, but sometimes Abu lets him sleep in the courtyard. It's just until we can get another hut built.'

'Baba does the gardening too but he has not found Ummie's roses,' Zeba said.

'Because of the earthquake, Dadi jan sleeps in Ummie's room now,' Asher told me.

'Is Dadi jan your grandmother?' I caught my breath. This was my father's mother, the person I was supposed to take after.

'Yes.' Asher stared at me as if he had just worked out something important. 'She's your grandmother too, is she not?'

I nodded. I had forgotten she would be here too. Perhaps she would be able to help me understand more about Papa, tell me stories of his childhood.

'Jamila says Dadi jan talks rubbish, but I don't think so,' Zeba said. 'She just sleeps a lot.'

My heart sank. Was my grandmother suffering from dementia?

Just then we heard a clanging sound. It came from the gate that faced onto the gali, the small lane.

'Come on,' Asher shouted. 'That will be Meena.'

'She has come for chai,' Zeba said.

I wasn't sure I was ready for another cup of Aunty's strong sweet tea so soon, but I was looking forward to seeing my cousin again.

12

Meena was in the courtyard, under the veranda, sitting on a stringed bed with her sleeping baby in her arms. Someone had put coals in an old oil drum and the blinds had been rolled down to keep the heat in.

'Ameera.' She rose, shifted the baby to one arm and hugged me with the other. 'How you have grown. How was your trip? Tell me everything.'

I stared at Meena in relief. Her welcome almost made me cry, it was such a change from Haider's and Jamila's. I sat down next to her, and Asher and Zeba joined us.

'The plane trip was okay,' I said. 'Papa booked me through Singapore —'

'How about the ride up the hill? Did you survive Abu's old Suzuki?'

I grinned. 'I thought I'd die on the mountain. One time Uncle had to back up twice before the car could make the turn.'

Meena laughed. 'I remember that. I bet it was Pindi Point near Murree.' Then her tone changed and became almost guarded as she asked, 'And how was Haider?'

'He never spoke to me.'

She shook her head. 'Haider and Jamila.' She said their names as though they were partners in a childish crime. Then she shrugged off the mood. 'We must go shopping. It is fortunate that I am living in Muzaffarabad and I can help at this happy time.'

I smiled politely, thinking she was referring to Jamila's wedding. She searched my face and must have found it lacking for her smile faded. 'Never mind,' she said. 'We shall have much fun together.'

Zeba spoke up then. 'Can I go shopping too?'

'I'm sure you can, sweetie.' Meena pinched her on the cheek.

'You were the person I remembered the most,' I said to Meena. 'Remember that day you took me for a lassi drink in the bazaar? I loved that.'

'We can do it again. You were such a sweet child, and you have not changed.'

Jamila came out bearing a tray and set out the inevitable pot of chai and cups on a small table in front of us. Did I imagine it or did she put those cups down with stronger force than necessary? I gave her a tentative smile but either she didn't see or she ignored it. She put chilli crisps and a plate of cake on the table too.

'I can help,' I said and stood up.

Meena pulled me down. 'Plenty of time to help. Be a guest for a while longer.'

'Can I hold Gudiya?' Zeba asked.

'Of course.' Meena passed over the baby. She was tightly wrapped and barely stirred as Zeba took her.

It sounded strange, calling a baby a doll. 'Is Gudiya her name?'

'Her real name is Fatima,' Zeba informed me, 'but I like Gudiya better.'

'So do we all.' Meena gave me a wink. 'My husband's mother was called Fatima. There wasn't much I could do about it. Since she died she has become an angel in my husband's eyes.'

'But we call Gudiya what we want, don't we?' Zeba said in Urdu.

Meena's gaze rested on her. 'You can practise your English with Ameera and you will be top of the class.'

All of a sudden Meena started talking about marriage — how good it was for families. Maybe she thought I'd lost my culture in Australia. In an effort to reassure her, I agreed. 'Marriage is a good thing; arranged marriages too.' She smiled at me, looking relieved. Then I added, 'But I want to go to university first, teach for a while, then marry.'

Her smile disappeared and she glared at Aunty Khushida who'd come out with a fresh pot of chai. Aunty kept her head lowered, but I could see her eyebrows furrowed into a frown. She'd obviously heard what I'd said.

'When you get married, Ameera,' Zeba said, 'I want to help with the henna. I can draw good patterns and I won't mess up the dots.'

'Are you coming all the way to my wedding in Australia?' I gave her a playful shake.

Zeba bit her lip. 'But Haider said —'

I didn't get to hear what Haider had said for Aunty

Khushida suddenly took the baby from Zeba. 'Go buy some milk,' she ordered.

'But I went this morning.'

Aunty Khushida pushed her with the palm of her hand. 'Buy some more — we have guests today.'

Zeba knew she was being sent away so the adults could talk, but her turned-down mouth was disappointed rather than sulky. I thought I should go too, let Meena and her mother talk without a guest listening in. I told them I needed to unpack.

As I left the courtyard I heard Meena speaking in Urdu. Her voice was little more than a hiss. 'Ummie, she doesn't know. Why hasn't she been told?'

I wondered what it was that Zeba needed to know.

Jamila was in our room hand-sewing a hem on a dupatta.

'I'll need to get some warmer clothes,' I said to her. 'I can't wear yours for the whole time I'm here.' My effort at a joke fell flat.

She stared at me for a few moments. 'No, we can go to the bazaar this afternoon. There should be a few shops open.'

I felt a sudden relief. This was an overture of friendship, surely? I was concerned about how I'd get on with Jamila, especially as we were sharing a room. We'd never written to each other personally — just the family cards at Eid — and we'd lived very different lives. Yet our fathers were brothers; surely there'd be some spark of familial feeling? Maybe this was the first indication of it. I unpacked my backpack; put my passports, ticket and money under my mattress.

'I could help you choose cloth for your wedding,' I offered.

There was a long silence. I could have kicked myself. This wasn't Australia where Muslim girls were more open. Probably Jamila hadn't even met her husband yet. Yes, that was it, I decided. She looked embarrassed and I resolved not to bring the subject up again.

After lunch — vegetable curry, chapattis, and more strong chai — Meena returned home. She gave me her mobile number before she left. 'Ring me anytime if you want to talk,' she said, then glanced at Aunty Khushida. I saw the meaningful look that flew between them, but couldn't decide what it meant.

Jamila and I walked to the bazaar. Asher and Zeba came too. I followed Jamila's lead and put my shawl over my head. It was so cold I was glad of its warmth, and glad to be walking. The way Aunty Khushida was feeding me I'd be as big as an elephant by the time I went home. Tariq wouldn't recognise me. The sudden lurch in my stomach when I thought of him surprised me and my hand found his necklace under my dupatta. When I got home I would start persuading Papa to give me what I wanted most in the world.

We passed a cement honour roll, the height of a triple-storey building, showing the names of men who had become shaheed, martyred in war. It had been split down the middle.

Asher saw me staring. 'The earthquake did that. Look.' He pointed to the bazaar ahead, its new tin roofs winking in the pale sunlight. 'Most of the bazaar is made of kacha tin shacks; all the real pukka buildings haven't been rebuilt yet.'

All around I could see rubble, half-built houses, tents where buildings should have been, debris that hadn't been removed. Muzaffarabad had been a beautiful city, but part of the mountain had fallen into the river. The city didn't look beautiful now.

'My school's just there,' Zeba said, and drew me over to show me. It was a tent school and looked forlorn, deserted.

'Not many of the schools have been rebuilt,' Jamila said. Her tone sounded bitter.

Before I could ask her about it, Zeba danced in front of me.

'Will you come tomorrow? You could teach English.'

I laughed, but Jamila said, 'You could teach a few days a week. I do.'

'Truly?'

She shrugged. 'So many of the teachers were killed. And twenty thousand children died. Muzaffarabad was called the City of Death.'

'We were in school when it happened,' Asher said. 'At eight minutes to nine. It was Saturday and we were reading. We could hear a noise as loud as a truck driving on the roof except it sounded like it was under the ground.'

'It was scary,' Zeba said.

Jamila glanced at Zeba. 'Zeba didn't go to school that day.'

'I felt sick,' Zeba added.

'It saved her life,' Jamila went on. 'The schools were so badly constructed, they collapsed as soon as the earthquake hit. Just two minutes it took, cement storeys falling onto the next floor below, like houses made from cards. The children did not have a chance.' She glanced at Asher. 'But thanks to God, Asher survived.'

'I was on the top floor as it came down,' Asher said. 'Then I crawled out of a window, just before the roof fell. Allah ka shukr hai.'

Tears welled in my eyes and I thanked God too. Papa had told us about the earthquake when he came back but he hadn't mentioned details like this. I wondered if Asher had nightmares. How long would it take to recover from a trauma like that?

'Haider helped the militants — they gave out food. Then the army came,' Asher said. 'They started digging out the children. They found my friend Saeed. He was still alive.'

He fell quiet and Zeba added, 'Now Saeed has only one arm and one leg. He does not play soccer any more.'

The bazaar was a rabbit warren of tin shacks, with power lines twisted dangerously together overhead. Even though it was cold, the smell of dust and smoke mingled with sweat and curry. Thin white chickens flew up in their cages as we passed. Spices were piled like pyramids of colour in hessian bags. In front of the meat shop I was accosted by children begging. I still didn't have any rupees.

'How come they know I'm the new one?' I said. I asked Jamila if I could change some money.

'The banks are shut today, but that man changes small amounts.' She pointed to a dingy shop.

Asher came with me. I didn't mind, for even though I may have looked like I belonged there, I knew I didn't. Everything was too strange. I spoke English but the money-changer couldn't understand me.

'Your Australian is faster than our English,' Asher said. 'And you use different words. Speak slower.'

I did, but I felt I was treating the poor man like a zombie. I reverted to Urdu, but I didn't feel as confident discussing money in Urdu. What if I misunderstood? But Asher said the amount I received for twenty dollars was fair.

'Do you know where to buy phone cards?' I asked him.

He took me to a small booth facing onto the lane. It sold everything that a deli would: drinks, ice-creams, fruit, and a prepaid Paktel phone card. It cost me six hundred rupees. Now I'd be able to send a message to Tariq.

This time when a beggar asked, I could give a few rupees.

'Do not give too much,' Asher advised, 'or they will tell their friends and you will be swamped.' He grinned at me. 'We learned that word "swamped" in English class. Our teacher said that if we use it, we will sound like natives of England.'

Asher was right about the beggars for by the time Jamila and Zeba found us there were more than before, like ants crawling out of a disturbed nest. 'Baksheesh, baksheesh,' they cried and moaned. The way they drew out the word it sounded like a cat being tortured.

'Baksheesh, gift for Christmas,' one small boy said in broken Urdu, his hand outstretched.

Then I remembered that it was 25 December — with all the travelling I'd lost track of the date. Most of the bazaar was closed today, but for Qaid-e-Azam's birthday, not for Christmas. How did that boy know I'd understand the word 'Christmas'?

'Ignore them,' Jamila said. 'They are just Christian kids. Their parents sweep the streets and clean toilets. If you touch them you will become ill.'

I thought about how different Christmas was at home, the shops gearing up for it months ahead, everyone getting presents, the parties, the lights in the streets. Here there was nothing. A picture of Mum came into my mind, sad at her parents' house because I wasn't there. I bent down to the boy and pulled out a ten-rupee note. How much was that? Just fifty cents?

'Too much,' Jamila snapped, but I'd already done it. I would give no Christmas gifts this year, but maybe I could give this boy a happier day.

13

Aunty Khushida was busy in the kitchen when we returned. I showed her the shalwar qameez Jamila had bought for me. I had offered to pay but Jamila had insisted. 'The money came from your father, do not fuss.' I wondered why they didn't give me Papa's money to spend for myself. Perhaps it was something to do with good hospitality.

Aunty liked the fabric. 'Smart, but warm. Accha, that is good. And a chaddar to match?'

I took out the shawl. It wasn't the dearest pashmina, but good enough for wearing out. Jamila had taken me to the family carpet and shawl shop to buy it. Inside the shop, we'd been able to relax and let our shawls drop to our shoulders. Uncle Rasheed was there, entertaining some men and haggling over prices. Papa had told me that buying a rug could take days in Pakistan. Haider was given the job of serving us and he didn't look enthralled. He hardly said a word to me at first and was short with Jamila. I'd seen through to a room behind the shop where boys were seated at a loom. 'So you make carpets here too?' I asked Jamila. 'Do the boys do it after school?'

Jamila glanced at Haider and he shut the door to the back room, then began pulling shawls off shelves for me to see. 'Our shawls are made from pashmina combed from the Changra mountain goat,' he told me, suddenly finding his voice. 'The Gujjars herd them. It is like silk, dekho, see.' He spoke in Urdu. 'The Moghuls used this in their carpets.' He showed me another shawl. 'This one is made from shahtoosh. It is the king of wool and comes from the hair of the antelope from Tibet. From here.' He pointed to his chest and grinned at me. It didn't seem like a cousinly smile and I looked away. He shoved the shawl under my nose. 'You could hatch a pigeon egg in this.' Jamila had said it was too expensive and directed me to the pashmina ones.

Now my aunt nodded her approval and turned back to the bench.

'Can I help?' I tried to look unmoveable as I packed my new outfit back into its brown paper bag.

Aunty sighed. 'Very well. You can chop the onions.'

I stripped off the skins and started chopping on the wooden bench. Aunty Khushida was soon breathing over my shoulder. 'Finer than that, child. The curry will stick in their throats.'

Maybe that was why our curries were never as good as Mrs Yusuf's, I thought. Aunty went back to shaping chapatti dough into rounds with her palms and flapping them back and forth in the air.

'So how is your mother? Such a sweet girl.' She sounded dismissive.

I thought of Mum at the mosque, sitting by herself. She was so out of the loop in the community at home, and I was beginning to feel like that here.

'She's fine.' I remembered the frightened look on her face as Papa pulled me away to join the boarding queue and corrected myself. 'She's well.'

'She was happy about you coming to us?'

The chapatti bashing had ceased and I looked up to find Aunty holding a piece of dough in midair. She was also watching me intently. I tried not to show how unnerved I felt: her eyes were pinning me to the wall.

'Yes. She wished she could come too,' I said. I hoped Papa hadn't told them why he'd sent me here. But if he had, that could account for Jamila's coolness towards me and all these questions.

Aunty Khushida seemed satisfied. 'Accha. Can you speak Urdu?'

'Of course. Papa taught me. I don't catch the meaning of jokes though, or understand deep discussions.'

Aunty nodded and pressed out another piece of dough with her fingers. Then she glanced at the onions I'd finished. 'So you do not cook Pakistani food at home?'

'We do, but I'm sure it's not as tasty as yours will be tonight.'

She smiled at me, the nicest one she'd given so far though it still seemed forced. 'We had better get you started quick-smart. Here, take this dough and slap it from side to side like this.'

I'd seen Raniya's mother and Mrs Yusuf making chapattis but Mum had never mastered the skill. She said you had to be born with a lump of chapatti dough in your hands.

'Not like that, like this.' Aunty showed me again. 'It is in the wrist. Relax your wrist.'

For the next half-hour I was harangued in the nicest way about my lack of culinary skills. Aunty didn't say it but I could tell she was thinking that even a child could do this, why couldn't I? With a prickling behind my eyes I realised I was probably the only seventeen-year-old girl in Pakistan who couldn't make the staple food.

'At home we buy naan from the local tandoor restaurant,' I said.

'We cannot do that here. What an expense.'

It was strange to talk about naan as an expense when she was putting real saffron in the rice. The pinch she used would have cost Mum ten dollars.

I tried again. 'I can cook Australian food. I can treat you to that anytime you want.'

Aunty looked unconvinced, and on second thoughts, after looking around the kitchen, so was I. The oven was used for storage. This was definitely a curry kitchen.

'I can make cakes,' I added lamely, my eye on the cereal boxes in the oven.

'We can buy them at the local bakery.' Then Aunty smiled. 'Come on, child, see if you can cook this chapatti. Place it on the tava like this — use the tea towel to press it here, and here. It must not burn. Haider does not like his bread burnt.'

Haider could go to hell for all I cared, but I did my best with Aunty Khushida hovering close by. Encouragement was not her forte.

Just then Jamila came in carrying folded tea towels. 'What is she doing?' she said quickly in Urdu. Whether she meant to or not, she effectively cut me out of their conversation.

'What does it look like?' Aunty Khushida gave her a sharp look.

Jamila came closer to inspect my work. 'We can't serve this one. Abu will think Zeba did it.'

'Even Zeba has to learn,' Aunty reminded her.

Jamila stared at me as if I had a disability. Her gaze gave me a sinking feeling in my stomach and I wondered why my cooking skills mattered so much. I was only a visitor who had offered to help.

I heard the gate open and realised the men had arrived home. Jamila prepared a tray of food for the men's room. She picked out the best chapattis that Aunty had made, with a glance at me that could have scorched them, and added covered bowls of chicken curry, orange-coloured saffron rice, raita and a little dish of mango chutney.

'The chicken curry is because it is the birthday of Qaid-e-Azam,' Aunty said. 'Remember he is the founder of Pakistan?'

I nodded, thinking about who else's birthday it was and what Mum would be doing today.

Jamila took the tray to the mejalis and Asher carried the plates and cutlery. He was old enough to eat with his father and Haider. Maybe if I wasn't there, the family would have eaten together. By the look on Jamila's face, this was one more job she had to do because of me.

We women sat around a tablecloth on the floor in the lounge. 'I like eating this way,' Zeba said.

The treat for me at dinner was to meet Dadi jan, my grandmother. She must have been asleep all afternoon for she shuffled out of her room with Jamila's help and sank onto the couch. She looked too old to still be alive, so wrinkled and tiny like a bird, with black-rimmed glasses. Everyone said I looked like her but I couldn't see any resemblance. She looked eighty; not like my other grandmother who still taught pottery and had exhibitions.

Jamila put a small tray on her lap holding a bowl of curry and rice and a spoon, then said in an undertone to me, 'Not everything she says makes sense so if you do not understand just nod.'

When Dadi jan was settled she beckoned me over. I went to kneel in front of her and touched her feet the way Papa had shown me; she laid her hand on my head in blessing. 'You are Ameera,' she said, as if she was telling me something new. 'It is a beautiful name — it means "leader".'

Papa had said it meant princess but I supposed that was the same. I smiled at her.

'You have grown into your name very well,' she said after scrutinising my face. I wondered what she meant; I didn't have any leadership qualities. No one at school did anything because I did it first. But Dadi jan was nodding at something she hadn't said. 'Ah, beti, you have such a look of my family. How is your father?' She spoke in Urdu and mostly I understood her.

'He is well, Dadi jan.' I spoke in Urdu too. 'The carpet business is good. He is …' I stopped; I couldn't say what Papa had been like the last year. 'He's fine.' It seemed I was destined to make lame, untrue statements whenever anyone asked about my life in Australia.

Dadi jan's birdlike eyes watched me for a moment and I thought Jamila's judgement of our grandmother's mental capabilities was wrong. She looked very alert to me despite those clumsy-looking glasses. She even seemed like someone I might be able to confide in. Then her next words killed that hope.

'So you have come all the way from Australia to live with us now. We are blessed indeed. I have never been so happy, not since before your father left. Now he has sent a part of himself to me. He is a good son.'

I glanced at Jamila, who was putting plates and cutlery on the tablecloth. She raised her eyebrows at me as if to say, 'I told you.'

Aunty Khushida said, 'Now, Mother, do not bore Ameera.'

Dadi jan looked annoyed; I saw the flash in her eyes before she quickly disguised it. I smiled, showing I wasn't bored. Then Zeba brought over a picture.

'Dadi jan, look. I have made you a drawing.'

'Hahn ji, child, it is very pretty.' She spoke lucidly to Zeba; she could tell it was a picture of me. 'Hassan should have come with you, Ameera. Such an important time and he has left it all to Rasheed.'

She dug her spoon into her curry while I wondered what she meant. I guessed this was one of Jamila's nodding moments and I smiled again.

'And your mother? She is well?' Dadi jan asked.

'Yes. She works as an English teacher. She teaches people who come from other countries.' I was annoyed I couldn't remember the word for 'migrants'.

'And Riaz? Is he behaving himself?'

I paused. It sounded as though my grandmother knew everything about our family.

'He is fine, but he doesn't go to Friday prayers much.' That was a safer response than the truth; that he didn't go at all and drank in nightclubs instead.

She leaned forward. 'Are you happy here, child?'

I hesitated slightly, then nodded. 'I am happy to be here for a holiday, Dadi jan.'

She stared at me while she chewed. 'Are you now?' she finally said.

'Yes.'

'You must come and talk to me one afternoon. I get lonely sitting by myself when Zeba is at school.'

Jamila said, 'Ameera may help me at Zeba's school, Dadi jan.'

'Very well, come when you can, Inshallah.' My grandmother leaned across her tray and took my face in her hands. It felt as if she was searching more than my features. 'Talk to me one day.' Her voice was low and I had to strain to hear her over Zeba's chattering to Aunty behind me.

Aunty called to me. 'Ameera, come eat, the food will be cold.'

After dinner Uncle Rasheed came in. 'How was your first day with us, beti?'

'Good, thank you, Uncle ji.'

Actually I didn't think I could remember a longer day. I was surprised I hadn't fallen asleep into my curry; Aunty's chai must have kept me awake. *At this rate*, I thought, *the month will feel like a year*. I had a sudden burst of longing for Mum. Was she thinking of me? At least Uncle Rasheed reminded me of Papa and that helped.

'If there is anything you need, then you must ask me or your aunt,' he told me. There was no talk of giving me money of my own and I didn't know how to broach the subject.

'Would you like to ring your father?' he asked.

'Yes, please.' Then I looked at my watch: 9 p.m. 'Won't it be too late there?'

He laughed. 'Not too late for Hassan. I often ring him after dinner. Try and see.'

Uncle Rasheed, Aunty Khushida, Zeba and Asher all listened while I dialled the number to Australia. Jamila stopped washing the dishes and came to hover in the doorway once I had connected. After ten rings Papa answered.

'Papa, I'm sorry to wake you, but Uncle Rasheed said it would be fine to let you know I arrived safely.'

'Accha, beti. It is good to hear your voice.'

No wonder my relatives were hanging around: they had a conference speaker on the phone. Papa's voice boomed into the lounge room. 'Are you having a good time?'

'Yes.' What else could I say? 'Jamila and I went to the bazaar and bought an outfit.'

'I hope you enjoy your stay. It will make me happy.'

'Papa, is Mum awake?'

He hesitated. 'No, she went to bed hours ago.'

'Could you wake her?'

I had an irrational urge to hear her voice; that if I didn't, something terrible would happen.

'That's not very thoughtful, beti. Ring in the morning.'

Mum wouldn't have minded being woken to speak to me, but I couldn't argue with all the rellies listening. 'Is she okay?' I said instead.

'Of course, why shouldn't she be?'

'Can you say —' I stopped. I'd been about to say 'Happy Christmas' but that wouldn't go down well in the present company. 'Could you tell her I was thinking about her today?' I wanted to know if she'd found the gift I'd left under her pillow.

'Zarur, of course, beti.' Papa was using more Urdu words than usual; I guessed he knew about the conference speaker.

Uncle Rasheed took the receiver from me and told Papa about some tribal rugs he had seen. I waited for him to finish, and then he hung up.

'I hadn't said goodbye, Uncle.'

'I thought you had, sorry, beti. There will be other times.'

A glance passed between him and my aunt, and suddenly I felt so tired I couldn't think a straight sentence, let alone speak one. I was horrified to find my eyes filling with tears.

'Best you go to bed now.' It was Aunty Khushida who tucked me in and when she left I hadn't even the energy to message Tariq.

14

The next morning I slept in again after being woken before dawn by the Azan. My tiredness must have been jetlag, and fortunately Aunty Khushida seemed to understand for no one dragged me out of bed. The children had already gone to school when I got up, but Jamila was still in the house: I could hear the thump of the mortar and pestle. I took my mobile and the Paktel card into the bathroom, inserted the card, then rang the prescribed number and followed the prompts. I rang home first, but Mum must have gone out: the phone rang through to the message bank. I blinked, forcing the tears back, and left a message for her and Papa. I hoped my voice sounded steady.

Now for Tariq. I keyed in a message that I had arrived safely and missed him; then pressed the send button. The screen went blank and the word 'Error' flashed. I tried again, and again. How would I contact him if the mobile never worked? Maybe the card was only for land lines. I couldn't ring him on the family phone, and if I went to a shop to ring it could get back to Uncle Rasheed. It was too risky. I washed myself and went back to my room to pray.

When I emerged Aunty seemed relieved to see me. 'Accha,' she said. 'Did you sleep well?' She hardly waited for my nod. 'There is much to do. Your father's sister, Bibi, and your Uncle Iqbal are coming for dinner tonight. We shall eat together and use the table. Meena will come too.'

'Will any of Aunt Bibi's children come?' I was looking forward to seeing more of my cousins if they were like Meena.

Aunty Khushida's face puckered in annoyance. I never seemed to say the right thing. 'Of course not.'

Dadi jan was sitting on a low stool peeling garlic. 'Come here, child,' she said. I kneeled in front of her and she laid her hand on my head. 'How are you?'

'I'm fine, Dadi jan. I had a good sleep.'

I thought I heard a snort from Jamila. She was picking stones out of a tray of rice — another thing we didn't have to do in Australia. Aunty was rolling chapatti dough; I wasn't asked to help her this time. Then I noticed the oven was open and everything had been taken out.

Aunty saw me staring. 'This would be a good time for you to be making an Australian cake.'

'Why?'

She stopped rolling and frowned at me.

'I mean, I'd love to make one. You think Uncle Iqbal and Aunty Bibi would like one? That's great,' I babbled, afraid I was sounding unhelpful.

Aunty put a bowl on the bench. 'Tell me what you need. If we are missing an item, Baba ji can get it.'

'Flour, baking powder, eggs, milk, sugar. What flavour would you like?'

'They like spice ones best,' she said after a moment's thought.

'Then ground cinnamon, cloves, a little ginger and nutmeg.'

Aunty's face cleared. 'Ji, we have all that. You can start now.'

Once the cake was in the oven I was given the split peas to take outside and clean. This involved picking out little stones and bits of grass and dirt. It was out in the courtyard that Haider found me. He started talking straightaway. I half-smiled at him; he was my cousin, after all, even though the family practised segregation.

'So, Cousin Ameera.' He sat next to me, quite close. Was he supposed to do that? 'You are a good actress.'

'Excuse me?'

'I know what you Australian girls are like. You might be able to fool my parents, but you can't fool me.'

My smile faded. Papa must have told them why I'd been sent here after all. 'What do you mean?'

He put his hand on my arm; I shook it off. 'How dare you,' I said. 'I'm a guest in your home. I'm your sister while I'm here.'

His eyes sparked at the word 'sister', then his gaze swept from my shoes back up to my eyes. That look made me draw my shawl closer around me. 'You,' he paused for emphasis, 'are not my sister. Your father never said how beautiful you are.'

His voice had a tone I didn't like and I stood abruptly. The tray of peas slid to the ground.

'Take care,' he went on. 'Your beauty is razor sharp, but I don't cut easily.'

He used the Urdu word for sharp, 'tez', and I had no idea what he was talking about. 'How dare you talk to me about beauty? Don't you care that I am Muslim? Where is your respect?'

He smiled slowly. 'But you're not pukki, are you? You're half-Christian and we all know what Christian girls are like. You girls do just what you want.'

Pure Maryam sprang to my mind. 'Christian girls are not like you are insinuating,' I said. 'Where did you get such a disgusting idea?'

'I see the DVDs from your country. If what they allow actresses to do is anything to go by, imagine what you all must be like in real life — like mangoes on a tree, ripe for picking.'

'I'm not like that and if you talk to me like this again, I'll tell your father.'

Haider laughed. 'And who do you think he will believe? A half-cooked Christian girl or his pride and heir?' He looked at me through his long eyelashes. 'Why have you come here alone?'

I wished Riaz or Tariq were there. Or even Papa.

'You're my cousin.' I said 'cousin' in the same way I'd say 'brother', hoping he'd leave me alone.

He smirked: 'Yes, cousin, but this isn't Australia. In Pakistan, cousins marry. You know that, don't you?'

Yes, I knew, but Mum didn't like the custom of cousins marrying. She thought it was incestuous and her family thought so too.

'Tell my father,' Haider went on. 'The most honourable thing for me to do would be to marry you.'

'Marry you?' Surely he didn't think I'd want to marry him.

I searched for a way to leave the courtyard without any more of a scene. I hoped none of this exchange had been overheard. I was about to pick up the tray of split peas and salvage what I could when his tone gentled.

'You can be coy if you like, but you can't tell me you don't know why you're here.' Then he stared at me as though some realisation had just come to him. 'So, you really do think you are here for a holiday?' He licked his lips. 'Remember this then: you could have me. Or you might wish you had.'

It was as if he knew all about me and Tariq. But if he did, surely he wouldn't pass up the chance to throw it in my face?

I'd had enough. I kneeled to pick up the split peas, and when I stood up he had gone.

15

That afternoon, when most of the work was done and Aunty was resting and Jamila had gone to the school, I took my phone outside. It would be dinnertime at home and I needed to speak to Papa.

It was Riaz who answered. 'Ames, we miss you around here. How ya doing?'

'I'm okay. How's Mum?'

'She's staying at Grandpa's and Gran's.'

'For Christmas?'

He paused. 'Yeah, I'm going over tomorrow.'

I thought of them all at the beach without me. Having barbecues, playing French cricket on the sand, eating ice-cream cones on the jetty. Mum always took halal meat for me and I could wear what I wanted. I missed Uncle Richard's hugs and teasing too. He was such a stirrer, but he never let my faith make a difference to him. I pulled my shawl tight around me.

'Can you give her my love?' I said. 'I don't know why she hasn't rung.' I couldn't stop my uneasiness pouring out. 'Haider isn't as nice as you.'

'Oh, really?' There was an edge to Riaz's voice but I wanted to tell Papa.

'Is Papa there?' I asked.

'Sure, and Ames ...'

'Yes?'

'Keep in contact.'

I smiled at his new protectiveness. 'Okay.'

He put Papa on. 'Hello, beti. Are you settling in?'

'Papa, I have to tell you something.'

His voice grew guarded. 'What is it, beti?'

'Haider touched me.'

Papa sighed. 'I told them to treat you like a daughter and sister. Riaz touches you.'

'That's different.'

'I'm sure he's just being brotherly.'

'Can't you say something to Uncle Rasheed?'

'Don't worry. Wait till you meet Bibi's eldest son. I know him better than Haider.'

Why was he so relaxed about this? He'd go ballistic if I said a boy had touched me in Australia.

'Papa, do they know why you sent me here?'

There was a silence, then, 'What do you mean, beti? I sent you on a trip to see the family. Maybe I'll send Riaz next — he can learn more about the carpet business.'

How could he have forgotten the Collinses party? His anger?

'Papa, Jamila's not happy, not like a bride should be.'

'She'll get over it.' It sounded as though he knew something I didn't.

'Get over what? Isn't she getting married any more?'

Maybe that's what the frowns and dark looks were about, I thought. Maybe her marriage had fallen through.

'I don't know for sure, but these things happen sometimes. Perhaps you can be a good friend to your cousin.'

'I'll try, Papa.'

'I'll say hello to your mother for you when she comes home from work. Bye now, beti.'

It wasn't until after I'd pressed the end button that I remembered what Riaz had said: that Mum was staying at Grandpa's and Gran's. Why did Papa say she was coming home after work?

'Ameera?'

I swung around. Asher. 'You're home.' I quickly flipped my mobile shut. How much had he heard?

'I've been home for ages,' he said, and watched me put my mobile in the pocket of my qameez. 'Have you heard? Aunt Bibi and Uncle Iqbal are coming for dinner.'

'Yes, I've made a cake.'

I tried to calm down. Surely Asher was too young to wonder why I wasn't using the family phone.

He grinned. 'They will like that. Jamila will not have a chance.'

'Why won't Jamila have a chance? She's helped make chapattis and curry.'

Asher was watching me. I thought I understood that furtiveness in his eyes: he didn't know what to say.

'Come on, tell me. What's our cooking got to do with anything?'

Very slowly, he said, 'When a family chooses a bride, they like to eat the girl's food so they know they won't be poisoned for the rest of their lives.'

So maybe Jamila's marriage wasn't arranged yet, I thought. Papa just thought it had been. Maybe her bad mood was due to nervousness. I nodded slowly at Asher, glad I'd worked it out at last. 'So who is the boy they want a bride for?'

Asher checked my face first, then looked behind him. When he seemed satisfied, he said, 'Shaukat, Aunt Bibi's eldest. He is a doctor. Jamila thought they would choose her.'

I could tell there was more he wasn't telling me, but it helped me to understand Jamila better at least. Shaukat must be the boy Papa had mentioned: his sister's eldest son. He wouldn't come to the dinner; only the parents would meet the girl and decide. I felt sorry for Jamila: it must be like sitting an exam. I could see what Asher meant about the cake, and I didn't understand why Aunty Khushida had pressed me to make one if it was going to outshine Jamila's curry.

Asher said, 'If I was Shaukat I'd want to marry you — you're prettier than Jamila and kinder too.' He flushed.

I stared at him open-mouthed. 'Asher, I'm not marrying anyone, so Jamila has a clear field.'

'Haider wants to marry you too.'

Asher didn't mean any harm but suddenly I felt as if I was standing on a lone rock with the tide rushing in and no retreat in sight. They had all been looking forward to Jamila's marriage and now it seemed I was here ruining it. No wonder she looked daggers at me.

Zeba came running out. 'Ummie wants you to come, Ameera. She has an outfit for you to wear.'

'Why can't I wear my own clothes?'

'Silly,' Zeba said. 'You have to wear a special outfit tonight. Aunt Bibi's coming.'

Asher was still watching me; it was rather an appraising look for a thirteen-year-old. A tremor shivered through me as I remembered his words: 'when a family chooses a bride'.

16

By the time I reached the house I realised how stupid my fears were; I'd let Asher's words transport me on a flight of fantasy. This was Jamila's night. Besides, if there was any misunderstanding and Aunt Bibi thought I wanted to get married too, I could easily put them right and say I was returning to Australia in a month to go to uni. Problem solved. Haider, I'd have to deal with later.

'Ameera!' Aunty Khushida called to me from her bedroom. 'Hurry, child.'

Zeba led me in. Dadi jan and Jamila were there too. Dadi jan smiled at me, but Jamila's eyes were puffy and red, and she turned her face to the wall when I attempted a smile. Aunty beckoned me closer. Then I saw the dress. It was laid out on the bed: musk pink, a high waist, gold shining through from underneath. The border around the hem was stitched in gold thread and was thirty centimetres deep at least. Instead of the shalwar there was the narrow pyjama worn in Bollywood movies called churidar. Gold high-heeled sandals stood erect on the floor. Aunty picked up the dupatta. It also had gold stitching on the border and hung in perfect folds; if it were on my head, my face would be framed in gold. I had never worn anything so exquisite.

Why give me such an outfit? I felt as though a cage was closing around me.

I glanced at Jamila. 'I can't wear this.'

Aunty's frown came into full play. She too glanced at Jamila, then chose to interpret my comment as polite incredulity. 'Of course you can. Your father has paid for it so there is no need to be embarrassed. He wanted you to look your best for your Aunt Bibi.'

Aunt Bibi had married well. She and Uncle Iqbal had houses in Islamabad and Karachi, though they lived much of the year in Azad Kashmir. I could understand Papa wanting me well-dressed to meet her. I relaxed a little.

'What about you, Jamila?' I said, trying to cheer her up, refusing to accept that her mood had anything to do with me. 'Do you have an outfit like this?'

Jamila clutched her hand to her mouth and ran out of the room. I looked to Aunty Khushida to tell me what was going on, but she pursed her lips and said nothing about Jamila. She addressed Zeba instead. 'Get Ameera's hairbrush, you can brush her hair.'

'I can do my own hair, Aunty ji.'

Aunty Khushida looked me full in the face then. The lines around her mouth were more pronounced and her cheeks sagged. Why did she look so tired and sad?

'There is so much about our culture you do not know, child,' she said. 'And I thought you would. It is very difficult.'

Her tone made me want to apologise. She sighed as if she knew this. 'It is not your fault. Like all of us, you are just a game piece.'

It was my turn to frown, but she turned away, not welcoming questions. 'Meena will be coming shortly to help you get ready.'

This time I didn't protest. Perhaps this was a custom for guests; it would be rude of me to refuse to take part. Dadi jan beckoned to me and I sat in front of her with my head bowed, thinking. After a long time Zeba came in with my brush. Had she gone through my backpack before realising it was on the dressing table? Dadi jan took the brush from her and began long slow strokes. Aunty Khushida took Zeba away and soon there was just Dadi jan and the brush. Mum hadn't brushed my hair since I was little, and she was always in a hurry so I wouldn't be late for school. Dadi jan brushed from the top of my head all the way down the length of my hair, as though she was dragging the worries out of my mind to drop them on the floor. My scalp tingled and my limbs began to slacken.

'There, child,' she said. 'There is no need for concern — all will be good. Inshallah.' Then she asked, 'Did you hear about my marriage, child?'

I turned slightly. 'I heard you had a romantic marriage. Did you run away together?'

She shook her head. 'They all think that — that Zufar brought me to Kashmir after we were married. But it is not true. I was abducted.'

I swung round to face her. 'Abducted?'

'Yes, I was stolen just like the tale of Omar and

Marui. Perhaps Zufar had heard of it and that gave him the idea.' She chuckled.

'But how could that happen? You would have been protected by your father, your brothers.'

'Ji, but it was a difficult time. It was sixty years ago — the time of the partition. Pakistan was being born like mountains rising up out of the sea. Like an earthquake it was, and just as many people died. There was much confusion and killing. My family was planning to travel across the border to India. We lived in Rawalpindi. Zufar had come from Kashmir to our shop in Rawalpindi selling rugs. He saw me by accident. I was fourteen years old and beautiful.' She smiled at me. 'I was like you once. Zufar knew better than to ask my father for a marriage settlement for he was Muslim and our family Hindu.'

'I didn't know you were Hindu.' I stared at her in wonder; perhaps her Urdu was really Hindi.

'Hahn ji. But then the partition happened and Muslim killed Hindu and Hindu killed Muslim. My family was on the train — it was full of Hindu and Sikh refugees. At one small place, Arifwala, the train had stopped. But on the station were many angry Muslims being incited by mullahs. They wanted revenge. Suddenly the mob fell quiet. A Sikh, drunk with opium, was hanging from one of the windows singing verses from "Hir and Ranjha" — have you heard of this poem?'

I nodded. 'Papa told me about it.'

'It was my favourite — I sang it to your father when he was small.'

I must have looked surprised, for she added, 'I could sing very well.' She continued, 'The Sikh sang the verses

117

where the poet criticises the corrupt mullah for denying Ranjha hospitality in the mosque when he fled from his family. When the mob heard those verses, they came to their senses and refused to obey the mullahs' instructions to attack the train. We left the station unscathed, saved by a song.'

Dadi jan paused and I held her hand. 'I never forgot it — that miracle — how one of our old tales could change hearts,' she said. 'For we all have the one heart even though they tried to split us in two. At the next stop, there was trouble again — too much fighting. My brothers were protecting our carriage, but I was pulled out through the window. There was a young man with a horse — a very fast horse as I remember.'

'Dada Zufar.'

'Hahn ji, he brought me to Kashmir.'

'And your family?'

'I never knew if they survived that trip to India. Once, when the children were grown, we visited Rawalpindi where I was born but there was no trace of my family. And they would have thought I had perished. Possibly, Zufar saved my life.'

'But that is romantic. It's better than a movie.'

She smiled wanly. 'At the time I did not think so. It took me a year to learn to love him.' She shrugged. 'What choice did I have? I was fortunate, I suppose, for he was a good man. He was the son of a khan and used to getting what he wanted, but he was kind to me.'

Just as I was wondering why she was telling me this, she leaned forward. 'Things do come good in a marriage, child, even when you least expect it.'

I stared at her, trying to formulate a question, for she was regarding me as though she expected one. The moment passed as Zeba burst in, leading Meena. 'Here she is. Meena will do your make-up and your hair, Ameera. Can I do your nails? I promise not to make a mess.'

Meena smiled at me gently, searching my face. Zeba jumped up and down as if nothing before had ever been so exciting, but I could share nothing of her joy.

17

Zeba said I looked like a princess. Asher stared when I emerged and whispered an actress's name: Aishwarya Rai. Maybe it was my green eyes. Meena had applied green eye shadow to accentuate them. She had arranged my hair so that the fullness of it fell down my back but little plaits on the sides kept it off my face. She had even bought lipstick and nail polish to match the exact pink of the dress. It terrified me to think of such attention to detail. Aunty Khushida smiled when she saw me but it was a smile tempered with sadness. She and Jamila were preparing the curries. Jamila also wore a new outfit but it wasn't as fine as mine. I felt a renewed pang of anxiety. Why had they dressed me up like this just because I hadn't seen Aunt Bibi since I was ten?

I tried to help Jamila cut up tomatoes but Aunty Khushida told me to sit down. 'You'll ruin your outfit. Meena will help.'

I sat on the couch and Zeba ran to get an English book so I could read to her. The book was a collection of folk tales. 'This one,' she said and pointed to a picture of a lake and a mountain.

'The Girl Who Cried a Lake,' I read.

'Mmm.' Zeba settled in close beside me.

The story was about a girl from Kyrgyzstan with unusual blue eyes who met a hunter and wanted to marry him. Her parents said he wasn't suitable, and arranged a marriage with a chieftain's son. At the wedding the girl began to cry. No one worried at first, for this is what brides do at weddings, but her tears wouldn't stop and soon she had cried a puddle, then a river, then a lake, drowning her family and the whole community. The young hunter found the lake and took a drink. It was warm and salty and so intensely blue that he realised his love had become a lake. He stretched his arms heavenward and grew into a mountain so that he could be near his love forever. I stopped, astounded at my feelings — that poor girl.

Zeba looked up at me. 'Aur hai, there's more,' she said.

I looked at the painting of the girl in a colourful Himalayan wedding outfit crying a stream of tears, and forced myself to say the last sentence: 'And that is the story of Lake Izzyk-Kul and the Tian Shan, the Celestial Mountains that surround it.'

It was a story I hadn't heard before and it reminded me of the tragic tales Papa had told me. Was it true, that a marriage between two people of diverse backgrounds could never work? Or were they stories to keep young people in line? Mum and Papa had their problems, I knew, but Tariq had a different personality from Papa. Surely love would give Tariq and me a different ending?

Just as Zeba put out her hand to turn to another story, there was knocking at the outside gate. Asher rushed to answer it. I wondered why Haider didn't go.

'Isn't Haider with your father?' I asked Zeba.

'He is at his friend's house. Aunt Bibi and Uncle Iqbal would not like it if he could see you all the time.' She gave me a knowing smile and my stomach churned.

I stood as Asher brought Uncle Iqbal and Aunt Bibi into the lounge. Uncle Rasheed and Aunty Khushida arrived to greet them. Aunty Khushida hugged Aunt Bibi the prescribed three times, but Aunt Bibi's gaze darted around the room … and rested on me. She pulled away from Aunty Khushida before the hugging was finished.

'Ah, so this must be Ameera. My, how you have grown, and much more beautiful than Hassan said.'

I fought the annoyance rising in my chest. Why was the way I looked always the first thing they saw here, the first thing mentioned? I never got this attention in Australia.

Aunt Bibi glanced at Uncle Iqbal and raised her eyebrows at him; then they both looked at me as if I were the only person in the room. In that moment I was in no doubt of their intentions. I had never been privy to an arranged marriage, but Asher's and Zeba's hints, Meena's concern, Dadi jan's story, Aunty Khushida's frowns, Haider's insinuations and Jamila's moods all became clear in the light of the excited look on Aunt Bibi's face as she launched herself towards me. I wanted to turn and run, but of course I behaved just as a good

Pakistani girl should. I bowed my head and sank to touch her feet; she laid her hand on my head, then hugged me. On the third embrace I feared she would never let go and I tried not to squirm. Then she relented and led me to the couch. I looked up at Aunty Khushida and saw Jamila behind her. Aunty's face was over-bright; Jamila's was a dark hollow.

'So, tell all about yourself,' Aunt Bibi said. 'I hear you have finished school and are quite grown-up now.'

I stared at her aghast but Papa had trained me well; politeness took over and I managed to answer like clockwork. 'Yes, my results will come out soon and I'll know which university I am accepted into.'

Aunt Bibi glanced at Uncle Iqbal. 'Yes, university. Of course there are many good universities here in Pakistan.'

My hands sweated in my lap. Aunt Bibi chose that moment to take one in her own. I tried to wipe mine as she took it, but only managed to create a fumble.

'Silly, let me hold your hand,' she said.

I tried to smile. I had so looked forward to meeting Papa's adored sister again. She was certainly warm and affectionate, but there was something else now: I felt my breath being sucked from me, my lungs collapsing. I could lose myself in Aunt Bibi's voluminous embrace, in her love, but would I ever be found again?

My fear must have shown in my eyes for when she lifted my chin she grunted. 'Everything will be good, beti. Do not worry. We will look after you. Accha, now tell me about Hassan. How is his business running?'

I couldn't remember afterwards what I had said. I just knew she hadn't mentioned Mum once. We moved to the table; the food came. I didn't remember much of that either, except that Uncle Iqbal's table manners were worse than Papa's. Then the cake came out, courtesy of Jamila. She was careful to smile at Aunt Bibi but Aunt Bibi didn't notice.

'Who made the cake?' Aunt Bibi sounded like a queen.

There was a silence until Aunty Khushida said, 'Ameera did.'

Aunt Bibi turned her gaze onto me again. 'So you can make cakes too.'

She made it sound as if I was used to holding garden parties in palaces and I thought a little honesty wouldn't go amiss. 'Yes, but I can't make chapattis.'

Aunt Bibi stared at me as she took that in. A glance at Aunty Khushida showed her with eyes tightly shut, waiting. Then Aunt Bibi chuckled. 'Who cares about chapattis these days? Shaukat has servants to cook.'

My eyes widened; any doubt I'd had was now dispensed with. Aunt Bibi had laid her hand on my knee as she said Shaukat's name and her bright eyes told me more than Asher's and Zeba's knowing looks ever had.

Aunty Khushida let out her breath with a whoosh and Zeba clapped her hands; Asher winked at me. Both uncles grinned stupidly. Meena's face was a question mark, and Dadi jan watched me with a wan smile.

The only unhappy faces in the room were Jamila's and mine.

124

I saw from the photos later that I had the right look on my face as Uncle Iqbal's digital camera flashed: not too eager, and a little frightened. It wasn't an act. I was truly becoming more scared by the minute.

Aunt Bibi produced a red chiffon scarf, which she threw over my head, and put a ring on my finger. Everyone was so kind and happy, but I felt as if I was caught in someone else's dream. Why would they think I'd want to get married at my age? Wouldn't Jamila be a better choice? At least when I got home I could get it sorted out. Papa could give some excuse. Better still: maybe I could fix it before I left.

18

Aunty Khushida was the first person I tried talking to the next morning, after I'd carefully taken off Aunt Bibi's ring and left it on the dressing table. Aunty was in her bedroom, ironing clothes on a table. She sounded relieved to be able to talk about it.

'Your father wanted you to settle first, get used to being here, maybe meet Shaukat. It would have happened naturally, but Bibi couldn't wait. She wanted it arranged straightaway — she thought she could win you over.'

'Papa knew?'

She glanced at me. 'He has been in contact with Bibi over this for years. The arrangement was that when you'd finished university you would come here to marry Shaukat. Only God knows why he suddenly decided to send you earlier.'

'So you knew too?'

'Not then. We were negotiating with Bibi for Jamila. Bibi didn't say Hassan was too. I suppose she was keeping her options open.' She fiddled with a shirt collar.

'When we found out, Jamila thought there was still hope, that they could choose between the two of you. That is what we thought, until you came.' She set the iron on the table. 'Once we saw you there was no doubt who they would choose.'

'But I don't want to marry Shaukat.'

Aunty Khushida looked up, her gaze almost fierce. 'Shaukat is a good man. Your father knows that — only the best for his little girl.'

'But can't I just go home and then Jamila can marry Shaukat?'

'It is not that simple. This is what I meant about you not knowing our culture.'

'But I do. I'm Pakistani as well as Australian.'

She shook her head. 'Didn't your mother explain?'

I stared at Aunty Khushida, thinking how Western Mum was. They probably thought I was disadvantaged having an Australian mother. 'She didn't know,' I said.

Aunty made a sound with her tongue and put another qameez on the table. 'Your father has sent your jehez, your dowry. Now do you understand? It is set in stone. And he has sent Jamila's so we can find a good man for her also.'

Shock made my mouth gape. 'Papa knew you wanted Shaukat?'

'He paid the highest price.'

I sunk onto the bed. 'I've been bought.'

'Do not think of it like that. Your father is looking after you. He said there was no one of Shaukat's calibre in Australia.'

Tariq is, I thought.

127

Aunty Khushida narrowed her eyes at me. 'Ameera, if you were to do something crazy like not accepting this shadi, it will be a great beizit, a dishonour, to your father and your whole family, us included.' She was so upset she'd reverted to Urdu.

I stared at her, dismayed. 'I'm trapped.' I whispered it, not expecting her to comment.

Nor did she for a full minute; she just pushed the iron over the shirt as if it were alive and cantankerous. Then she said, 'We all feel like that sometimes. Life is not the romantic nonsense you see in films. A daughter has a duty.' She glanced at me as she set the iron on its heel. 'And this is not a bad situation. Jamila would give her eyes to swap places with you.'

'Perhaps you could swap us at the wedding. Who would know?'

She checked my face to see if I was joking. 'Stupid girl — everyone would know as soon as Shaukat looked in the shadi mirror. Do not worry for Jamila. With what your father has sent we can arrange a first-class match for her also. Besides, it is good for girls to learn early that they cannot always have what they want.'

She turned back to the ironing and I went in search of Jamila. She was lying on her bed. I sat beside her rigid form. She didn't stir but I knew she was awake. Above her bed was her bookshelf: rows of English Mills & Boons. Mum never liked me reading romance novels when I was younger. 'You mightn't realise they're fantasy,' she'd said once, 'and expect too much.' We both knew I'd have an arranged marriage, but I'd expected a choice, a discussion at least.

I wondered how to start with Jamila. 'I'm sorry.'

She rolled over as though she'd just noticed I was there. Her stare reminded me of a cat's; on them it's called baleful. 'What is the point of being sorry?' she said.

'I didn't know. Honestly, I didn't willingly come here to ruin your life.'

'Well, you have. You have stolen my husband.' Her eyes filled.

I didn't know what to say. I was expecting anger and nastiness, not these tears. She dashed them away and sat up.

'You have taken the one thing I wanted. I adored Shaukat even as a child. When he married the first time, I was too young to be considered.'

He'd already been married? No one had told me that, but then what had I been told?

'When she died, I hoped,' Jamila continued. 'For years they did not arrange another marriage. Then Ummie started the negotiations. Aunt Bibi did not tell us your father was doing so also. When we found out, my hope was that Aunt Bibi would take a dislike to you, then they would remember me. But look at you: English-speaking, Western, pale-skinned — the perfect wife for a doctor. You can even make cakes for all the other doctors' wives.'

I chose to ignore the sarcasm. 'But I don't want to marry.'

'And that is supposed to make me feel better? I lose him, you get him but you do not want him. Ha, it is almost funny.'

'Jamila —'

'If I knew he would be happy I could bear it, but you do not even care or understand. All you want is to return to Australia. I suppose you have a boyfriend — all Westerners do.'

I kept silent. Now was not the time for confidences. She was too hurt, and hurt people hurt back. 'I am sorry and I'll try to fix it,' I said instead.

She looked at me with something close to pity in her eyes then. 'You are so Western, you know nothing. This is Pakistan. There is nothing you can do. It is arranged. Bas, khatam, finished.' She cut the air with her hand at each of those final words.

I left her alone.

Even then I didn't fully realise my position; the cement had not yet set around my feet. I tried Uncle Rasheed next. After all, he was Papa's representative in Pakistan. I knocked on the mejalis door, relieved to find him alone and watching cricket on a small TV. He was sitting cross-legged on a rug, carpeted cushions behind him, and in front of him a bowl of peanuts that he was systematically shelling. He reminded me so much of Papa that I felt a familiar prickling behind my nose but I controlled myself. Now was not the time to cry.

I told Uncle that I was thankful for his excellent hospitality, but I wanted to go home as soon as possible.

Just like Papa, he thought before he spoke. 'Beti, you understand about marriage, do you not?'

I nodded. 'I always knew I would have an arranged marriage, but in Australia with my family.' I stopped, hating the way my voice broke.

Uncle Rasheed watched me while I composed myself. I thought he'd say what babies Australian girls were, but instead he gestured for me to sit on the rug with him. Then he murmured, 'Hassan should have come with you, but he thought it best this way. You see, your father wanted you to settle first before he said anything about a marriage, but your Aunt Bibi — she is impulsive. She said she could make you want to stay with the force of her love.'

I remembered the night before with an internal shudder. 'Force of love' was a good description of Aunt Bibi.

'I am sorry it has been handled clumsily,' Uncle went on. 'To tell you the truth, I believe girls should be told of their marriage and be allowed to accept it or not.' I looked at him in hope; was he taking my side? 'But your father was adamant. He feels Australia is a difficult environment to bring up a Muslim girl and I must admit it has been easier in comparison to raise girls here.'

I understood. Papa was phobic about protecting me from bad influences. He even censored what I watched on TV. There were no such problems here. Everything on Pakistani TV was censored already; there was no kissing, even between married couples on sitcoms unless they were married in real life.

Uncle Rasheed offered me a peanut he'd shelled, but I declined. 'I would have had an arranged marriage in Australia, when I was older.'

'Hassan thought it best to marry you earlier, to keep you safe. Shaukat will certainly do that.'

'I was safe in Australia.'

Uncle Rasheed put aside the peanuts and shells. 'Beti, you are an unusual girl. Men will be attracted to you for the wrong reasons in a place like Australia. Every time you went out of the house, to school, to friends' houses, Hassan was in pain for he could not properly protect you.'

'But Australia is safe.' Even as I repeated it I thought of the incident on the street that day after the movies. But none of us was hurt.

'Nowhere is safe for a girl like you, beti, except in marriage.'

'What sort of girl is that, Uncle ji?'

He flicked a peanut shell from his vest and regarded me. 'Just accept this. I can see you have been brought up well enough.' He hesitated; was he thinking that I could have been brought up better without Mum's influence? He continued, 'You are an obedient and compliant daughter. Your father wants this for your benefit.' Then he cornered me with his gaze. 'Honour him by accepting this marriage that has been arranged for you.'

I shut my eyes. Arranged? This wasn't an arranged marriage: this was marriage by force, and I still didn't believe Papa could condone it.

'I want to speak to Papa,' I said then.

Uncle pulled himself up. 'Very well, beti.' His voice sounded weary.

19

It was too early to ring Papa so I went outside to the courtyard and sat there wrapped in two shawls. How could this be happening? I hoped Papa would make the whole problem disappear. Everyone (excluding Haider and Jamila) was kind; they thought I was pretty and sweet. I cringed. Sweet meant soft. Uncle Rasheed had said I was compliant; that meant I had no backbone. It suited Papa to have a daughter he could control but couldn't there be a balance? Why couldn't I still love my family, love God, but marry who I liked? Why was loving God judged by how I obeyed my father? I knew that was how Papa thought. What if he wanted me to do something that God didn't will for me? Was there such a thing?

While I was waiting in the courtyard, I had another run-in with Haider. His sudden presence startled me and I blinked as I looked up at him.

'We don't need to fight,' he said.

He spoke in Urdu. Why? To keep putting me at a disadvantage? I made to go but he put out a hand and held me, drew me nearer. 'Ameera.' His voice was pleading. 'If we were seen together, Aunt Bibi would call the wedding off.'

He was so close I could feel his breath on my cheek. I tried to squirm out of his grasp. 'Let me go.' *No one must see us like this.* What could he mean anyway? Aunty Khushida had said the arrangement was set in stone.

He didn't seem to hear me. 'We could have a love marriage. Then both Jamila and I will be happy. Wouldn't you like to make me happy?'

The sleazy tone had crept back into his voice; he probably thought it was romantic. I almost slapped his face but fear stopped me. What would he do if I retaliated? I wasn't sure what sort of an enemy he would make and I still had a month to stay here.

I said the next thing that came into my head. 'Why would I choose anyone anyway, least of all you?'

I shouldn't have sounded so revolted for his eyes became slits and his hand circling my arm squeezed tighter.

'Your beauty stings like a bee.' That sounded like a song lyric and I almost smirked. 'Get used to the idea. One way or another there will be a wedding. The choice of groom is yours.'

What sort of a choice was that?

That afternoon when Aunty and I were preparing the evening meal, Uncle Rasheed and Haider rushed into the house and turned on the TV in the lounge. Pictures of Benazir Bhutto flashed across the screen and I watched, horrified, as her last moments were played out. It reminded me of when my family had sat glued to the TV after the September 11 attacks. I was only ten but I'd picked up on Mum's and Papa's tension and sadness.

Uncle wasn't fond of Benazir but still he was shocked. 'Couldn't America have kept her alive?' He shook his head.

'That poor family,' Aunty Khushida murmured. 'How many more will die for democracy?'

I suddenly thought of Mum and how worried she would be. That was when the phone rang. It was Papa. Uncle Rasheed spoke to him for a while and then called my name. He handed me the phone. I waited for Papa to speak.

'Hello, beti. I just heard. Rasheed says you are safe there.'

He was talking about the assassination but all I could think of was the wedding. 'Papa, why didn't you tell me?'

His voice was teasing. 'No how are you, Papa? I am safe, Papa?'

I ignored him. 'Papa, Uncle Rasheed told me that you planned this wedding for me.'

There was a silence. Then, 'I didn't want you to know yet. I wanted you to find out gradually, so it would be a surprise.'

'It's not a surprise, Papa. It's a shock. Why didn't you tell me?'

'Would you have gone?'

'What about Mum?'

'She doesn't know. I thought it best to keep the happy news from her for a while longer — she wouldn't understand.'

'Papa, I don't understand either.' This time I didn't care that everyone could hear the conversation.

'Beti, Shaukat is the best a father could give his daughter. You will thank me. In a year's time, Shaukat will bring you home to visit us and you will be very happy, fulfilled.'

'A year?' My voice squeaked. 'You know I want to go to uni.'

'You can still attend university there. Shaukat has agreed.'

A coldness crept over me; this was what betrayal felt like. 'You've spoken with him?'

'He is looking forward to the wedding. I have been sending him your photos since you were fifteen.'

Any strength I had drained out of me. 'Papa, when would you have told me?'

'It is best if people are finding things out when they are ready for them. I am sorry this has been revealed prematurely.'

'I want to come home.'

'There is no need for that. Rasheed says the police have the situation in hand, the army too. You will be safe if you stay in the house.'

'The wedding, Papa. Can't you call it off?'

Papa's voice changed. There was steel under his words. 'I'm sorry you feel that way but it has been arranged in your best interests. I have given my word, and I want you to obey your uncle in all aspects of the marriage just as you would me.'

I was confused. I could hear the voice of the father I knew but what he was telling me came from a stranger.

'Are you listening to me, beti?'

I was silent.

'Ameera?'

'Yes, Papa.' But I hadn't promised; I had only agreed I could hear him.

Uncle Rasheed took the phone from me. He spoke about the elections, how Benazir's party couldn't win now unless they postponed them. I didn't care about any of it. I drifted like a sleepwalker to my room.

Jamila was in there, knitting this time. 'Didn't do any good, did it?'

I shook my head. Then I regarded her. Had I imagined it or was that a note of sympathy I heard?

I hadn't been in Pakistan a week and my whole life was crumbling. It was couched in nice terms but it boiled down to this: I was sentenced to a forced marriage, a prison sentence in a third-world country, married to someone I'd never met. Uncle Iqbal had buck teeth, most probably Shaukat did too. Papa would have been blinded by the fact that Shaukat was a doctor. My father revered doctors.

All the next day I lay in bed until even Jamila grew worried. I missed the drama of Benazir's funeral, how the coffin was mobbed, the pictures of her at different ages in the paper. Schools were closed. Militants took over the streets, even in Muzaffarabad. No one went out if they didn't have to. There were riots in Sindh and Jamila said the country was on the brink of civil war. I just went back to sleep.

The day after, it was safer to be outside and Meena visited.

'Come on, you have to get up,' she told me. 'We women all have to go through difficulties at some stage of our lives.'

Her words sounded flippant, but her eyes were kind. I sat up and hugged her; she was the closest I had to an older sister. I missed Mum so much. Mum would agree with me about the marriage, but how would that change things? A woman in Pakistan didn't seem to have a lot of power. There were six of us in the house if you counted Meena, but what could we do against Papa who had made up his mind?

'What about you, Meena?' I asked. 'What was your arrangement like?'

She bit her lip, wondering what to tell, I guessed. 'Abu did it the correct way, Ameera. I'm sorry, but Abu would not have done as your father has. Abu and Ummie showed me photos of boys they had visited. I remembered some from childhood. Together we narrowed it down to two and I was allowed to meet the families and the boys. Then we chose Haroun.'

It was the way I had imagined it happening for me too.

'But, Ameera, although you haven't had a choice, if you were offered Shaukat, you would choose him.'

138

'How do you know?'

'He is a good man. If I was old enough at his first marriage I would have liked to be chosen myself.' She was stroking my hair. Then she shifted her position and said, 'Ameera, Jamila would like you to go to school today. You can teach English.'

'How? I'm not trained.'

Jamila broke in. 'There is a book. You only have to follow the exercises and say the sentences so the children can repeat them. Then they write them. It will be good for the kids to hear a true English accent.'

I checked her face for sarcasm, but didn't find any this time. Meena watched me, a half-hopeful smile on her lips. 'And good for you, Ameera.'

She was right. I was hemmed in — even by their kindness. I had to get out of the house to think more clearly, and I couldn't go alone. There still had to be a way out of the marriage. I just had to make a plan. And get word to Mum and Riaz.

20

On the way to Zeba's school I thought about Haider. Perhaps he had a point: if we were caught together Aunt Bibi would call off the wedding. Then I could go home. I didn't trust everyone's praise for Shaukat. How often had Jamila or Meena seen him? He may not be my idea of a good man. I would have to be careful dealing with Haider though. He was like a faulty power line: you never knew when it could burst into flame.

Zeba's chatter broke into my thoughts; she was using a lot more English words now. 'Ameera, my friend is Tariqah. She has an aunty in Australia. She sent Tariqah a toy possum.'

My gut churned at the name. Tariqah would mean the same as Tariq: the morning star. I'd looked it up on the internet after the party. Tariq was my morning star, and I'd imagined waking up every morning and seeing his smile. Would that ever happen now?

At the school, girls in blue dresses, white shalwars and red jumpers rushed up to us as we entered the gate. Tariqah was one of them and Zeba introduced us. She had a cute smile and a plait that she swung across her shoulder. Soon she put her arm around Zeba and took her off to play. The whole school was made up of tents, even the principal's office. Surely they would have to close down soon because of the cold?

Jamila introduced me to the principal, Mrs Malik.

'We are very happy to have a native speaker of English helping in the classes,' Mrs Malik said formally.

'I am happy to help.'

She was busy; she kept glancing at her desk. A boy hovered nearby, ready to run an errand. A handbell rang and Jamila took me to Zeba's class tent.

'Why don't they rebuild?' I asked.

'It takes time. The government offices are first to be rebuilt. The schools are not the highest priority.'

'They should be.'

Jamila gave me her first genuine smile. 'I agree.'

All the girls stood as we entered. Jamila introduced me in Urdu and then in English. 'This is Miss Ameera. She is an English teacher from Australia.' I raised my eyebrows but didn't correct her. The girls chorused a 'Good morning' and then stared at me. Jamila smiled and left.

'Please sit down. Who can tell me what page you are up to?' I was determined to speak in English since it was an English class.

No one answered, not even Zeba, but at least they all sat down on the cheap blankets. The only furniture in the tent was the teacher's small table and chair — more evidence of the devastation of the earthquake.

I picked up a book from the desk. 'Which lesson?'

A girl at the back stood. 'Please, Miss, we study page twenty.'

'Good. Open your books to page twenty.'

A few girls understood and then the rest followed them. The older ones helped the younger ones. Even though this was Grade 4, there was a wide range of ages. It was a world away from what I remembered of primary school at home. The girls listened to everything I said, and were polite. I was careful to speak slowly, remembering Asher's warning about my fast speech. When I asked them to repeat sentences after me they did. I felt I'd travelled back a hundred years. As they leaned over their exercise books, writing the sentences, I counted them — fifty-seven. When they finished they formed a line so I could mark their work.

One of the older girls said in English, 'You is very beautiful, Miss,' and then blushed.

She was the only one who dared to speak to me directly and I didn't have the heart to correct her grammar. I told the girls to read from the textbook while they waited in line, and so I became a teacher.

At recess Jamila came to take me to the staff tent for a cup of tea. One of the office workers had made chai and was pouring cups for us all. Jamila introduced me to some teachers but I doubted I'd remember their names. Some of them hadn't completed their teaching degrees but were learning on the job. It was either that or close the school, I was told. Another teacher had recently come from the Jesus and Mary Convent School in Murree, the school Benazir Bhutto had attended, and discussion soon centred on the latest news.

The woman on my right was called Nargis. She had a bruise under her eye, almost hidden by heavy make-up. 'Are you married?' she asked me.

'No.' I glanced over at Jamila who was watching me. I turned back to Nargis. 'And you?'

'Yes.' But it was barely a sigh. She touched the bruise on her face.

Jamila moved closer and gently laid her hand over Nargis's. 'Nargis has been married a year.'

Nargis smiled at her; it was a brave smile full of a meaning I wasn't privy to. Before any more could be said, another teacher leaned over and introduced herself.

'I am Asma, Zeba's class teacher. She is telling me you come from Australia.'

'Yes.'

'I have family in Melbourne. We hope to visit at Eid next year. Could you take a parcel for me?'

I glanced at Jamila. 'Of course.' Then I suddenly thought of the phone. I didn't care if Jamila heard. 'Do you know how to send messages to Australia on a mobile phone?' I asked.

She smiled. 'You have to leave off the zero and put plus six one. Then you can ring mobiles and send messages.'

'Thank you.'

The time at the school did stop me from dwelling on my own problems. Seeing the kids in tents in the cold and yet still willing to learn made me want to help. On the way home, I said as much to Jamila.

'Yes, it fills your heart,' she said.

I asked her about Nargis. 'Is she in a difficult marriage? She didn't look happy.'

Jamila glanced at me before she answered. 'Nargis is the victim of a forced marriage.'

Before I could stop myself, I said, 'That's what's happening to me.'

Jamila swung around on me. 'You are not being forced. You are having a marriage arranged by a loving family. Nargis was sold into slavery. Her evil husband beats her and uses her like a dog. That will not happen to you.'

The anger in her eyes made it difficult to remember the smile she'd given me at the school. I didn't agree about my marriage, but she'd shocked me into silence. All the same I felt sorry for Nargis.

'Can anything be done?' I said eventually. 'In Australia there are refuges for women whose husbands abuse them.'

Jamila's lip curled. 'This is not Australia.' After a moment she relented. 'I have heard of a refuge in Islamabad for women who are beaten, but how can Nargis go there? If her husband found out, he would kill her.'

'What about her parents?'

'Her father just tells her to be a better wife and not annoy her husband.'

There was nothing to say in the face of such injustice. Yet was my position any better because my husband was said to be a good man? Was Nargis told that too?

When we returned home, Aunty Khushida was busy in the kitchen. Dadi jan was with her, peeling garlic for the evening meal. I put on an extra shawl and went into the garden with my phone hidden in my pocket. It was colder and there was snow now on the mountains. Baba ji was out there near the Persian garden, weeding in an old heavy coat. I sat in the pavilion and keyed a text to Tariq: `family aranging marrige 4 me. Dont kno what 2 do`. It went through this time.

Then I rang Riaz. He didn't answer the first time. The sound of the fountain calmed me while I waited. I kept trying and finally he answered. 'Ames, you okay?'

'No.' I swallowed a sob. 'They're arranging a marriage.'

'For Jamila?' There was hope in his voice.

'No. It's for me.' It came out as a squeak.

'Shit, so it's true.'

'You knew? Why didn't you say anything?'

'I heard Dad on the phone one night. It sounded suss but I wasn't sure. Who's the guy? Not Haider?' The disgust in his tone echoed my own feelings.

'Shaukat.'

There was a slight delay and I panicked. 'Riaz?'

'I'm still here. Can you hear me properly?'

'Yes.'

His voice was different now, almost eager. 'Find out if you like him.'

'But —'

'I'm serious. Just listen. I've heard good things about him. Maybe he'll come to Australia to live and you'll get us back and a good marriage as well.'

'I'm barely seventeen. I don't want to be married.'

'Just check it out. Dad wouldn't do something to hurt you.'

'This hurts. I wasn't told. Isn't the marrying age eighteen in Australia?'

'I think it's younger in Pakistan.'

'But wouldn't it be illegal if I didn't consent?'

'Not there probably.'

Then I took a chance. 'Riaz, I can't do this. I love Tariq.'

There was a silence so long I thought I'd lost him. 'Are you still there?'

'I'm here.' I could imagine his face, how he'd screw up his eyes as he thought. 'Look, if you still feel like this in a week ring me back and I'll see what I can do.'

'Can I speak to Mum?'

'She's at Grandpa's.'

'Still?'

'She hasn't come back yet. She didn't like the way Dad sent you over there so quickly.'

'Wait till she hears about the wedding.'

There was a silence again.

'Riaz?'

'Yeah, but what can she do? She doesn't understand as much about Dad's background as she thinks.'

'Can't you do something? Talk to Uncle Rasheed; or find out if it's illegal and scare them with that?'

'I don't think it'll work, but ring me later, okay?'

'I won't be changing my mind,' I told him.

Speaking to Riaz had unsettled me so much I couldn't face helping in the kitchen. I went to my room instead. I was wishing Mum had a mobile, and thought I should have asked Riaz for Grandpa's number so I could speak to her.

In my room, I noticed my backpack was in a different spot by the low dressing table. A few of my things — my brush and make-up — were on the floor. *That Zeba*, I thought, *I really must tell her she can't go through my stuff*. I picked up the bag and then stiffened. The quilt on my bed looked dishevelled as though someone had slept on it. Had Dadi jan rested in here while we were at the school? I checked that my passports and ticket were in their usual spot under the mattress. My hand brushed against the rope support ... nothing. I moved my hand down, maybe they'd slipped. Still nothing. I stood up and pulled the mattress off the bed. The rope bed was bare. My return ticket and passports were gone.

I raced to the kitchen. 'Aunty Khushida, my passports and ticket are missing.'

Aunty Khushida was stirring onions in a large pot on the stove. She wiped her eyes but didn't answer. I thought she hadn't heard, then I saw her face. On it was a mixture of disapproval and concern.

'Aunty ji?'

She glanced at me but didn't stop stirring. 'It is better this way. At the moment you are not thinking wisely. Maybe you will try something dangerous, to return by yourself. It is better that we keep you safe.'

'But —' Then I stopped. Would I try to go home by myself if they kept on with arranging the wedding? I hadn't considered that; at that point I still believed the wedding could be stopped.

Aunty Khushida gave me a longer look. 'You Western girls can go where you want, walk by yourself down the street. You cannot do that here. Especially not since Begum Benazir's assassination.'

'Who took my passports?'

'Your uncle has them in his safekeeping, for when you need them.'

'You took them, didn't you? While we were at school. And Meena? Was she part of the ploy to get me out of the house? Jamila knew they were there.' My voice was rising and dangerously close to being disrespectful. *How could they betray me like that? How could Meena?*

Aunty Khushida stopped stirring and turned to face me. 'Meena knows nothing of this, nor does Jamila. It is for your benefit only that your uncle and I have acted.'

My words dried up. I walked back to my room and sat on the bed. I stared at the flaking paint on the wall outlining the crack that ran from the ceiling almost to the level of the bed. I thought of myself as half-Pakistani. Was our Pakistani culture in Australia so different? Maybe Mum had unconsciously made me more Australian than Pakistani, for if this was Pakistani culture then everything that made me who I was fought against it. I dropped back onto the bed. People's faces swirled in my head: Aunty Khushida, Uncle Rasheed, Dadi jan saying it would be all right, Aunt Bibi suffocating me in a hug, Jamila smiling for the first time, Haider squeezing my arm, hurting me, Zeba pulling at me to come and read to her, Asher watching, always watching.

I lay there and must have finally slept for I dreamed of Omar and Marui — how he came on his camel to her humble village to abduct her and carried her to his fort in the desert. She refused all his attentions and gifts, and pined for her home and her childhood sweetheart. Her brother and cousins finally found her and took her home but Marui's starvation and pain of longing in Umarkot had taken its toll. Now she was dying. 'To die among you is sweeter than to live in a beautiful palace among strangers,' she said to her family. She died like a beautiful desert flower that grows then withers after the rains.

21

Things went from worse to disastrous. The next morning, breakfast was strained. Jamila was quiet, but it was an uneasy quiet. Even Zeba and Asher didn't say a word, as if they could sense an impending storm. I felt as if I had run a marathon; I was wrung out from a restless night thinking about the folk tales, and Dadi jan's marriage and how she was abducted. Tariq had told me the Koran said marriage had to be willingly entered into, but my relatives didn't seem to agree. As we sat together uneasily, munching on greasy parathas and eggs, Uncle Rasheed came in.

'Beti ji,' he addressed me. I looked up. So the veneer of politeness was to be continued even after he had taken my passports and ticket. 'I hear you have a mobile phone.'

I felt as if I'd been submerged in freezing water. I shot a look at Asher, but he half-shook his head.

Uncle Rasheed sat down. 'Hassan says he gave you one. Do you have it, beti?'

There was no point lying. 'Yes,' I said.

'I think it best that I keep it for you.'

Did he find this easy, I wondered. He scratched his beard, perhaps a sign of discomfort, but his face was as impassive as if he'd asked me to get the milk from the fridge. I didn't reply.

'Ameera.' It was a warning, but I took a chance.

'Uncle, Papa said the phone was for my safety. If I should get lost I can ring you.'

'You will never be alone here, beti.' Perhaps he meant to sound caring but to me it was a threat.

'You can use our phone to call home,' Aunty Khushida said. She glanced at her husband. I knew that look: Mum used it on Papa when she thought he might lose control.

'Get the phone, beti.' Uncle Rasheed's voice had a sudden edge to it, like Papa's often got: the hint of anger lurking.

I stood to go to the bedroom and had a sudden terrifying thought: what if Tariq should ring? He'd said he wouldn't but what if he changed his mind? And what if Uncle Rasheed answered it? There was Riaz too — I mightn't be able to ring him back and he'd think I was happy about the wedding. And Mum. I'd been considering getting Grandpa's number and asking her to change my flight or something. Oh, why hadn't I thought of that before?

And what if Uncle Rasheed went through my contacts list? There wasn't enough time to delete it but maybe there was time to send a message.

In my room, I sat on my bed and quickly texted Tariq: truble. dont rng or txt. I started a message to Riaz — no change — when I heard Aunty Khushida's footsteps. I pressed the send button, deleted all messages and turned the phone off, just as Aunty's hand came over my shoulder to take it.

'Your uncle cannot wait all day,' she said. Perhaps she could see how miserable I was for she didn't say anything else, she just left with my phone.

Now I had no means of contacting anyone privately. It was like being trapped in a nightmarish story of thwarted love. There was no way around any of it. I couldn't ask them to call the wedding off. I couldn't even talk to them about it: they had such a different view of it from me.

It was lunchtime when I showed my face in the kitchen. Aunty Khushida was cooking a chapatti. She pressed hard on it with a tea towel and the tava clanged against the stovetop.

'We need to go shopping today,' she said when she noticed me. 'Meena will come too.'

I was silent and she went on without looking at me. 'The wedding will be in two weeks.'

That got a response. 'Two weeks?'

She turned to face me with weariness etched in every line of her face but I didn't care. 'Aunty, how can you do this? I haven't consented. I haven't even seen the bridegroom.'

'Bibi does not want you to see him, she wants to surprise you. And we have talked of this before. It is your father who has said to have the wedding early.' Then she added, 'You will be happy.'

Papa had said I would be happy with the marriage too but I didn't believe any of them.

Aunty Khushida put the chapattis on the table wrapped in a bright cloth. 'Just accept this. It is a happy time.'

I stared at her, at the sadness in her face that belied her words. If it was a happy time why was she worried? Then I found myself saying something I never thought I would to her. 'Aunty ji, I'm frightened.'

This seemed to be a situation she knew how to handle. She came to me immediately, put her arms around me. 'Ameera, we women are always frightened at this time, frightened and happy both. But you need not be concerned. Shaukat is a good man, trust us. And Bibi, she will always treat you as if you were her own.'

'We'll live with Aunt Bibi?'

Aunty Khushida took time to consider her response and I grew worried afresh. 'Normally you would stay with your Aunt Bibi after the marriage since Shaukat has a clinic in the tribal areas, but in the circumstances we feel it is best that you go with Shaukat and get to know each other from the start.'

'The tribal areas?'

'He directs a clinic near Khala Dhaka, Black Mountain,' she added.

It meant nothing to me.

'It is near Mansehra.' She sighed noisily. 'Oh, Hassan.' She said it low and roughly and I realised it wasn't me she was annoyed with. Still it was small consolation.

By the time Meena came I had composed myself. Jamila had gone to school for the afternoon session. It seemed I could only help at the school when I wasn't shopping for the wedding. The shopping trip was a blur of sparkling material, shawls, dupattas, shoes and gold jewellery. Meena was kind to me and never left my side.

'I was so excited when it was my turn,' she told me. 'The jewellery alone was incredible. Imagine trying on all that gold.' She glanced at me and put an arm around my shoulders. 'Ameera, all will be good.'

She sounded like Dadi jan. How did they know it would be good for me? They didn't know about Tariq. But even if I hadn't met Tariq, I was sure I'd be upset with Papa for doing this. Would he have organised it this way if I hadn't been caught at the Collinses party? Maybe I was being punished after all and needed to submit to Papa's discipline. That's what Raniya would say. I thought of her and Maryam. How differently I had imagined my wedding: my friends giving me advice on clothes and colours, Mum taking me shopping, me overjoyed about the young man we'd chosen together: Tariq. In time I could have persuaded Papa to accept him. Instead, I was in a strange place, far away from my family and friends, being forced into a marriage I didn't want.

I lost count of how many gold shops we visited. They were all on the one street. Most only had a bench to sit on, some gold in the window, and a cabinet inside with more gold. In the last one, a man with a hooked nose bigger than Papa's brought some velvet-covered trays from a safe in a back room.

'Memsahib,' he said to Aunty Khushida, 'this is the latest we have. Twenty thousand rupees. You will not find anything as fine as this necklace in all of Muzaffarabad.'

If Aunty Khushida was impressed she kept it hidden. She sighed loudly. 'It is no different from any of the others. We shall have to go back to the first shop.'

I must have looked horrified: I was tired of gold shops. Maybe my expression convinced the man Aunty Khushida was genuine.

'All right, Memsahib, for you only fifteen thousand rupees for this beautiful piece.'

Still Aunty Khushida didn't look convinced. 'Come, we must go.' In a lower tone, she hissed, 'Stand up.'

Meena and I obeyed.

'Madam, thirteen fifty. I cannot go any lower or I will be selling below cost price.' He sounded genuinely worried.

Aunty Khushida flopped onto the bench. 'Oh, I suppose we can look at it again. Thirteen fifty?' She raised her eyebrows at the man and he nodded sadly.

'Let me buy you Pepsi,' he said, 'and then I am showing you earrings and bangles to match.'

'Thank you,' Aunty Khushida said with satisfaction, and a boy was despatched into the street.

I went to look at the pieces in the window. I wasn't interested in the gold necklace Aunty Khushida was about to buy me to wear at my wedding. Yes, it was beautiful but I hadn't chosen it. Nothing about this wedding was of my choosing. It took a moment for me to notice a young man holding out a paper bag. I frowned. *Wasn't it a boy who was sent for refreshments?*

'Missahiba, for later,' he said quietly, then in a louder voice added, 'Mittai, sweets for the bride.'

Aunty Khushida smiled at me, and the young man gave her and Meena a paper bag of sweets too. The bags were made from the pages of old exercise books showing sums worked out in large pencilled numbers. I glanced at the young man, but he half-shook his head. I shrugged and stuffed the bag into my handbag.

'Have a sweet,' Meena said to me. She took out a piece of barfi and nibbled from the corner. 'Mmm, delicious.'

'I'll eat them later,' I said. The young man smiled slightly as he swung back out to the street.

22

Back at the house, I slipped the bag of sweets into my backpack. I'd give them to Zeba later. Aunty Khushida had taken all our purchases to her room where she had a lockable cupboard. I sat on my bed to think. The stupor I'd felt in the shops had worn off. Now I thought about the sum of money that had changed hands in the gold shop. Aunty Khushida hadn't bought just the necklace but also earrings, bangles, a nose ring and teeka — the piece for my forehead — and that was just for the wedding ceremony. She'd bought another set of jewellery for the party at Aunt Bibi's house after the wedding. She must have spent fifty thousand rupees. It was frightening, as if every rupee raised the bounty on my head.

There had to be something I could do. I wondered if Haider was home. I put on a shawl and headed out to the mejalis. But just as I had my hand up to knock on the door, I checked myself. What did I think I was doing? 'If we were seen together,' he'd said. But there was no one here to see us. Did I want a confrontation with Haider when Aunty Khushida might not hear? Stupid idea.

Just as I was turning away, the door opened. 'Ameera, what are you doing near the men's room, hmm? Come to me at last?' How differently Tariq said my name. Haider made it sound cheap.

I turned to face him and cleared my throat. 'Do you know of any legal reason why this marriage shouldn't go ahead?'

He half-laughed. 'Like what? If Shaukat has another wife? That doesn't matter here.'

'I mean is it legal to marry a girl against her will?'

His eyes narrowed. 'When I spoke to you before, I didn't think the marriage was arranged.' He smiled slowly. 'But now it is too late. I have lost you and you have lost me. Such is life.'

I tried not to show how much his tone disgusted me. 'It is fixed then, with Shaukat?'

'All pukka and fixed, baby cousin. Shaukat is the lucky devil to lay you first. Or is he the first?'

He stepped closer and this time I didn't think about the consequences: I slapped his face and raced back to the house. I entered through the lounge and tried to slow my breathing. No one was there. Dadi jan must have been resting. There was no noise in the kitchen either so maybe Aunty Khushida was in her room. I looked out to the courtyard; Haider hadn't followed me as I'd feared and I tried to stop worrying about how he might retaliate.

I desperately wanted to speak to Mum. Surely I could remember the number if I tried. I crept over to the phone and dialled the number for Australia, then Adelaide, but no, I couldn't remember Gran's and Grandpa's number. At home we pressed a button on the caller list. Instead I punched in Maryam's number, hoping I had it right. I glanced at the door: still all clear.

Mrs Yusuf answered in her uncertain English. 'Yes?'

'Mrs Yusuf, this is Ameera. Is Maryam there?'

'Please speak up. Who is it?'

'Ameera Hassan.'

'Ah, beti,' she reverted to Urdu, 'how are you? How is your aunt, your uncle?'

'Theik hai, fine.'

'Is the weather cold?'

I didn't have time for this. 'Please, is Maryam there?'

'Ji, I will call her.' She sounded surprised that I could be so rude.

It was a whole minute before Maryam came. 'Ameera!' She was squealing.

'Maryam —'

'I've missed you.'

I felt mean but I couldn't waste any time. 'Maryam, tell Tariq and Riaz the wedding is in two weeks. Can you ring my mother?'

I couldn't tell if she heard me or not for her sentence overlapped mine. 'Tariq has spoken —'

I didn't get to hear the rest for Aunty Khushida was suddenly beside me, ripping the phone from my hand. She listened a moment then said, 'I am sorry, Ameera cannot speak now,' and pressed down the receiver. Then she fixed me with a look that I hadn't seen her wear before. It made me shrink backwards out of her reach.

'If you do this again I will be telling your uncle. In future, ask permission. You can be ringing your father, but no one else.'

She was waiting for a response; I nodded. Her face told me how much trouble I was for her. But I knew what Mum would say if she heard what was going on. Maybe Riaz had told her by now.

'Come, child, I need help in the kitchen,' Aunty Khushida said. She sounded calmer.

In the kitchen she handed me a bowl of peas to shell. I sat on the low red wooden stool I liked, with flowers hand-painted on it. Zeba had said it came from Swat. Aunty began to cut up okra on a board.

'I know this is difficult for you,' she said. 'You are not from here. But you must relax and enjoy this time. It is like being chosen to be a princess.'

When I didn't comment she carried on. 'If you win a prize in school it is because you have worked hard; you do not ask for it, you do not choose. This is the same: you have been chosen for the prize.'

I stared at her, amazed. 'But this is different, Aunty — this is my whole life. When I marry, my life will be totally … changed.' I almost said 'ruined' but switched it in time.

She smiled at me as if I had seen her point at last. 'Ji, that is correct. Inshallah, everything will be changing for the better.'

'What if I don't want it to change?'

Her smile died. She pointed the knife at me. 'You must be fixing your attitude and accept this situation. Your father has paid much money for you to be having a good and happy life.'

She dropped the okra into a saucepan and thumped it onto the stove, then glanced back at me. 'Hurry with those peas. Everyone will be coming soon.'

After dinner, while the newsreader reported more riots in Sindh, I sat with Dadi jan. She held my hand. 'I am very happy that you are living with us.'

A fresh surge of feeling for her rose up, making my eyes fill. 'Dadi jan, I don't want to get married but no one will listen.'

Her magnified eyes regarded me through her glasses. Kids at school in Australia would call them Coke bottoms. 'Do you remember the story of Hir and Ranjha?'

'Yes. Hir was finally allowed to marry who she chose but was killed for leaving her first husband.'

I wondered why Dadi jan had brought that up. None of the folk tales about lovers had happy endings. Was that my destiny too — to have a tragic ending?

'But what did she say in the ceremony?' There was a twinkle in Dadi jan's eyes.

I thought for a moment. 'She withheld her consent.' Then I added sourly, 'But it did no good, they married her without it.'

'However, she had a clear conscience before God when she refused her husband.'

I sucked in my breath. I hadn't thought that far ahead. I would have to sleep with Shaukat, and for the rest of my life. This was what I had saved myself for: not for a man I loved but someone I had to marry because Papa said so.

Dadi jan leaned towards me and whispered, 'Child, refuse your consent. I did.'

I was shocked. 'You, Dadi jan?'

She smiled. 'I knew the old stories.'

'But you were still married.'

'True, no one took notice of a girl, but I did not feel guilty when I refused Zufar later.'

'You did that?'

She gave a slight twist of her head. 'At first. Until I liked him.' She chuckled and I was struck by how she hid her wicked humour behind wrinkles and near blindness.

'He must have been a patient man.'

'Hahn ji. A good man will not force you, child.'

By the time I went to bed I had the seed of a plan.

Jamila was brushing her hair at the dressing table. Her sorrow at losing Shaukat was beginning to ebb and at times she had a faraway look. I wondered if she and Aunty Khushida were discussing suitable men she could marry. Her distraction now suited me: I could think about how to turn my plan into action.

I turned my back to Jamila and quietly counted what was left of the money Mum had given me. If I changed it all, I might have enough for a bus fare to Islamabad. Then I could catch a taxi to the Australian embassy. They would help me get a flight home — Grandpa would pay for it. *Once I get to Islamabad I'll be fine*, I thought, *but getting out of Muzaffarabad might be tricky*. I could go to school with Jamila, then say I was taking Zeba to the bazaar to buy make-up for the wedding. Of course I wouldn't take Zeba, and by the time Jamila realised she was still at school I'd be on the bus.

It was the happiest I'd felt since I'd arrived. Amazing how satisfying it was to be able to do something constructive. I climbed into bed and pulled the heavy quilt over my shoulder. The embassy would ring Mum. I would see Tariq again.

23

In the morning I asked to go to school with Jamila. A glance passed between her and Aunty Khushida and I saw a slight nod from my aunt. Maybe they thought getting out of the house would be good for me. I put on extra underwear and took another shawl in a shopping bag. I didn't want to arouse suspicion by taking the backpack. 'It gets cold in the tent,' I said to Jamila. I squashed my make-up into my handbag.

Aunty Khushida had made puri halva for breakfast. It was semolina and parathas, one of my favourites, and something we couldn't buy readily in Australia. I only ate it when Mrs Yusuf made it. How different it could have been if it was Tariq's family I was marrying into. Mrs Yusuf would enjoy teaching me how to cook her favourite dishes. I shook my head clear: I had to keep firm in my resolve and that didn't involve thinking about what might have been. I pictured Tariq smiling at me that night at the party when he looked directly at me. Tariq, who had written *Piari Ameera*, who would change my wooden and ceramic necklace into gold. But only if I returned home.

I went to the school with Jamila and taught English in Zeba's class. I don't know how I managed to keep my mind on the job. I kept thinking about what could go wrong. Maybe the buses were on strike — would that happen in Pakistan? Probably not. What if I didn't have enough money for the fare? Or someone noticed I was alone and told the police? I'd have to make sure that didn't happen. Pretend I was with someone else — that was Papa's answer to travelling alone.

The girls were all talking before I realised they weren't doing their work. 'Girls, be quiet.' They stopped playing around at once and returned to writing in their exercise books.

At the end of the lesson, I drew Zeba away from the others. 'I'm just going down to the bazaar, I won't be long. You can go home with Jamila.'

'You can't do that.' She looked horrified.

I had to think fast; some of her friends were looking at us. 'Asher will bring me back.'

'Oh.' She smiled. 'Can you buy me a surprise?'

I hated telling her a fib. 'I'll try,' was all I said. I hugged her. I'd grown fond of her and she'd be upset when I didn't return.

She ran off to play with Tariqah and I was free for the first time in weeks. It was both a heady and scary feeling. In the bazaar I changed my money in the same place as before. The man smiled at me as though he remembered me and I hurried out. I asked a woman for directions to the bus station; then thought it best to get a taxi and not draw attention to myself by walking alone.

The taxi driver studied me in his rear-vision mirror until I covered my nose with my shawl.

At the bus station I bought a ticket to Islamabad at a newly erected ticket box. The man there stared at me but didn't ask any questions. So far so good and I still had money left. I went into the makeshift waiting room for ladies and sat near a woman with two teenage daughters. Papa would have been pleased with me: we looked the perfect family.

'Are you going to Islamabad?' the woman asked in Urdu.

I nodded.

'Where is your father?'

I looked out the door as if he was there watching over me.

The woman smiled at me. 'Are you studying?'

'Yes, I have just finished matriculation.'

Her frown reminded me that the school year in Pakistan didn't finish until March. 'I mean for the year.'

Her face cleared. 'Zaitoon is studying in eighth grade and Gulshan is studying tenth grade, like you.' She smiled indulgently at her daughters.

I nearly corrected her about me being in tenth grade until I remembered that tenth grade is the matriculation year in Pakistan.

Gulshan smiled shyly at me. 'Are you from London?' she asked.

'No.'

'You speak with an accent, I just wondered.'

I expected the mother to tell her off for being nosy but I could see she was just as curious as her daughter.

She leaned closer and I didn't feel safe any more; I could see the speculation in her eyes. I mumbled some excuse about needing to see my father and left the room, even though I knew it was the wrong thing to do. Any father would expect his daughter to stay in the waiting room until he came to collect her.

Outside, a large group of men from the mountains had congregated. They had long beards, black turbans and Kalashnikovs and their stares were hungry and antagonistic. Those riots on the news the night before, could they happen here? I bought a bottle of Coke from a boy with an esky on makeshift wheels and hurried back to the waiting room. The woman wasn't as friendly this time, but I caught the girl Gulshan slipping me furtive smiles, so I returned them. I took out my book and tried to concentrate on the story. I must have read the same page ten times, and I checked my watch constantly. Once I was on the bus I would be safe, on my way back to Mum and Tariq.

There was a shout outside. The woman began collecting her bags and telling her daughters what to do. I stood up and followed them out. A harassed-looking man was directing women onto the bus first. He must have thought I was with the woman and her daughters for he flapped his hand at me to sit with Gulshan.

'Where are you from?' she asked when we were settled.

I didn't think it would hurt to tell her. 'Australia. I have been visiting relatives and now I am going home.'

'I wish I could go to Australia,' Gulshan said. 'Is it like Islamabad?'

I hadn't seen much of Islamabad that night I arrived. 'Maybe,' I said. 'Fewer people. It's clean, and Australians wear different clothes.' It was difficult to describe in a few sentences. My mind followed my heart. 'My mother is waiting for me there.'

'She didn't come with you?' Gulshan was all consternation.

'Australians are very independent,' I said.

Gulshan stared at me in wonder. 'Your father isn't here either, is he? He allows you to travel alone?'

'I am not alone, I am with you.'

She smiled at me then. It wasn't like her mother's smile, for her mother probably thought I was a fast and modern girl, but a smile of awe. 'Of course, you must be my sister for this trip.'

She seemed to feel she was part of an adventure. I didn't share her elation; I just couldn't wait for the bus to go. What if Jamila realised I'd left the school and came to find me? *Stop being stupid*, I chided myself. *How could Jamila know where I am?*

It wasn't Jamila who came; it was Haider. I saw him before he saw me. He was checking through the windows of the bus next to mine, then a young man directed him to my bus. I sank low into the seat and covered my face. There was no time to get off; besides, there were so many people pushing their way on that I'd cause a scene going against the tide. I prayed it wasn't me he was after.

Then he was on the step, talking to the man who'd directed me to my seat. The man pointed me out. A muscle moved near Haider's jaw as he saw me. He made a point of saying loudly, 'This is the wrong bus, Cousin. Come with me now.'

Gulshan's mother turned to look at me. She seemed slightly worried but Haider sounded reasonable. What would he do if I refused? Would the bus stay there until I got off with him?

'I have the money returned from your ticket,' he said then, as if he could read my thoughts. How polite he sounded and all so no one would know what I had tried to do. The family certainly stuck together.

I stood and excused myself to Gulshan.

'Are you all right?' she whispered.

I nodded. Disappointment was welling up inside me. The frustration at being so close to getting away must have showed in my eyes for she clasped my hand. 'I'm glad I met you.'

Haider turned away as I came down the steps and I followed him. We must have looked like a married couple: me walking a few metres behind, him confident that I was following. He led me a different way home, through an old shaded part of the bazaar I hadn't seen before. It looked like hardware shops: I saw ropes and chains and tools. The open drains had a pungent smell and I draped my shawl over my nose. This part of the bazaar was like a maze and soon my sense of direction evaporated. There were no women; it was almost sunset, 5.30 p.m., a time when they were at home cooking. I hurried to keep Haider in sight. Suddenly he stopped. He turned to face me and waited until I was close. I paused just out of arm's reach. He might have been the only familiar person in an unknown environment but I was still wary of him.

He closed the gap between us and moved forward, forcing me back against a wall. What he did next came so suddenly I had no warning. He slapped me across the face so that my head hit the wall behind me. I almost blacked out, and slid to the ground.

He pulled me up to face him. I knew what he'd do then — I saw it in his eyes — but I couldn't move my head; it was wedged between his hands. He put his mouth over mine. I tried to struggle, but he kept me still with the length of his body. I thought I'd die of the shame of having his tongue in my mouth. I bit down hard. His head swung away.

'Leopard bitch.' He held me with one hand and wiped his mouth. 'Quiet rivers run deep after all. Lucky Shaukat.' It was as if the mention of Shaukat reminded him of his job at hand. 'We must not damage this beauty for Shaukat, my little flower.'

He hit me across the head, so hard I thought my neck would break. His fist punched into my stomach and I doubled over and fell to the ground. I curled up as he kicked my backside and my back again and again. Then he stopped. I opened my eyes to see why. He had crouched beside me, his shoe centimetres from my face.

'You have to walk home, so I can't give you the beating you deserve. But let this be a warning, dear Cousin. If you try to dishonour our family again, trust me, I will kill you. Do you understand?' He put a hand under my neck and pulled my hair so I had to raise my head to look at him. 'Samajti hai? Do you understand?'

I grunted. It was all I could manage. Why didn't someone come? Surely there were men closing shops for the night — wouldn't they have heard me? Or hadn't I called out? I had no energy to scream now. Haider dropped my head to the ground then hauled me up. Now my lesson was over, he could afford to be magnanimous. He put my shawl over my head — I couldn't lift my arms — and gave me my bags. 'Chello. Walk now.'

Periodically he checked I was behind him. I didn't think I'd manage the incline to the house. My pace became slower by the minute yet I made it. Haider was by the gate when I finally limped inside. His face was a blank mask and I was determined not to show him how much I hurt. I staggered past him into the courtyard. I didn't dare stop there, it was too cold. I needed a warm shower. I went straight to the bathroom to avoid Jamila telling me off for leaving the school.

It was Jamila who noticed later that I couldn't walk properly. If I'd been hurt like this in Australia, Mum would have taken me to Emergency and called the police. But no one here even mentioned it; I didn't even know if Haider had told them where he'd found me. In silence Jamila rubbed ointment onto my buttocks and back. She checked my head and muttered once. Apart from a red mark on one cheek, my face, as Haider had promised, was untouched.

I couldn't put food into my bruised stomach — I was sure it would come straight up. Besides, my head throbbed, so I went to bed. I was reminded of a film I'd seen: *Not without My Daughter*. I'd always thought that woman could have made it easier on herself by not fighting — they would have accepted her in time — but now I understood how she must have felt: as if a conveyor belt in a sawmill had been turned on and there was no getting off.

I lay half on my middle and half on my side, the only spot that didn't hurt so much, and felt the ointment seeping into my muscles, making them burn.

24

The next day all Aunty Khushida could talk about was the bus arriving in Muzaffarabad from Srinagar. It captured her attention even more than Benazir Bhutto's assassination. A bus service had begun between Indian Kashmir and Pakistani Azad Kashmir and for the first time in sixty years relatives would be able to visit each other.

'I have never seen my cousin who lives in Srinagar,' Aunty said. 'Now I can.'

I wondered if militants would attack the bus. It would only run once a fortnight: no doubt a test to see if anyone dared use it.

I sat gingerly at the breakfast table. Zeba catapulted into my lap and I gasped with pain.

'You were late yesterday,' she said, 'and Asher couldn't find you.'

So Asher hadn't let on that I'd never arranged to meet him. How interesting. Zeba studied my face. I touched the cheek Haider had slapped. Was there still a mark there?

'Did you get me something?' she asked.

I squinted at her, wondering what she meant.

'My surprise.' And she smiled. I was forgiven if I had a surprise.

I thought of the bag of sweets from the gold shop. 'You have to hop off and then I can get it.' It hurt again when she jumped down. I pushed myself up and tried to move normally, but she noticed.

'Do you have a sore back, Ameera?'

'Must have been how I slept.'

Why did I cover it up? I thought of the chance that they may know about the beating. I couldn't bear to tell Uncle Rasheed and then find out that he had ordered it.

'Dadi jan gets a sore back in her sleep,' Zeba said, and so I was dismissed.

I found reaching down difficult, but I sat on my bed and dragged my backpack closer so I could pull out the paper bag. I looked inside and smiled: the sweets were barfi, made from condensed milk and almond flavouring. Mrs Yusuf made barfi at Christmas; it was square, like the coconut ice that Gran made. There was a lot in the bag so I took a few pieces out, then my hand froze. My fingers had touched plastic. I checked inside and found a mobile phone and a compact charger. I remembered the young man's face as he gave the bag to me. 'For later,' he'd said quietly. He'd smiled when I'd said I'd eat them later, as if I was repeating part of a code.

There was a note too. *Dear Miss Ameera Hassan*, it said. *I am in Special Services with the Australian High Commission and I go by the name of Frank. We have been contacted by a person in Australia who is worried about you. Please ring this number and tell me if you are in trouble or if you are just on holiday here. Please keep this phone secret. Learn the number and destroy this letter.* Below was his signature and the number. It had two sets of triple digits and would be easy to learn. There was a password too.

How weird was that? How did the young man in the gold shop know to give it to me? Suddenly I realised how stupid I'd been to think I could leave by myself. Any one of the people I'd seen could have tipped off Haider: the money-changer, the taxi driver, the ticket-seller. My family probably knew everyone. It would have been easy for the messenger to simply watch out for the new Australian girl.

'Ameera?'

It was Zeba. I quickly stuffed the phone into my handbag as she came into the room.

'I have something for you, Zeba.'

She came to sit with me on the bed. 'Mmm, almond barfi. My favourite.'

She chattered on about sweets at weddings and Eid, and which flavours she liked the best, but I couldn't concentrate. Tears sprang into my eyes; help was coming after all.

It was late afternoon before I managed to ring Frank. I sat in the pavilion by the Persian garden. It must have been his personal number for he answered immediately. 'Frank here.' He sounded efficient.

'This is Ameera Hassan. You gave me a phone?'

'Ah, yes.' His voice was like my Uncle Richard's, earthy and strong. It made me feel he could do anything. 'Right.' He paused slightly. 'Your mother has rung me and says you have a problem.'

'Mum? I've been here over a week and I haven't been able to get in touch with her. Is she okay?'

'Sure, but very worried about you. She wanted us to send mercenaries in to get you,' he chuckled, 'but I'm the closest she'll get. At least I was in the SAS. Besides, helping you has to be done legally. Now, she's been trying to contact you every day apparently, but your relatives always say you're out.'

I stood up. 'No one told me Mum rang.'

There was a pause. 'I'm afraid they're blocking your mother's calls. She says her husband would have asked them to do that. For your benefit, no doubt.' His tone was dry.

'But that's terrible. I'll ask —'

'Ameera, don't say anything to them.'

'But —'

'How will you explain how you know?'

I could see his point and stayed silent.

'Your brother thinks there's a wedding being arranged,' he went on. 'Is that true?'

His straight talk made it easier to admit the truth. 'Yes, it's for me.'

'Are you happy about that?'

'No. I want to go home.'

'But they're not listening?'

'No. My family here say it's a wonderful opportunity.'

176

'And you don't agree?'

'No.'

'Right, that's all I needed to hear. It's an offence to marry a girl without her permission. It's not supported by Islam or by the judicial system in Australia, or here now either.'

I felt a lightening sensation in my head. 'It's illegal here?'

'Yes, since the government passed a bill last year. That doesn't stop it happening though, but it does mean we can get you out of there.'

I caught myself holding my breath. 'Truly? When?'

'It's tricky — we have to get police assistance and that can take a while, especially now with Benazir Bhutto's assassination. When's the wedding?'

'Less than two weeks. I think they're even skipping the engagement party to make it go through quicker. Actually, they act as though I'm already engaged, but I didn't consent to anything.'

I remembered Aunt Bibi putting the red dupatta over my head and the ring on my finger: that had probably been the engagement. At the time I'd had no idea.

He made a sound I didn't catch.

'Is there a problem?' I asked.

'There are always problems. Look, we'll do our best to get there in time.' He asked for my address. 'Is that where the wedding will be?'

'I think so. Part of it anyway.'

'I don't suppose you have your passport?'

'No, my uncle took both my passports.'

'I'll try to pull some strings. I'll text information through.' It sounded as though he was writing notes. 'Okay, keep this phone hidden and on silent, and check for messages. Oh, and Ameera?'

'Yes?'

'Do you know a Tariq Yusuf?'

I hesitated.

'He seems to know you.' There was humour in Frank's voice.

'He's my brother's friend.'

'Hmm. Actually I've spoken to both of them. So are you happy if Mr Yusuf and your brother are included in the progress of your situation?'

'Yes.'

'Your mother wanted to come to Pakistan but I have persuaded her not to.'

I started to protest but he cut in. 'It'll be easier for us to get you out without your mother to worry about as well. We've found mothers are powerless to stop a wedding and she may be put in danger. Do you understand?'

My voice was small when I answered. 'I think so.' How good it would have been to see Mum. My eyes were tearing up and I blinked them clear.

'Ring whenever you feel worried, okay? But only use this phone. Have you been threatened at all?'

'My cousin beat me up yesterday.' There was a silence on the other end. 'I tried to run away,' I added.

'I'm sorry to hear that.' Frank's voice was quieter. 'But there's something I want you to do.'

'Yes?'

'Don't try to run again. From now on you must go along with the wedding plans.'

'Why?'

'So they won't be watching you all the time. If they think you've accepted the marriage, they'll relax and it'll be easier to get you out. Trust me on this.'

Two different men had told me that in the space of twenty-four hours. Even Aunty Khushida had said it. Could I trust Frank any more than Haider and Aunty? I had to; he was my only option. 'Okay,' I said.

'Good girl. Now don't worry. The British Forced Marriage Unit makes the run up your way every week. We'll sort something out for you.'

Relief and surprise almost made my knees sag. There was actually a department for this?

'I'll ring your mother now to get a photo. Any message?'

My voice choked up suddenly as I answered. 'Please tell her I miss her and I wish I was home.' It was all I could manage.

There was a short pause, then he said quietly, 'Hang in there. And try to look happy.' Then he rang off.

I sank onto the pavilion bench. In all my wildest imaginings I hadn't expected this. I wondered if the phone would cope with me ringing Tariq. If I could hear his voice, even just for a moment, maybe I could be brave until Frank came.

I entered the number of Tariq's mobile and held my breath. I heard the dial tones, counted five, six, seven ... was he there? Then a click. 'Hello.'

I would recognise the vibrancy of that voice anywhere. 'Tariq.'

'Ameera.' He hesitated as though he was shutting a door. 'Are you okay?'

I closed my eyes. What a relief to hear my name just the way he said it, with that slight roll of the 'R', the 'A' like the fluttering of a prayer. I forced myself not to cry. 'Not really, but I just spoke to the Australian embassy. They'll try and get me out of the country, but I'm scared —'

Tariq cut in. 'What of?'

'If they don't get here in time, of Haider.'

'Is Haider the ... the groom?' His voice couldn't conceal his pain.

'No, he's another cousin, and he thinks he's responsible for keeping me in line.'

'Tell your uncle.'

'I don't think that will help. They all think the marriage is a great idea, and don't know why I'm so ungrateful.'

'Ameera, this kills me. I wish I was there.'

I hardly hesitated. 'If you were here I'd be happy about a wedding.'

There was a silence while he must have wondered how brazen I'd become. But I wanted him to know. 'Tariq, it's you I love.'

It was like a dam bursting. 'And I will love you no matter what happens. Will you remember that?'

'Yes.'

'Whatever happens — even if you decide you should go through with the wedding —'

'I'll never —'

'I'm sorry, I have to say this. My background isn't so different from yours and I know the pressures. No one should be forced to marry, but if you do it for your own sake, and you're happy about it, I can live with it.'

His words made me cry. 'Tariq, don't say that. I don't want to marry anyone else.'

'Then I'll do all I can. All I think about is what you must be feeling.' His voice broke then. 'I love you, Ameera. I hope that will comfort you in whatever happens.'

We were both quiet a moment, then I said, 'Thank you for the necklace — it helps.'

'You're welcome.' They were light-hearted words but his voice sounded wobbly.

I didn't want to but I ended the call in case the credit ran out and I wasn't able to ring Frank later. I sat in a trance afterwards. Tariq had made me feel stronger. I prayed out there in the garden, even though it was cold and it hurt to kneel, and then went inside with my shalwar damp from the grass.

That night there was a message for me:

```
Tariq helping me send this. Have contacted
embassy. They have experience helping
girls out of the country. Do everything
frank says. We wont ring this no, too
risky for you. All the family here
praying. Can't wait to see you. All my
love mum.
```

25

The next morning I put Frank's advice into action. I thanked Aunty Khushida for the trouble she'd gone to for me. Her mouth opened and shut twice before she managed to respond. 'Accha, that's good.' Then she looked at me long and hard. I smiled at her.

'Bibi wants to take you shopping,' she said eventually.

'What time shall I be ready?'

Aunty Khushida was lost for words except for one phrase: Al hum du lillah. She whispered it as a prayer. I thought I shouldn't overdo it; for one thing, I felt like a hypocrite, and secondly, it didn't take much to remind me that this wasn't a game. If it all went wrong I could be stuck here for good. I didn't even know how Frank was going to 'get me out' as he called it. I just had to trust that something would happen before the wedding.

Meena came with us to the bazaar. I remembered to cover my head when the Azan sounded, and tried to look interested when gold brocade material was laid out in front of me. Aunt Bibi shook her head and the shopkeeper flung out more clouds of cloth like sails on a summer's day. I lost count of how many lengths of fabric she bought. I wasn't asked what I liked. Aunt Bibi would put a bolt of cloth against my face and Meena would say how much it suited me and that was it. Then we were off to the tailors. Aunt Bibi had to pay double for having the outfits sewed quicker.

'She's only just arrived from Australia for the wedding,' Aunt Bibi explained. She enveloped me in a hug and I felt myself slipping down a dark tunnel. I chanted God's names in my head to mask the fear, to remind me I was still me.

I wasn't consulted about the designs either. I could sew well and was usually interested in fabrics and designs, but Meena had that all sorted. She gave the tailor pictures of shalwar qameezes from fashion magazines. 'Copy these,' she said. It took ages to explain which cloth went with which design. The man wrote it all down in an old exercise book, making painstaking curls with a blunt pencil stub. I watched in a haze, managing to smile when Aunt Bibi glanced at me.

My wedding suit was bought ready-made: a gharara, red and gold, with a shawl to match. Instead of a shalwar there was a long divided skirt. The embroidery on the dupatta was sewn with thread spun from pure gold. My soul was being sold, and only Frank's voice in my head stopped me from telling Aunt Bibi I couldn't do this any more.

Shoes were bought with the same intensity. David Jones would make a killing if 160 million Pakistanis lived in Australia, I thought wryly. There was a pair of shoes for each suit; Meena had kept a swatch from each piece of cloth to match the colours. Make-up was given the same attention: for each cloth, a different lipstick, eye shadow, nail polish. Everything matched and everything was haggled over. We went to henna shops, sweet shops, bangle shops, underwear shops, although there was nothing in Muzaffarabad like the lingerie shops back home. I tried not to cringe when Meena waved a cone-shaped bra in front of my eyes. I wouldn't have wanted Tariq to see me dead in it.

Meena and Aunt Bibi were laughing as if they were at a party. For the first time I let myself wonder what it would be like if I went through with the wedding. Papa would be happy with me. I hadn't allowed myself to think about the alternative yet: that if I stood Shaukat up at the ceremony, I would be disowned. I would lose my whole Pakistani family, my identity. Could I be brave enough for that? And was it bravery or disobedience? Would God disown me too? I knew Mum and Riaz, Grandpa and Gran wouldn't disown me. Nor would Tariq. The thought of him brought a true smile to my lips.

There was so much to carry, Aunt Bibi paid two boys to take it all to her house. I was glad for my back ached: I still hadn't recovered from the beating. She returned with me to Uncle Rasheed's and she and Aunty Khushida chuckled together in the kitchen. I was struck by the sound: it was the first time I'd heard Aunty Khushida laugh since I'd arrived.

After supper Uncle Rasheed came to watch TV with us. He smiled at me. 'I hear you enjoyed shopping today, beti. Inshallah, you will enjoy the next days very much — the happiest of a girl's life. I am glad to be making you happy.'

I stared at him; he really meant it. Frank's idea was working, but a fresh wave of fear crashed onto me. What was I doing? I felt as if I was drowning myself and it would be my fault when the sea closed over me and the air ran out.

'Ji, beti,' he said. 'You will be thankful. You come from a different place but our hearts are one. You will be happy with us. It is good you are seeing this at last.'

Aunty Khushida smiled at me too. They probably thought I'd just been acting like a spoilt kid and now I was being mature about it. Dadi jan, Asher and Jamila watched me unsmiling. Were they fooled? I wasn't sure.

Haider wasn't fooled. He waylaid me in the courtyard next morning after prayer time. I'd taken to praying in the garden; I felt closer to God in the cold air under an open sky. I'd never prayed so much. If Papa had seen me he would have said sending me to Pakistan had worked out for the best, but I was praying for an escape. I had been taught that to obey Papa was also following God but now I was confused. Was it possible to keep God's blessing if I defied Papa? I was deep in thought when Haider grabbed my arm. I couldn't help my reaction. The trembling started in my legs and relentlessly moved up my body until I could hardly breathe. How brave was I now? Faced with danger, I turned into a rabbit. I hoped my fear didn't show but I swear he knew. He smiled in that sleazy way of his but anger sparked in his eyes too.

'I can't believe you have learnt your lesson so quickly,' he said. 'I thought you would need more persuasion.'

I fought down my disgust as I saw he had been looking forward to teaching me more lessons.

Then he said evenly, 'Who is Mr Tariq Yusuf?'

My eyes opened wide while my mind raced. He couldn't have heard me on the phone the other day. Then I remembered my old mobile. He must have checked my contacts list. There were no messages so he couldn't know anything for sure.

'He ... he is my best friend's brother. She doesn't have a phone and he gives her my messages.' I hoped none of what I felt for Tariq had slipped into my voice.

Haider pulled me closer and my shawl slipped. It was as if I was paralysed — I made no protest. 'So, Shaukat is getting damaged goods.'

Haider had said he would kill me if I dishonoured the family. The initial affront of him ripping into my privacy was swiftly overcome by terror. Dread burst in my chest like a bomb. 'No.'

Haider laughed, but then he stopped and stared at me. The violence I feared hadn't flowered yet but his laughter unnerved me. He put his hands around my neck. His fingers seemed gentle but I knew what they were capable of. 'So beautiful,' he murmured and stared at me through his lashes. My stomach churned as he quoted an old proverb: 'A lie has no legs to stand on.' I felt the pressure of his thumbs on the arteries in my neck. 'If you are lying, and you ever contact this Tariq, I will kill him too.'

Nervous reaction made me grin stupidly. Surely he was joking. 'In Australia?'

'You are so ignorant.' His face was close to mine. 'Sunno, listen, all you have to do is be a good girl and all will be well.' Then his fingers found Tariq's necklace under my scarf. 'What's this stupid thing? Wood?'

He yanked at it. My throat constricted and I gagged. I thought I'd be strangled after all, but mercifully the thread broke. The beads scattered on the ground; I heard them bounce away from me. I forced myself not to pick them up or he would know how much the necklace meant to me. Instead, I stood staring past his shoulder and he pushed me away as if I was the one who had been restraining him.

When he had gone I salvaged what I could of Tariq's necklace and retreated to the Persian garden. I sat on the bench in the pavilion shaking, and it was nothing to do with the cold. The beads were clenched in my hand; the tears still hadn't come.

'Meri bachi,' said an ancient voice. 'My child.'

I looked up; it was Baba ji. He shuffled closer and handed me more beads and then put his hand on my head in blessing. He was just a gardener, yet at that moment he reminded me of Grandpa and his hand on my head felt like the brush of an angel's wing.

26

Everyone was busy over the next week.

Food for the wedding was organised with the local barbers. It sounds weird but traditionally Pakistani barbers always cook for weddings. Aunty Khushida and Meena had bought the outfit Shaukat would wear at the ceremony, just as Aunt Bibi had bought mine. It was hanging in Aunty Khushida's room. Once I went in to look at it. It was long and elegant with a Nehru collar, cream with gold stitching, pure silk. I could imagine it on Tariq. I began to wonder what Shaukat was like. Would I even get to meet him or would Frank turn up first?

So far Frank hadn't made contact again. A week wouldn't seem so long to him but for me it was the length of my life as I knew it.

Haider put up lights around the outside walls. I made sure I was never in the garden or courtyard at a time he could be home and so managed to avoid him. He may have broken my necklace but there were enough beads left to make an anklet, and I wore it in defiance.

The week before the wedding was called 'mayon'. Cousins and aunts I'd never met before came to the house to sit with me and sing songs. From that night Meena put me in an old yellow shalwar qameez and I wasn't allowed to leave the house. Each day she pulled the curtains in my room to darken it and I was only allowed to drink milk, eat fresh fruit and sweet dishes to help cleanse my skin: the Pakistani version of detox. At least I was safe from Haider, but it meant I couldn't ring Frank for I was never alone.

Every day of mayon I was given a beauty treatment. The first day Aunt Bibi and her married daughter, Fozia, came with a special paste called uptan, made from oil, turmeric and flour, and spread it over my face and hands. Then Aunt Bibi blessed me. The uptan was like something from the Body Shop, but it didn't smell as good and I was sure it'd make me look jaundiced. Meena waved my objections aside. She was the one who spread the uptan over my body every day until the wedding. She never made a direct comment about my bruises the first time I lay on my stomach, just clucked.

Aunt Bibi came again another day and by her air of excitement I could tell that Shaukat had arrived home. She was looking at me as though I was about to receive the biggest blessing ever. I suddenly thought how disappointed she'd be when I disappeared. Right then I wouldn't have minded if Frank turned up on a magic carpet. There were only a few days left: where was he?

Two days before the ceremony all the women of the house went to Aunt Bibi's to sing songs for the groom and to put uptan on his face and hands. Jamila was chosen to put henna on his little finger; I felt sorry that all she reaped from her dreams was a little finger. Of course I wasn't allowed to join in the fun. So when they were all at Aunt Bibi's I took the chance to contact Frank.

He answered immediately like last time. 'Frank here.'

I was so relieved that I started to babble. 'I was wondering how everything's going. I haven't been able to ring — someone's been with me all the time.'

'Sorry I haven't contacted you. I've been waiting for something good to tell you.'

His voice sounded tired and my heart sank. 'There's a problem?'

'I'm afraid so. The Australian passport's under way but it's the police assistance that's holding us up. This has to be done legally — you understand?'

There was a pause and I spoke quietly into it. 'Yes.'

'The police have been caught up with extra work because of the riots since Bhutto's death, but it's easing now. We just have to get the paperwork through. I'm trying my best, Ameera.'

I was sure he was but would his best be enough? To my mind the marriage was the end; there was no life after that.

'What will happen if you can't make it?' I asked.

'If we can't get there in time, then keep the mobile with you and we'll get your new contact details. Do you know where you'll be living after the wedding?'

I didn't like the way he said that, as if the wedding was going to happen. 'I can find out.'

'Do that just in case. And, Ameera, we will get you

190

out. I'm sorry if it's after the wedding, but can you …'
He stopped and sighed with what sounded like
exasperation. 'This is a hard job. Look, I'll say this
straight. Maybe the groom won't force himself. Do you
follow what I'm saying?'

'I think so.'

Dadi jan had said the same: refuse the groom. At least
until I liked him. But didn't a marriage have to be
consummated to be valid? The walima — the wedding
party two days after the ceremony — was expressly for
celebrating just that: the consummation of the wedding.
Just two days.

'Will you hurry though?' I said it before I could stop
myself. Then I whispered, 'People are kind but I'm …
I'm frightened.'

'We'll be there as soon as the police paperwork comes
through — it's the last thing. You have to be strong —
one way or the other we'll get you out.'

But would he be too late? No other man would have
me if the wedding had been consummated. I couldn't ask
that even of Tariq.

I sniffled as I put the phone in my handbag, then blew
my nose. A faint noise made me glance at the doorway.
Asher stood there staring at me. How much had he
heard? I couldn't read his expression. I closed my eyes,
imagining the consequences if they found out about
Frank. What would they do? What would Haider do?
My eyes flew open, then I remembered that Haider
couldn't come in here.

I relaxed and smiled tentatively at Asher. 'You didn't
go to Aunt Bibi's?'

'I am here to look after you.'

He hesitated in the doorway, then came in slowly. He was young enough to know he was allowed, old enough to want to be barred. I checked his face. He had none of Haider's anger. Would he tell Uncle Rasheed that I had another phone? But his eyes were guileless.

'I wish you weren't leaving,' he said. Then he grinned, a boy again. 'You would only have to wait ten years then you could marry me.'

'I'd have grey hair by then.' I followed his lead; he was playing this light. Maybe he hadn't noticed the phone.

'All this fuss over a wedding. So much money, and I have friends at school who still live in tents.'

Surprise made me gasp.

'One of my friends says it is disrespectful to have a wedding so soon after Begum Bhutto's death.'

I wished I'd thought of that. Maybe I could have had it postponed.

'Perhaps your parents feel it's okay since it was already arranged,' I said.

'Abu says life has to go on — weddings, births, deaths. It is the life cycle and we can't stop everything for a tragedy or the militants have affected us after all.' Then he said, 'Why were you crying? Don't you want to marry Shaukat?'

Could I trust him? I hesitated but the need to let my feelings out was strong. 'No. I don't expect you to understand but where I come from people meet each other before they are married. They marry because they want to, not because they're told to.'

'You didn't know you were going to be married when you came, did you?'

I shook my head.

'Haider said you would be trouble because Uncle Hassan had not told you.'

There was no doubt Haider thought I was trouble even now, when I was pretending I was enjoying myself.

'It is not fair,' Asher said. 'You do not want to get married and Jamila does.'

I attempted a grin. 'They should just swap us, eh?'

'It is not possible. Aunt Bibi likes doing things in the old way — she is having a big mirror after the nikah and in it Shaukat will see you for the first time.'

I sighed. 'I was joking.'

He sat on the bed and sighed with me. 'When I get married I am not going to force my wife or daughters to do anything.'

'No? How will you manage that?'

'I shall be the boss.' He stared at me defiantly.

I smiled at his innocence. He still didn't understand the force of the culture we were born into, how it often made people act differently from what they wanted.

'Asher, do you know the address of Aunt Bibi's house?'

'Everyone knows where Iqbal Iman and Bibi Zufar live. Do not worry, the limousine will take you there after the wedding. Everything will be done for you.'

That was what I was afraid of.

'And Shaukat — where is his clinic in the mountains? Have you been there?'

Asher shook his head. 'It is near a place called Oghi on the border of Khala Dhaka.'

'Is it far?'

He shrugged. 'Many hours by car, more in winter. He comes across the mountains from Mansehra to visit Aunt Bibi and Uncle Iqbal.' Then his face brightened. 'He has a first-class car, I saw it yesterday — a Toyota Prado. It is four-wheel drive. Only the foreigners from aid agencies have cars like that.' Then it was as if he couldn't contain himself and I wondered if this was why he'd come to seek me out. 'There are so many surprises for you, but there is a special one tomorrow.'

'Seeing Shaukat at last?' I said dryly.

'No, another special surprise.'

Asher's eyes brimmed with it but he wouldn't tell me. I just hoped it wasn't a surprise like the one Papa had sprung on me.

27

The next day was the mehndi ceremony during which the groom's female relatives draw henna patterns on the bride's hands. 'Mehndi' is the Urdu word for henna, which is a symbol of joy. I felt as if I was in a trance, as if all this was happening to someone else.

As I was being dressed in a lovely but simple unembroidered green outfit, Jamila told me about the fun at Aunt Bibi's the day before. I saw speculation in her eyes and wasn't sure what it meant. Was it jealousy? Awe? Pity? By then my imagination was running wild; I wasn't sure of anything except that the sand in my hourglass was running out. Every time there was a knock on the gate I'd tense, wondering if it was Frank, but it was always more relatives I'd never met.

Aunt Bibi, her three daughters-in-law, Fozia and a menagerie of distant female relatives arrived bearing pots of henna paste prepared by Fozia. 'Fresh is better than bazaar-bought for such an important occasion,' Aunt Bibi said. Meena and Jamila were there as well as numerous cousins I didn't know. Zeba was vying for the front seat and asking to do some patterns, but Fozia was an artist, apparently, and had been elected for the task. I hadn't been allowed to have a shower the whole week because of the uptan treatment. Now I had to sit on the little Swati stool in the bedroom with my head lowered while Fozia brought the henna in on a round tray decorated with gold tinsel. She danced, and the other women clapped and sang a song about the groom.

Oh my beau! Thy mare is so lovely;
Graced with the saddle, a saddle worth thousands
    of lakhs,
I be thy sacrifice, O thou darling of thy mother;
Come marching through the garden,
Beating kettledrums.

Then Meena and Jamila led the women from our family to sing a song in return:

The daughter's mother and father weep
Like the clouds of the rainy season.
Why do you weep, my parents?
This is what befalls the whole world.

There was a lot of laughing, and jokes were thrown back and forth, though I didn't catch the meanings. I understood the song about the parents weeping. Mum would be crying if she knew this was happening. Not Papa though.

Then all the women danced while Fozia kneeled on a cushion and drew designs on my hands. She used the

Kashmiri leaf motif that Australians call paisley, along with dots, lines, flowers and arches. Even a few hearts. What a joke. There was nothing about this wedding that engaged my heart, except that it was breaking for Tariq. Henna was meant to mark the bride for happiness, but I felt stained.

'Shall I put the groom's name?' Fozia asked.

I shook my head in horror and hoped I just appeared shy.

When Fozia was finished the dancing stopped and Aunt Bibi called my name. 'Ameera, we have a surprise for you.'

So Asher was right. I knew some families allowed the bridegroom to visit the mehndi ceremony, though he wouldn't see much of the bride for her head was always kept lowered. I wasn't ready to see Shaukat and stubbornly I refused to look up.

'Ameera.' Aunt Bibi's voice bubbled with joy as she called me again and there was a hush in the room. Curiosity won. I looked up, and my breath caught in my throat. It was Papa. He was smiling at me with tears in his eyes. I stood and the women made way for me. I couldn't hug him for I'd ruin the henna: it took hours for the dye to set. There was so much I wanted to say to Papa but I couldn't speak in front of an audience or I'd dishonour everybody.

'You look truly Kashmiri, beti. I have waited for this day.'

Aunt Bibi flittered around him like a peahen. 'Wait till you see her tomorrow, Hassan — you won't recognise her.'

'Why have you come, Papa? Is Mum here?' He shook his head at Mum's name. 'I have come to see you married — to make sure this actually happens.'

The women laughed easily, but I wondered why he'd said such a thing. Did he guess I may try to escape?

'It makes me so happy to see you like this, to see you embracing our ways.'

'Can I talk with you alone?' I asked.

Aunty Khushida nodded and I took Papa into the courtyard. Though it must have been cold, I didn't notice. We sat on a stringed bed and, encouraged by the tears in his eyes, I begged for his understanding.

'Papa, I don't want to marry. If you can't stop it I will refuse my consent. No one listened to me, and now I just have tomorrow to say no.'

Papa closed his eyes and when he opened them I was struck by the hurt and disbelief I saw there. 'Rasheed said you were happy about the wedding now.'

'They don't know how I feel. They don't understand, but you're my father. You want me to be happy.'

'Of course. That is why I have arranged the wedding with Shaukat.'

'They wouldn't even let me see him.'

'We thought it best under the circumstances.'

'Papa, you understand, don't you, that I can't marry tomorrow?' I saw how it could all happen: I could go back with him. 'You and I could travel home. We can be together again, just the four of us.'

Papa stood up and looked away; when he turned to face me, the softness was gone. 'There is something you must understand: this cannot be undone. I have arranged it out of love so you will be happy. You don't understand how settled you will be after marriage, you have to trust me.'

'Everyone wants me to trust them, but why can't someone trust me and my feelings?'

'Feelings?' His face screwed up as though I'd said a foreign word. 'You are being foolish now. Do you not think your elders know more than you about how to organise your life? You must trust your elders.'

My resolve was slipping. I'd never been able to defy Papa. 'What can be done?'

'Not what you are asking. And believe me: afterwards you will be glad.'

'But —'

'There are no buts. Listen carefully: if you do not obey me tomorrow you will incur God's wrath. Which will you choose: a marriage lived in paradise or an eternity of damnation?'

I gave it one last shot. 'But, Papa, God doesn't condone marriage when the girl refuses. There's even a law against it here.'

He slapped me and I held my cheek in shock. 'This is evil talk. Who have you been listening to? The Koran tells children to be obedient. Is this obedience?'

I wanted to say marriage was different, that this wasn't a case of being disobedient, but a dart of doubt pierced me. What if Papa was right and I had to obey him to ensure God's mercy? By all accounts Shaukat wasn't a bad man; my life shouldn't be a nightmare like Nargis's was.

Papa took my quietness for acquiescence. He put an arm around my shoulders. 'I hope I don't need to remind you about your duties as a daughter. This is not all about you. A marriage is for the whole family.' He paused. 'But I am also thinking of your future and your happiness. Tomorrow will be a happy day, you will see.'

Aunt Bibi flapped outside and drew us back into the lounge. By then I was weeping, but no one took any notice. I'd just had a huge surprise; tears of joy were expected.

Long after Papa had gone to the mejalis with Uncle Rasheed to eat, the singing and dancing in the house went on, late into the night. All I wanted to do was go to bed and never wake up.

28

I woke on the morning of the ceremony feeling sick. Jamila was in the bathroom so I checked the phone. There was a message. Frank had left it late; would I be able to get away now? But the message said how sorry he was that the paperwork wasn't through.

> we have to come after the ceremony. will you
> be at grooms parents house?

It was a while before I could reply. So I was going to have to go through with the wedding. In my heart I would be refusing Shaukat, but did that count in God's eyes? Then that doubt washed over me again. Would God want me to marry to keep Papa happy? Then Tariq flooded my mind — how could I even think of not marrying him?

> will be at grooms parents house. walima there
> in 2 days time.

I gave Frank Uncle Iqbal's full name; he'd be able to find them by asking in the bazaar.

I tried not to dwell on what the walima was for. I'd be a false bride, for although they could force me to marry Shaukat they couldn't force me to sleep with him.

Meena came in then to wash off the beauty treatments I'd been subjected to all week. I was to be treated as a princess all day; she even showered me. Any enthusiasm I'd tried to conjure up before the wedding was gone, yet no one minded. This was how a bride was supposed to be: sorrowful at leaving her parents' home. But it was all wrong; this wasn't my parents' home; Mum wasn't even here. All their kindness couldn't disguise the fact that I was being made to do something I didn't want to do.

It took hours to get me ready. At first I sat in my old clothes and girls and women looked in to say hello and wish me God's blessings. A hairdresser came, and a make-up artist — Meena wasn't chancing her talents on this important day. She did my nails though, hands and feet. The henna had been washed off before I went to sleep and the patterns were clear and tasteful.

Zeba sat cross-legged on the bed and watched my transformation. 'I hope I am as beautiful as you when I get married,' she said.

The make-up artist scrutinised me before she got started. 'You have used bleaching cream for many months, yes? How are you so fair?'

Meena laughed. 'Ameera is Australian — she doesn't need bleaching cream. Nor cover fluid.'

'Your eyes — you use the contact lens for green colour?'

I shook my head.

'They're real,' Zeba said proudly.

'Incredible,' the woman said, and went to work with her powder, lipstick, eye shadow and kohl.

After the make-up, the jewellery was put on. The teeka was pinned to my hair with strings of tiny pearls. It hung cold and heavy on my forehead. Then the huge nose ring, the nath, was inserted. The gold ring was too thick for the hole already in my nose and Meena had to push it through with a piece of ice on the other side. I felt a sharp pain: 'Ow!' She wiped away the blood. Precious stones dripped from the ring and a gold chain travelled into my hair as a safety chain. The gold necklace came next, then earrings, bracelets, a ring for every finger with a chain attached running up to my wrist. Every piece made me feel more weighed down, as though someone was pressing the air out of me. I was sure I wouldn't be able to hold my head up.

Meena held a mirror in front of me. The make-up was so thick I looked like a Moghul painting. It wasn't me at all. In one way that was easier to bear, for I could imagine this was happening to someone else: the girl in the mirror.

Meena helped me into the red and gold gharara that had been brought over the night before. It was so long and heavy it was difficult to walk in. She pinned the dupatta with the gold fringe to my hair. With the dupatta covering my face, I would look like the perfect bride.

Dadi jan came to bless me; she looked graceful in an ice-green sari. 'My child,' she said.

I clung to her. 'Dadi jan.' I was desperate. She was the eldest woman in the house; if anyone could stop the wedding, couldn't she? Didn't Uncle Rasheed still listen to her advice? I had never told Dadi jan why I couldn't marry Shaukat. I did then. I whispered in her ear, not sure she would hear me. I pulled back to look at her face and her eyes widened. She clutched my arm.

'Remember Hir and Ranjha,' she whispered. 'Remember what we spoke of.' She touched my head but gave me no other encouragement. All she said was, 'May God be with you, child. He knows what is best and will guide you.'

Then we heard the sound that thrilled the heart of a happy bride but was like an arrow through mine: the barat, the groom's procession with the drums and horns and the shouts and joyful songs of the young men in the party.

Zeba was up at the window, squealing. 'Look at Shaukat! He is on a white horse. It's huge and it's dancing! He has a turban like a prince and gold tassels covering his face. Ameera, come look.'

Fortunately Meena said it wasn't seemly for the bride to be caught staring at the barat, for I couldn't have forced myself to go near that window. The music that made the girls in the room dance was a funeral dirge to me.

'Come now,' Meena said. She led me to the lounge where a table stood with two brocade chairs opposite each other. Apparently, the marriage hall that Meena had been married in was destroyed in the earthquake. There was a wooden screen that I could sit behind on a couch. The family couch had been changed for a red and gold one; they must have hired it.

'No one will bother you here,' she whispered. She kissed me and there were tears in her eyes. 'May God bless you.' Then she added, 'Don't worry, you are so beautiful Shaukat will fall in love with you as soon as he sees you.'

She must have seen the fear in my eyes for she hugged me before she went out to greet guests. I sat there stunned: her words had had the opposite effect from what she'd intended. This was a loveless marriage on my part; I hadn't counted on Shaukat having feelings of his own.

Every now and then Zeba came to check on me. Each time she stared at me in awe before she spoke. She gave me a running commentary on my own wedding. 'So many guests have come. They are sitting under the shamianas, the big coloured tents. There are carpets from Abu's shop everywhere and another beautiful couch for you and Shaukat to sit on after the nikah. The barbers are cooking the chicken curry and rice.'

Then Papa was there. When I saw him I couldn't help myself: I burst into tears.

'My beautiful beti,' he crooned.

It was the first time in ages that he'd called me beautiful, but I didn't want beauty if all it did was catch me the most eligible man in the family. Papa held me and I cried harder.

'You will miss your life in Australia but you will be happy,' he said. 'And so will I.'

All I wanted was Mum, but I couldn't voice the accusation that Papa was deliberately keeping her from me. Had she rung again without them telling me? Did she even know that this was my wedding week? Don't say anything, Frank had said. And so I remained silent.

Meena was there then with a box of tissues. She patted under my eyelashes. 'It is time for the nikah. Are you okay?'

I sniffed and nodded. My body was taut like a rabbit's ready to flee, but there was nowhere to run.

The maulvi came in with the wedding papers. He had a long black beard and a white turban, and in the way of religious men kept his gaze averted from me. Papa guided me to the table and I sat; he stood behind me as the witness. The maulvi spoke swiftly in Urdu and I missed some of what he said. He mentioned the dowry Papa had provided, then there was talk of the mehr, the bride price. Some for me, but also Shaukat was giving Papa money — some payable before, and the rest after the marriage was consummated. I felt the cage snapping shut, squeezing all the air out of me. Papa's comment about the marriage being good for the family — this was what he had meant. It was a business deal and I was just a pawn.

I heard the word 'talaq' and realised the agreement included a provision that allowed me a divorce if necessary. The idea was so the bride could feel secure, but I tried to imagine me divorcing Shaukat. The fallout would be nuclear and Papa would lose his money. My head began to ache.

Then the maulvi was asking me a question; the room fell quiet.

'Pardon?' I said.

'Ameera Hassan Zufar, do you accept this marriage?'

I didn't think, I just said, 'No.'

The maulvi's discipline splintered and he glanced at me. I imagined I saw concern in his face. He was my only hope and I started formulating an argument in my mind. Surely he couldn't in all conscience marry me if I objected?

Both Papa's hands came down heavily on my shoulders; his fingers dug into my flesh. I steeled myself not to utter a sound. He gave a short laugh. 'She is stressed today and didn't hear you properly, Maulvi Sahib. Please ask again.'

The priest licked his lips and stared at the paper in front of him. 'Ameera Hassan Zufar, do you accept this marriage?'

I was silent.

Papa spoke. 'Is it true, Maulvi Sahib, that a child invokes God's wrath if she doesn't obey her elders?'

'The Holy Koran talks of obedience, yes, but —'

'See, beti, this stubborn childishness must stop. Soon you will see how fortunate you are.'

The maulvi nodded at that. 'This is a good match, child.'

I wasn't going to get out of it. The maulvi thought I was nervous. He could never understand the culture I had come from, nor about Tariq. No one understood about Tariq or how I thought love was more important than good connections and honour. With tears in my eyes I spat one word, 'Fine.' It could have meant anything.

I was supposed to be asked for my consent three times and to say 'qabool kiya', 'I accept', each time, but

Papa released my shoulders and the maulvi quickly recited a chapter of the Koran and some other things I didn't understand. Then he declared Shaukat and me man and wife.

I was still in shock when the maulvi laid a paper in front of me to sign. It was written in Urdu. Papa pointed out the line where I was to sign. Below it was another signature: Shaukat had already signed. Shouldn't the girl sign first? I sat staring at his writing, the only tangible indication that he was real and from this day would be my husband. It was a firm hand, with a flourished line underneath, but like most doctors' handwriting, entirely illegible. I decided to make mine illegible too so no one would know I had willingly signed. I scribbled Ameera Tariq, not because I would have taken Tariq's name if I'd married him, but because he had possession of my heart. Not all of me was marrying Shaukat. It was my last token of defiance. In the presence of God and in my heart I refused Shaukat and I prayed God would be merciful and help me in the days ahead.

Papa witnessed my signature. As he put the cap on his fountain pen, he said in an undertone, 'I never thought I'd see you act like this. You have been spoilt by your mother. If there was any doubt about my decision I know now I have done the right thing for you. Now you are Shaukat's problem and he will pull you into line.'

His words hit me with the force of a backhander and fresh tears squeezed out of my eyes.

Then he straightened and smiled at Aunt Bibi as she looked in the room. 'Are you ready?' she asked.

I breathed heavily as I stared at the table and tried to compose myself. This was the moment I dreaded. Aunt Bibi, Uncle Iqbal and their close relatives brought Shaukat in to sit opposite me. I had my head lowered so he couldn't see my face. I could hear other relatives crowding into the room too. Aunt Bibi put the mirror on the table between us and a red silk scarf was thrown over our heads so that we were alone beneath it. Someone handed Shaukat a Koran under the scarf and he read from it in Arabic. His voice was deep and it never wavered. Even one sign of weakness might have made me feel better, but no, this was a man who Papa thought could look after me properly.

'Look at her in the mirror, Shaukat. Here is your bride.' There was a chorus urging him on. I kept my eyes shut. My lip trembled. 'Ameera, look at Shaukat.' There was singing, but I didn't open my eyes. I felt the veil pulling on my hair as it came away. Then I was lifted to stand and my own dupatta was raised. I opened my eyes, the table was gone and Shaukat was in front of me. He took my hand and put a ring on my finger. His hands were warm and he had a faint smile on his face as though he was amused by the whole show.

The people in the room practically cheered, excited to be present when the bride and groom saw each other for the first time. My breath was coming too fast; I thought I'd faint. His skin was almost as fair as mine, no buck teeth, trimmed moustache, grey eyes, almost the same height as Tariq. His Pushtun nose wasn't as hooked as Papa's and gave strength to his features. In that maroon turban adorned with pearls he looked so refined. Mum would say he was handsome, and that was the problem: he was closer to her age than to mine. He even had flecks of grey at his temples. What was Papa thinking? I'd thought Tariq was old, but Shaukat looked twenty-five years older than me. He could have fathered both of us.

A plate of sweets on a silver tray was held out to Shaukat. Our first act as a married couple was to eat from the same sweet. Shaukat chose a piece, took a bite and held it for me to bite as well. I didn't refuse; I was too stunned. We chewed together and a camera flashed. My glance flickered to him once or twice; he was watching me. Had he been told I'd be a difficult bride? It didn't look like it. He seemed pleased with what he saw, almost as if I was familiar to him. Maybe age gave him that poise, that ability to make others feel more at ease. Strangely, that made me more nervous than ever.

part 3
A Lake of Tears

29

Aunt Bibi and Uncle Iqbal led Shaukat outside. Meena took my arm and guided me to the shamiana, the tent where Shaukat and I would sit on display. There were hundreds of guests, but fortunately I didn't have to greet anyone. I glanced up once when we reached the tent. Shaukat was seated on the couch, watching me approach. It could have been the heaviness of the bridal dress but I felt as though I was fighting a high tide to walk towards him.

'Are you okay?' Meena asked.

I nodded but I knew what it was: I didn't want to be there. I didn't want to sit on that couch by Shaukat to show all those guests I was now his wife. *If only it were Tariq.*

Meena helped me up the step to the stage, and Shaukat practically lifted me the rest of the way. Relatives swarmed around us congratulating us. None of the men spoke to me directly but I heard the comments: perfect match, Allah ka shukr hai, thanks be to God, may you be happy. Everyone was happy for Shaukat. He still hadn't spoken directly to me and to my untrained ear his Urdu sounded like everyone else's. Then he answered one of his friends in English, which made me forget to keep my face lowered. Shaukat had a cultured English accent; he must have studied at an English university. He caught me staring and I looked away, my face burning.

The guests were still eating. We'd missed the first rush on the tables that typically occurs at weddings. Now many were sitting and talking; some young girls were dancing to the band that had accompanied Shaukat. Food was set on a low table in front of us: Kashmiri pilau with saffron, sultanas and peas, tandoori chicken, rice, naan and other curry dishes but I couldn't bring myself to taste anything. The babble in the tent was incessant and the tightness in my head wouldn't clear. Different groups of relatives stood behind us for group photos and a man with a video camera roamed around. No one asked me to look up and smile. I probably looked as sad as any true bride.

Meena and Jamila managed to steal Shaukat's shoe and made him offer money to get it back; a custom I'd heard of but never seen. He gave three thousand rupees, handed over in crisp new notes. 'I've never known a groom to be so generous,' Meena whispered, happy for me.

We must have sat there for hours while guests gave us their best wishes. I gleaned some new information: the death of Shaukat's first wife was a tragedy, she had a brain tumour, they had no children. My headache persisted.

Finally it was time for the ruksati, the leaving. Meena helped me down from the stage. Uncle Rasheed held a Koran over my head while Papa recited some verses. Then he said the words that gave me to Shaukat. The band sang sad songs of separation. Papa hugged me and I saw the tears in his eyes. That started me off too.

Aunt Bibi had hired a doli to carry me to the car. Male cousins lifted it while Shaukat walked alongside. I felt myself floating above it all, watching it happen to the girl in the mirror. Shaukat lifted her out of the doli and put her in the back seat of the car. Uncle Rasheed, Papa, Aunty Khushida, Meena, even Asher and Zeba were there, waving and wiping their eyes. Shaukat sat in the back beside the girl in the mirror; he took her hand to hold it between both of his and she let him.

I wished I could float away forever but there were still games to be borne at Aunt Bibi's. All their immediate family members were squashed into an entertaining area. First I was introduced to Shaukat's three younger brothers, their wives and children. My brain was so muddled I didn't have a hope of remembering their names. Shaukat and I sat on another sumptuous couch and Aunt Bibi placed a tray of milk and water on a coffee table before us. Then she dropped in a ring. 'Find it,' she cried in glee. I cared little about the game yet I found the ring and Shaukat smiled. Apparently whoever found the ring first would prove to be the dominant partner. No wonder he was amused.

Then Aunt Bibi brought in a bowl of kheer, a rice dessert. Shaukat put his right hand into the bowl and fed me kheer with his fingers. His fingers were smooth and deft: he didn't spill any pudding on my skin. A bowl of water was brought then. Shaukat wiped his hands and, to my horror, kneeled before me, took off my shoes and washed my feet. I didn't know about that custom. One of his relatives took the dirty water and sprinkled it in every corner of the house, for good luck. I knew what these games were for: they were to make us feel more intimate. I began building a retaining wall inside me.

One of his brothers sang a song accompanied by another playing a tabla. It was a Rumi song Tariq would have liked:

> *May these vows and this marriage be blessed.*
> *May it be sweet milk,*
> *this marriage, like wine and halvah.*
> *May this marriage offer fruit and shade*
> *like the date palm.*
> *May this marriage be full of laughter,*
> *our every day a day in paradise.*
> *May this marriage be a sign of compassion,*
> *a seal of happiness here and hereafter.*
> *May this marriage have a fair face and a*
> *   good name,*
> *an omen as welcome as the moon in a clear*
> *   blue sky.*

How beautiful the song was, and how sad that I couldn't enter into the spirit of it for this was the wrong marriage. At the end of it I caught Shaukat regarding me with that faint smile. I hung my head so he wouldn't see my regret.

After this, the whole family — or so it seemed — took us into a bedroom. It was decorated with beautiful carpets and the bed was covered in cushions, richly red and gold. The whole room shouted one word: bride. All the clothes Aunt Bibi had bought for me in the bazaar were there. So were Shaukat's clothes for the next day. Appalled, I stared at his freshly ironed suit hanging on the wardrobe. I'd imagined we'd have separate bedrooms.

Aunt Bibi said how glad she was to have me as her daughter and hugged me so tightly that I thought I'd suffocate and my problems would be solved there and then. No one had talked to me about being with Shaukat on this night. It was all left for me to find out by myself. My friends and I had giggled about sex but we hadn't discussed the serious stuff. I had never dared ask Natasha what it was like. How I missed Mum; she would have told me what to do.

Shaukat was taken out of the room and Fozia helped me out of my bridal outfit and put me in a soft shalwar qameez. She took down my hair, then, with a reassuring smile, she left. I didn't like the qameez she'd chosen — it was transparent and I had no underwear on. I decided to change it. I had my back to the door and my arms in the air, painfully struggling into a new top, when Shaukat walked back in. I was mortified. The tears welled up as I tugged in vain at the shirt.

'Ameera.' His voice sounded concerned. He stopped me and examined my exposed back, putting experienced fingers on my bruises. It was a professional touch and I calmed myself.

'Who did this?' As he spoke he pulled the qameez down so I was covered and guided me to face him.

I wondered what he would say. So many men thought that if a woman got a beating she deserved it. 'Haider.'

He tensed slightly, and although his next words were even, I could tell more depended on my answer than his tone implied. 'Did he do anything else?'

'No, he just beat me.' I was too ashamed to mention the kiss. Shaukat stared at me and I felt unnerved, scared he'd question me further, so I babbled on. 'I tried to run away.'

Shaukat's forehead creased in confusion. I was suddenly struck by how much of it could be seen without his turban. His hairline had receded as much as Papa's. Now was the time, I decided, to tell him how it was. 'When I came I didn't know about the wedding.'

'What?' His face jerked as if I had slapped him. 'Your father didn't discuss it with you?'

'Never. I'm sorry but I didn't want to be married today. I tried to refuse so you wouldn't have to be upset, but no one listened. It's nothing against you,' I added quickly. 'I'm just too young, I want to go to uni, I want to live in Australia. And I miss my mother.' It all tumbled out and I had just enough presence of mind to stop before I mentioned Tariq.

Shaukat stood staring at the floor, rubbing his hand slightly on his shirt. Then he reached for me. Maybe he wanted to comfort me but I wasn't taking any chances. I stepped out of his way and delivered my wounding shot:

'And I don't feel married at all. I feel like a prostitute — bought.'

He stared at me, the creases between his eyes deep cuts. I had finally pricked that poised veneer. 'I am sorry you feel like that.' He sat heavily on the bed. 'I never intended this. I thought you wanted the marriage. I have been looking forward to it for two years. I feel I know you.'

It was my turn to be shocked. He half-smiled as he looked up at me. 'I have seen all your family videos since you were fifteen. You were lovely even then.'

My mouth fell open. 'Those horrible videos. Even the ones at the beach?'

'The very ones. Your father sent copies to Mother. She made sure I saw them. I was willing to wait until you grew up, until you finished university. You were just going to visit this time, and we would meet. It was to be a surprise from your father. Then I was going to visit you when you were older — the engagement would have been in Australia.'

The thought of someone knowing so much about me — as if through some spyhole in the sky — was unnerving. It was unforgivable of Papa. The shock made me sharper than usual. 'My father stands to gain from this marriage, doesn't he?'

Shaukat glanced at me. 'That's the way of all marriages here in Pakistan.' He frowned as though I should already know that.

'But this one?'

Shaukat sighed. 'Your father's business is failing.'

'That can't be true. Papa never told me that.'

'He told me,' Shaukat said firmly. 'He needs money to expand — more stock, a bigger building, he wants to import more, hire workers. Apparently Riaz doesn't share his passion.'

'What do you get?'

Shaukat raised his eyebrows. 'I get you, that is all I wanted. And the possibility of a visa to Australia should we wish to live there.'

'Through marriage with me?'

'Yes, but I chose you for other reasons. You are the daughter of my favourite uncle. Your father and my mother have a close relationship.' He stopped. 'I still can't understand why he didn't involve you in the preparations.'

I knew why but I wasn't going to tell him about Tariq and the party.

'Ameera.' He stood in front of me. 'This must be difficult for you, coming straight from Australia.' He touched my hair and stared at it falling over his fingers. A sigh escaped him as if he'd made a decision. 'Even if you had wanted to be married today we wouldn't necessarily — how shall I say this — do what they think we are doing.' He indicated out to the entertainment area and grinned at me. He was so different from Haider that I smiled. He sobered immediately. 'You are beautiful when you smile. I'll wait as long as it takes for you to be ready.' Then he added with a wry grin, 'Within reason, of course. I'm looking forward to a family.'

Dismay made my smile vanish. 'A ... a family?'

'Isn't that why people marry?'

Another thing I hadn't thought about. 'Not yet,' I said without considering his feelings.

'No.' He crossed to a chest of drawers and took out a letter. 'Your father gave me this. It was opened — I hope you will forgive me for reading it as I needed the information to prepare my wedding gift.'

Gift? I had no gift for him, not even the traditional one he was expecting when I was 'ready'.

He handed me the letter. It was from SATAC: my matric results and acceptance into the University of Adelaide for a Bachelor of Education. I sank to the bed to read it.

'Your results are good, but not quite good enough for medicine.' He was teasing.

'You know I didn't want to do medicine?'

'Your father talked to Mother about it one night — he was worried.'

What didn't Shaukat know about me? Tariq; he didn't know about Tariq. I would never tell him and at least I would have something of my own.

'This is my gift.' He handed me a piece of paper and joined me on the bed. 'I took the liberty of enrolling you in the university here in Muzaffarabad. It's one of the best, a beautiful campus and there's a student teacher centre. When we live in Islamabad, it will be easy to transfer.' I sensed he was watching me. 'Your father said this would please you the most.'

I stared at the entrance slip to the University of Azad Jammu and Kashmir.

'You can stay with Mother when classes start,' he added. 'I'll return on weekends while I still have the clinic.'

Tears welled in my eyes. So Papa had tried for me, but it was Adelaide University I wanted, not Muzaffarabad, and Shaukat couldn't give me that. He expected me to be happy and I tried to smile. 'That's kind.' I was still too shy to say his name to his face. Then I thought, *Won't I be gone by the time lectures start?*

'Even if you fell pregnant, you could still study,' he said. 'Mother would love to look after the baby.'

This was a big concession, I knew, but I stiffened. Twice now he'd mentioned children. I knew that in Pakistan the bride was expected to produce a boy by the first anniversary.

He ran his forefinger around each of my eyes. 'You are tired.' He stood up. 'I'll come back later and sleep on the sofa bed. No one need know what we have decided.'

'Thank you.' This time I truly was thankful; I smiled at him and meant it. He drew me up and put his arms around me. I tensed, but felt nothing. It was like being hugged by Papa.

'Ameera, there is plenty of time for us to know each other. If I'd known you weren't happy, I would have postponed the wedding until you were older, but now it's done. We will make it work, for, whatever you may be thinking, we are a match.'

I sat back on the bed as he took a packet of cigarettes from a cupboard and left the room. I didn't even think then about the fact that he smoked; I could only think of how he would have called the wedding off. All I had needed to do in order to go home was to meet him before the wedding. No wonder they wouldn't let me see him.

30

The next day we returned to Uncle Rasheed's for a family dinner. Papa was still there; I wasn't sure of my feelings towards him any more. One moment I remembered how I loved him; in the next, anger rose up at what he'd done. He looked at me keenly, then said, 'Are you all right?' I couldn't work him out. Why not ask me that before the wedding? Comments like that showed he loved me, yet he had married me against my will. He could slap me one moment and hug me the next. It was so confusing. I told him I was fine. He smiled benignly at Shaukat. I was married now; no doubt they all presumed I wasn't a shy virgin any more and that was the most embarrassing thought of all.

Everyone ate together: another concession to my married state. Dadi jan laid her hand on my head as I sat beside her. Even Meena's husband, Haroun, was there. I had never met him before, and when he smiled at Meena I could tell he was gentle and loved her. He wasn't much older than Tariq.

I wished I had a gift for Meena and told her so. 'You helped me so much yesterday. I don't know what I would have done these last few weeks without you.'

She hugged me. 'You're my favourite cousin. Be happy. That would be the best gift you could give me.'

She said it as if I had a choice. If I didn't love Tariq, could I be happy with Shaukat? I looked over at him, laughing with the older men. He fitted in well with them. Would he grow strict like Papa? A movement at the door caught my attention. It was Haider. He walked in slowly, his expression surly. My stomach clenched and I glanced at Shaukat. He was watching me, his eyebrows raised, the faintest of smiles teasing his mouth. I understood: there was nothing to worry about now — Shaukat was the eldest cousin and I was his wife. When I glanced back at Haider I saw what I hadn't noticed at first. He had a black eye and made no sudden movements. He didn't offer any congratulations.

After the meal, I went to my old room to finish packing. Zeba came with me. 'I will miss you,' she said.

I hugged her. 'I'll miss you too.'

'Can I come for a holiday?'

I paused. I hadn't let myself think too far ahead, but if this were a normal marriage, these were the things that would happen. What would Zeba be told when I disappeared? That I was an evil runaway bride to hurt Shaukat and the family so much? I stared at Zeba in dismay. I would dishonour Shaukat, dishonour all the men in the family.

'Ameera? Can I?' Zeba said.

'Of course.'

She was satisfied and ran off. Asher came in then. He watched me zip up my backpack. 'Shaukat is a lucky devil.'

I tried not to smile at his pseudo-adult talk. He walked further into the room until he faced me. I hadn't realised before how tall he was: he was almost the same height as me. Then he cleared his throat and uttered this amazing speech: 'Now I will be your brother, your happiness is my happiness, your sorrow, my sorrow. You only have to tell me if Shaukat hurts you and I will help you.'

I stared at him, wordless. I could imagine Riaz saying that, but why would Asher think it was necessary?

The wedding dragged on. It was a festival for the guests, but a funeral for me: the death of my dreams. Frank was my only hope to resurrect them.

The party at Uncle Iqbal's and Aunt Bibi's the next day was lavish. I wore an outfit not unlike the one I had on the night I first saw Aunt Bibi and Uncle Iqbal: churidar pyjama, high strappy shoes. The qameez had a bodice that sparkled with pearls and zircon and was like a dress with a full skirt that would have flared if I twirled. Only Shaukat now would see me twirl.

I was slightly in awe of Shaukat's public reserve. Though he said we were a match, I couldn't see what we had in common except genes and looks. I yearned for Tariq's warmth, his humour, the stories we shared, the music. I doubted Shaukat would approve of Junoon, and what about David D'Or and the Idan Raichel Project? Papa would have had a fit if he knew I listened to Israeli music, but Tariq believed music should transcend cultural differences. Papa didn't like any modern music: he said it put too much emphasis on love and distracted people from their faith. Like Papa, Shaukat probably admired traditional raag singing and sitar playing.

Papa was tender towards me at the party. He could afford to be: I had done what he wanted. 'I'll be leaving tomorrow, beti,' he said, then paused. 'There is some sacrifice in marriage, especially at first, but I know you will be safe now.'

What was I to say to that? Dadi jan had said it took a year for her to love my grandfather. Would that happen to me? But if all went to plan I wouldn't be here in a year. Shaukat and I would stay with Aunt Bibi for a while and then Frank would come for me. I tried not to think about what would happen then; instead, I concentrated on how what Papa had done wasn't right. Even Shaukat had been shocked when I told him — surely he'd understand why I had to leave. The word 'dishonour' reared its terrifying head again, but I pushed it into the attic of my mind and locked the door. If I thought too much about it I'd be lost. I had never entirely understood Papa's preoccupation with honour and shame and how the balance worked. How could my choices possibly affect a whole family of strong and independent men like Papa, my uncles and Shaukat? But I felt the flutter of fear all the same. I had witnessed Papa's anger whenever he thought his wishes may be flouted.

Be strong, Frank had said. But he knew nothing of my family. Tariq had wanted me in Australia, but would he still want me at the expense of my family's shame? He understood honour and he wasn't even Pushtun. But would he put it above love for others as Papa did?

I had plenty of time to think, sitting on yet another gorgeous couch next to Shaukat in Aunt Bibi's garden. This was the day the whole community was invited to congratulate us. My thoughts were interrupted by a girl's voice. I looked up: it was Gulshan from the bus.

'I'm so happy to see you,' she said. 'Are you well?'

I nodded.

'I am glad — that day on the bus I was worried. Your cousin looked so … severe.' Then she glanced at Shaukat. 'You must be very happy.'

I could tell she was curious: why had I been on the bus when I had a marriage to look forward to? Did she remember me saying I was going home?

'So it worked for the best?' she went on.

'Yes, thank you.' I didn't want Shaukat hearing this. She took the hint and moved towards the food tables.

A young man approached to give us sweets. They were in bags made from old exercise books. I glanced up quickly; yes, it was the young man from the gold shop. He didn't even look my way, nothing to arouse suspicion. Did he know I wanted to run away? Anyone who looked at Shaukat would never suspect it. I opened my bag — there was a folded note inside. I didn't dare wait till later to read it for the sweets would be taken from us and given away. My dupatta acted as a screen and I opened the note.

Dictated for Mr Frank: Coming within three days to groom's home. Eat this note, it is rice paper, sorry about the ink.

I grinned at the humour the scribe had managed to capture. It sounded like Frank. I pulled out a piece of sweet with the paper underneath and took a bite.

'Hungry, Ameera?' Shaukat leaned closer.

For one horrified moment I thought he wanted a bite too; he'd feel the note in his mouth. I opened the paper bag while I forced myself to hold his gaze. 'Would you like some?'

He settled back against the couch and smiled. 'I'm all sweeted out.'

I swallowed the barfi and the note. I felt dizzy. It was going to happen: Frank was coming. Soon, before Shaukat got too attached. Then I chided myself for thinking of Shaukat's welfare. Thoughts like that would only make it harder.

That night there were too many goodbyes from relatives and friends of the family whose names I would never remember. Some of Shaukat's friends had even come from London for the walima. Shaukat told me I'd learn all the names over the years. 'There will be enough weddings and funerals, don't worry.'

In our room I caught Shaukat's gaze following me as I emerged from the ensuite where I'd got changed. The look in his eyes worried me. I wondered how long I could hold him to his promise to wait. How long did he think it would take? A month? A week? A few nights?

In the morning I was delivered a bitter blow.

At breakfast, Aunt Bibi floated around the dining table. Two of her sons and their wives lived in the house; Fozia and her husband were visiting. Shaukat and I were still the guests of honour. A servant brought in eggs and toast and set them near me. I wasn't used to servants and, to be on the safe side, I murmured 'thank you' every time something was put in front of me.

'Why can't you stay a few more days, Shaukat dearest?' Aunt Bibi said. 'Ameera must be exhausted. You will be so busy at the clinic, and we need the sound of little feet in this house again.'

My hand froze over my knife. The talk of leaving even overshadowed Aunt Bibi's reference to babies. I had been expecting a quiet day of cleaning up.

Shaukat's glance at his mother barely concealed his exasperation. 'We need to go, Mother. I've been here a week and I have a surprise for Ameera. Don't worry, we'll be back in a few weeks.'

Aunt Bibi pouted as though time without Shaukat would be a deprivation, but her next words dispelled that idea. 'Ameera and I have so much to do together, don't we, darling?'

She came behind my chair and squeezed me. It felt as though I'd married her, not Shaukat. If she knew the appalling thing I was planning, she wouldn't love me at all.

Shaukat mistook my silence. 'She's okay, really,' he said to me, teasing, 'you just have to pace yourself.' He grinned and Aunt Bibi smacked him playfully over the head. In that instant I wished he could have been horrible like Haider.

'Please don't go today,' Aunt Bibi crooned.

Involuntarily I made a sound. 'No.'

'See?' Aunt Bibi said. 'Ameera doesn't want to leave either. Wait for a few days.'

Shaukat frowned, trying to read my face.

'Could we stay longer ...' I paused, then added his name for the first time, 'Shaukat?'

Aunt Bibi beamed, but Shaukat's frown deepened. 'It's not possible. I have something planned.'

'A surprise?' Aunt Bibi was coy. That should have been my line, but nobody noticed.

Shaukat's face cleared. 'I'll tell you about it later, Mother. But we're leaving today.'

Aunt Bibi clicked her tongue, but I could see she wasn't really upset with him; it was all a game. I couldn't join in the fun: my mind was racing. I'd have to let Frank know.

'What time are we going?' I asked.

'After breakfast.'

I stared at him. 'So soon?'

He got up from the table. 'I want to be there before nightfall.'

Frank wouldn't be able to come in time; I knew it as surely as I knew the wind would be cold outside.

Back in our room, Shaukat tackled me about my response. 'Why so glum? We're going to my home, temporary as it is, but nothing will change if that's what's bothering you.'

'No,' I said, and the next words slipped out without thinking: 'I trust you.' I wondered if that was true or just a hope.

He studied my face. 'That's a good start.' I wasn't sure if he was being sarcastic. 'Please pack your things.'

I hadn't thought about going to Shaukat's home and had no idea how to pack all my new things so quickly. I let Aunt Bibi organise it for me. She had a present for me — a travelling jewellery box made of maroon leather.

'You can leave most of your gold in Iqbal's safe,' she said, 'but you'll want to take some pieces to show you're married.'

Shaukat strode out to see to the car and Fozia packed his clothes for him. 'You never know when you'll have a dinner with his friends — he has so many,' she said.

Within two hours we were in Shaukat's Prado, speeding across the border of Azad Kashmir into the North West Frontier Province. I hadn't had a chance to text Frank properly, just a few quick words when I was in the bathroom: leaving 2day 4 oghi. hope u can cum.

Later I would let him know where we were.

31

Shaukat's house was in the shadow of the tribal area called Khala Dhaka. To get there we had to cross mountains and rivers, including the Jhelum of Hir and Ranjha fame. At the highest part there was snow on the side of the road and Shaukat stopped the car so I could touch it when he realised I'd never seen snow before. I was struck by its brittleness, like dead water. I didn't linger long — I could see he was itching to keep driving. At least it was an easier ride in the Prado than in Uncle Rasheed's car, even if Shaukat's driving was little better. He leaned on the horn before blind corners and took incredible risks with passing trucks, but we reached the town of Mansehra alive.

He took me a longer way, so I could see 'the sights'. 'There's the Indus River. From now on we are travelling the Karakoram Highway, the ancient trade route from China.' I wondered at the pride in his voice. 'There is little medical help in this area,' he explained. 'What hospitals there were fell with the earthquake. Only one built by an aid agency withstood the shock.'

We arrived at the house late in the afternoon. Shaukat tooted once and the gate mysteriously opened. He drove in and a man with an assault rifle shut the gate. Servants were lined up Jane Austen style by the time we reached the front door. One man hurried to help with the cases.

Shaukat introduced them. 'Mrs Rahmet looks after the house for me. Aslam,' the man now carrying both cases on his head, 'is the chowkidar and gardener. He'll go to the shops for you too. Ibrahim is my driver — he'll drive you where you need to go. I trust him completely.'

Ibrahim hadn't smiled at me like the others; he was closer to my age. He kept his gaze lowered but I didn't miss the flush of pride at Shaukat's words.

Shaukat glanced at the man with the gun who was now sitting on a stool near the gate. 'That is Risaq Abdullah — he is our security guard.'

'Is that necessary?' I asked. I imagined Frank trying to get past the man and his rifle.

Shaukat made a face. 'Ever since the earthquake, the government has put security guards on clinics and non-government organisations. A precaution against terrorist activity, imagined or not.'

'Daktar Sahib!' A young man hurried along a walkway at the side of the house. 'Mubarek ho. Congratulations.' He nodded at me. 'Please be coming to the clinic, Sahib. It is an emergency we cannot handle.'

Shaukat turned to me. 'Settle in as best you can. Mrs Rahmet will show you your room, and she'll cook dinner. I won't be long.'

I thought how it would always be like this married to a doctor: he would always be rushing off to help someone.

233

Mrs Rahmet smilingly gestured me into the house. It was large and airy with marble stairs leading to rooms on a second floor. The lounge room had brown leather couches and a huge Kashmiri rug, its silk thread shining in the lamplight. From the family business, no doubt. Shaukat's office was downstairs. Aslam deposited Shaukat's suitcase there. I glanced inside and saw a bed and my spirits lifted. Aslam carried my suitcase up to my room. It had a view of the mountains. They were closer than I'd thought. I went to the window. There was a fort not far away; I could make out tiny figures like toy soldiers and flags fluttering against the glow of dusk.

Mrs Rahmet began unpacking my things and I stopped her. 'You are busy enough,' I said in Urdu.

Her smile disappeared. 'Daktar Sahib said I was to look after you,' she offered.

'We can do it tomorrow. I'm tired now.'

This she understood and the smile returned. As soon as she was gone, I took out the phone and texted Frank: in oghi at rahman clinic near mansehra.

I hoped it was enough. I didn't know how far we were from Mansehra, maybe thirty kilometres. I pressed the send button but nothing happened. The error sign came up and I checked my coverage. None. I raced down the stairs and into the garden. The security guard stood up as I emerged. I backed away from him and out of sight around the side of the house. I tried again but still no success.

'Memsahib?' At first I didn't realise the guard was talking to me. 'Kya bat hai? Is there a problem?'

I stuffed the phone into my pocket and turned to face

him. His features were severe. I didn't doubt his loyalty to Shaukat but would that extend to me? His job would involve keeping me safe by Shaukat's terms, not letting me do what I wanted.

'No problem, thank you.' I walked past him into the house.

Mrs Rahmet met me at the door. 'Just ask me, Memsahib,' she said. 'Whatever you need, I am getting it for you.'

'Thank you.'

I retreated to my room. A housekeeper, a driver to take me everywhere — no driving lessons for me, I could tell — a security guard to watch my every move. It was like being in gaol. Could I risk the phone in Shaukat's office? Uncle Rasheed's conference speaker had put me off land lines. What if it rang through to the clinic? Mrs Rahmet would hear every word or at least know I'd gone in there. She would tell Shaukat. Besides, a call from a land line was probably traceable. Frank had said to only use his phone. I walked up and down in front of my window. How would I ring Frank? If I didn't contact him, he'd think I had fallen for the groom.

That night Shaukat delivered his surprise. He had also delivered a difficult baby and he was tired. He didn't come in until 9 p.m. and that was when we ate. Mrs Rahmet had left the curry on the stove for me to dish up.

When we sat down to the food, I said in conversation, 'You like babies.'

'Yes. Unfortunately my first wife was too unwell … there were miscarriages …' His voice trailed off and I felt like kicking myself. 'I did my paediatrics in London,' he went on. 'Too many babies die here and they don't need to. Every little bit helps.'

He took more curry and rice and picked up his fork in his right hand. Mrs Rahmet had put knives as well as forks on the table; I wondered if that was for me. When he'd finished, he wiped his mouth on his serviette and leaned back in his chair.

'I'm taking you on a trip. I thought you'd like a honeymoon.'

I stared at him. 'That's not a Pakistani custom.'

'But it's a Western one. I thought it would make you feel more … at home.'

'At home' weren't the right words. Actually a honeymoon terrified me: concentrated time with him and one thing on his mind? No, thanks.

'We will go by train to Karachi so you can see all of Pakistan, and the beach.' He paused to let that sink in. 'I know you like the beach, and when we arrive back we have been invited to a party at Mansehra.' Then he added more quietly, 'Our first together.'

He cocked one eyebrow at me and I realised I hadn't thanked him. He was waiting for a flicker of excitement perhaps, but I was appalled. None of this was panning out as I'd expected. Surely I needed to stay in one spot for Frank to find me?

Shaukat carried on. 'I have booked our own berth on the Tezgam. We can get to know each other more.'

Did he think I was such a hopeless case that it would

take two thousand kilometres to get to know each other? But then I remembered he would have booked this before the wedding and I felt a begrudging respect for someone who'd plan an activity just because he thought I'd like it.

'You don't seem glad.' His tone was dry.

'Thank you, that will be good.'

But I didn't fool him. How long would he keep persevering with a bride who wanted nothing to do with him?

He came up the stairs with me to my bedroom. 'I had better sleep in here tonight or there will be talk.'

In panic I looked around the room and saw that the couch was actually a single bed. 'Of course,' I said matter-of-factly, but I couldn't staunch my rising panic. I felt like a frog in a pot of water that was being heated so gradually I wouldn't know when it was too late to jump out.

I dreamed of Tariq. We were fleeing on foot from Oghi. He held my hand so we wouldn't be parted. Shaukat, Haider and Papa were on horses chasing us. We reached the river. We could hardly breathe we were so tired but we managed to swim across. It was so wide and cold that all I could do on the other side was shiver. Tariq lifted me and ran with me in his arms, but the track was up the mountain and he couldn't run fast enough. A white stallion reared in front of us; I couldn't see its rider. Tariq dodged to the left, but Papa was there. Behind us was Haider, holding an assault rifle.

Tariq turned to face the rider on the white horse. 'This is my true bride — she gave her heart to me and you stole her. Let her go.'

'No!' It was Haider who shouted. I saw the rage contort his face and he fired the gun.

We were falling down the mountain. Tariq tried to grab me. I reached for him, but I couldn't catch his hand. 'Tariq!'

I snapped awake. Shaukat was sitting on my bed, his brow furrowed in concern. 'Ameera.' He took my hand. 'It was just a dream.'

I sat up, my chest still pounding. 'A nightmare.' I swallowed.

'It must have been. Do you have them often?'

I shook my head. 'I'm sorry I woke you up.'

'I was already awake.' He still hadn't smiled.

My eyes were drawn to the window. It was early morning; I could see the silhouette of the fort against the lightening horizon.

'Ameera?'

I pulled my gaze back to him.

'Who is Tariq?'

The words were even but I could imagine a detonator on every one.

My breath came in fits. 'If Haider said anything to you, it wasn't true.'

Shaukat pushed himself up from the bed and his voice rose as well. 'I didn't give Haider time to tell me anything, and I wouldn't have listened if he had.'

'Then where did you hear that name?' Fear made me whisper.

Shaukat watched me for a moment then sat on the bed again and placed his arms either side of me. 'From your own lips. You said his name in your sleep.' He leaned back and folded his arms. 'Now you had better tell me who he is. There can be no secrets if this marriage is to work.'

He looked grim and I nibbled my bottom lip. Was he threatening me? What if I told him and he beat me like Haider had done? I had betrayed myself with my own mouth, how stupid was that?

'You said you trusted me,' he prompted.

I was silent.

'Do you respect me at least?'

That I could nod to.

He waited, his head on one side; he knew I would speak eventually. That familiar feeling of impotence was so debilitating. I heard Frank's voice in my head: go along with it, easier to get you out.

'Tariq is my brother's friend and my best friend's brother.'

'And? A girl doesn't call a man's name in her sleep because he is her brother's friend.'

There was steel between Shaukat's words and I felt a hot prickle behind my eyes.

'He ... I hoped to marry him.'

I shut my eyes. I felt Shaukat stand up; heard him walk across to the window. I checked what he was doing. He had his back to me, leaning on the windowsill.

'So, it all makes sense at last,' he said. 'The early wedding, your reticence. I presume your father found out you had a relationship?'

I didn't like his tone. I sat up straighter. 'No, there was no relationship. I was at a function and someone told Papa a lie about my behaviour. He wouldn't believe me.'

'Instead he deceived me.'

Shaukat's voice rose on the 'me' and I gulped down a sob. I could sense his anger, even if he was suppressing it. Haider would have hit me by now. Shaukat swung around and faced me. I shrank into the pillows and pulled the bed-clothes around me. He strode over and yanked them back, then he hesitated. For an instant, I saw horror flash across his face. He slumped onto the bed at my feet.

'You don't have to look so terrified. I will not beat you. What good will it serve? No, I am just sorry for us both. Sorry you had to be tormented. I've lived in England; I understand how easy it is to meet the opposite sex in a Western environment and how alien this must seem to you. And me? It just makes my job harder.'

I didn't know what he meant by that. Did he mean what a challenge I'd be?

He sat quietly rubbing the bridge of his nose, then turned to me suddenly. 'If, as you say, there is no relationship, there is nothing to hold you. You will forget this young man. I presume he is younger than me?'

'Much. I didn't realise you'd be so old.'

I could have clapped my hand over my mouth, but Shaukat laughed. There had been an element of hysteria in the room but now the atmosphere shimmered and changed.

'I am only forty-one — I'm in my prime,' he said. Then he went on: 'I mean this, Ameera. What you feel for

this boy will die, for now you are in a real relationship —
with me. It will flourish because you will feed it.'

Was that an order?

'You will grow to love me because I will be the one
who is meeting your needs.' His eyes were bright, his
voice had risen again. 'It may take a while but it will
happen. The day will come when I am the only man you
will want to see come through that door.' He indicated
the bedroom door.

I stared at him, astounded.

Then he said more quietly, 'You mentioned Haider.
What does he know about it?'

'Nothing. I think he found Tariq's name in my phone.
He said if I contacted him, he'd kill him as well as me.'

'Haider.' Shaukat said his name the same way Meena
had that first day. 'There is nothing else? No other
secrets I need to be armed with in order to protect the
family honour?'

'No.' My voice was small; was he making fun of me
now?

He moved closer and leaned over me. 'Now, my wife,
we will go on a trip to Karachi and have a good time.'

It sounded like a command, as though he could order
my heart. There was no talk of the marriage being illegal,
of the possibility of annulment, and I suddenly
understood why: he wanted the marriage. How different
it would have been if I'd told him I wasn't a virgin. He
would have packed me straight back to Papa then. But I
couldn't have uttered that lie, not even to save my life.

Now Shaukat knew everything about me, except one
thing: I was planning to leave him.

32

The Tezgam was not as fast as its name suggested and there was a lot of waiting on side tracks for faster trains to pass. For a seventeen-year-old it was deadly boring but Shaukat wasn't fazed. It reminded him of boyhood trips, he said. I wondered if it was the same train Dadi jan had been abducted from sixty years before.

The window was so dirty that it was difficult to see much through it, but what I did see surely couldn't be the best of Pakistan. Shaukat's 'honeymoon' was like travelling through the country's private backyard. There were so many poor people living in boxes and tents by the tracks; rubbish tips that children in rags scrounged through. On a dusty track I saw a donkey cart with a load so heavy it had tipped backwards and the donkey was suspended in midair, still trapped in its harness. The image of the poor thing stayed with me for days.

Shaukat bought papers and magazines at Lahore, and we talked, and I even showed him how to play canasta, though it didn't work so well with only two players. He went out into the corridor a few times and I smelled the smoke on him when he returned. So many men in Pakistan smoked but I wondered how a doctor could. I also wondered if Papa knew.

Shaukat had booked a two-berth cabin with an adjoining toilet. The toilet looked Victorian and it was disconcerting seeing the tracks flashing below me when I used it. More disconcerting was what would happen at night. I needn't have worried. After we'd been served a lukewarm curry swimming in oil, a railway worker came in to make our seats into bunk beds. I chose the upper one; it felt safer.

Karachi was warm at least. We stayed in a house by the sea belonging to Uncle Iqbal's family. Hired help had made it ready for us; there was even a car to use. Shaukat slept in a different room the first night but his glances made me nervous. When would he think the time was up? Every night he hugged me before he left the room and I kept as still as if it was Haider with a knife at my throat.

By the fourth day he still hadn't made a move but I couldn't relax. We went to a restaurant for dinner and walked along the beach. I wore a purple silk shalwar qameez that fluttered in the breeze. Shaukat wore a suit jacket, undone, and he'd removed his tie, but his cologne never managed to mask that combination of smoke and antiseptic. I couldn't help thinking what this trip would have been like with Tariq, how I'd have welcomed his every embrace.

Shaukat took my hand that night and showed me the stars. He told me I was lovelier than the moon. I knew what he was doing and I guarded my heart against it: he was wooing me.

The evening after we returned from Karachi I dressed for the party. Ibrahim drove us to the house of a young Pushtun man who worked for an aid agency, and as we arrived young men shot guns joyfully into the air and yelled congratulations to Daktar Shaukat. There were some Western people there too but I kept my dupatta on my head. Shaukat took me to a lounge room where the women were sitting. I was glad: I didn't like the guns. They were so loud that the floor of the lounge vibrated through my feet; the noise made my heart thump.

A European girl was shaking in her chair. 'I wish they would stop. My sister was killed by gunfire in a war in our village. It sounded just like that.'

'You are Daktar Shaukat's bride?' one older lady said to me. She pinched my cheek. 'Lucky girl.'

I smiled politely.

A girl called Rebekah introduced herself to me. She was from Canada and only a few years older than me. She was doing a cross-cultural degree at uni and working with World Vision was her field experience. 'We're trying to get goats for people in Siran Valley now,' she told me. 'They lost all their stock in the earthquake.'

'There are still thousands of people in tents in Azad Kashmir,' I said.

'In the mountains here too. Houses are being rebuilt but not fast enough.' She regarded me. 'Your husband has been good — he'll treat people we send even when they can't pay much.'

The host's sister brought in dessert: it was kheer, rice pudding. The last time I'd eaten kheer Shaukat had fed it to me with his fingers. How sensual that would be with someone you loved.

'So you came here to get married?' Rebekah asked.

I hesitated too long and she noticed. 'We must spend some time together while I'm here. We could go shopping.'

I brightened. 'That would be great.' I missed time spent with my friends. Surely Shaukat would let me go shopping.

Rebekah gave me her card. 'Ring me when you're free.'

That was a joke. I would always be free, except for waiting on Frank.

'If you need anything, just call,' she added. 'It must be difficult going to a new country to marry, and missing your family.'

My eyes teared up and she leaned closer. 'I'll come to you,' she said.

We heard the men in the next room playing instruments and singing.

'They'll be dancing too,' said the sister of the host. 'Then they'll smoke their hookahs.'

'Water pipes?' I asked, thinking Riaz would call them bongs.

'Yes, my brother has some new apricot tobacco. My grandmother loves it.'

'As long as that is all he has,' said the lady who had pinched my cheek. 'When those boys get going, anything could slip into the hookahs.' She rolled her eyes and I presumed she meant hashish. Surely Shaukat wouldn't smoke hashish; he was a doctor.

I was tired by the time the call came to go home. The trip to Karachi had been wearing even though we'd sat all day in a compartment, and I hadn't slept well on the train. Shaukat was already in the front seat of the car with Ibrahim, so I climbed in the back. It was a quiet ride home if I ignored Ibrahim's Indian pop CD. When we arrived, Ibrahim helped Shaukat out of the car and supported him as we walked inside.

'Is there a problem?' I asked.

Ibrahim said, 'No, Memsahib. Daktar Sahib, he will be fine in the morning.'

He didn't seem worried, but I was. Surely there wasn't alcohol at the party? Maybe there had been hashish in the hookahs after all. Ibrahim helped Shaukat to the bed in the downstairs office. Shaukat moaned and I hovered, wondering what I should be doing.

Ibrahim suggested I go to bed. 'Do not be worrying, Memsahib, I have seen this many times before.'

He shooed me off like a child and I climbed the stairs to my room. What did he mean, he'd seen it before? He'd seen someone else like that? Or did he mean Shaukat?

My thoughts were tangled before I finally slept and so were my dreams. I dreamed I was being attacked by a masked horseman. He was holding me down and I couldn't breathe. I tried to scream but his mouth was covering mine, choking me. I woke and found it wasn't a dream. Someone was crushing me onto the bed, an unshaven face scratching my neck. I thought it was Haider, come to take his revenge. I cried out, 'Shaukat!'

'Yes,' his voice answered above me. 'I knew you'd call for me. It's me you love.'

This wasn't the self-possessed Shaukat I knew; his voice was slurred and he stank, not only of smoke and sweat but something nauseating.

'Shaukat, stop.'

He pulled the bedcovers back with one arm and dragged at my shalwar. The drawstring came loose as he tugged and suddenly my legs were bare. 'You are my wife, my beautiful wife.'

'No! You promised.' I scratched his face, tried to push him away, but he was too heavy. In trying to wriggle out from under him, I became trapped. My legs were apart and he pushed hard against me. There was a sudden tearing pain and a burning rasping sensation that I thought would never end. Shock made me tense every muscle and even my breathing stopped. I just wanted to block what was happening from my mind.

There was nothing left. This was the ultimate betrayal of my love for Tariq. Even if I got away, he wouldn't want me now. He had said he could cope if I married — he had set me free; this was why. I wanted to float away, high above the bed. This wasn't happening to me. It was the girl in the mirror lying there.

I had begun to think of Shaukat as a good man, but this Shaukat was crazed, a brute. Was this what Papa had wanted for me?

Finally Shaukat shuddered and grew still. He was a dead weight so I eased my way out from under him, grabbed a quilt and fled to the bathroom. I locked the door, turned on the shower, pulled off my qameez. I slapped the flannel over my skin in a fever, trying to wash off every trace of him. But I couldn't get rid of that sickly smell. I sank to the floor and sobbed. So that was all it was — why we girls kept ourselves pure — just so a man could plant his seed in us.

That thought stopped my sobs. There had been no talk of birth control at Aunty Khushida's. Even Meena had never mentioned it. No doubt they all hoped I'd get pregnant and forget about going to uni.

Frank was too late.

I woke to the sound of Shaukat knocking on the bathroom door. 'Ameera. Let me in.'

'No. Keep away from me.'

'I won't hurt you, I promise.' I gave a snort. 'I want to see you are all right.'

When I didn't answer, he said, 'I can get a screwdriver and take the door off.'

Stiffly I stood. Sleeping on a tiled floor had made my body hurt even more. I wrapped the quilt around me, unlocked the door, then retreated to the corner of the bathroom.

When he saw me he sighed. 'I'm truly sorry.' He glanced back at the double bed; a red spot was visible on the sheet.

'You raped me.'

Shaukat smiled uneasily at me. 'Rape? I'm your husband.'

'It was still rape. I was forced to marry you and now you forced me to ... to ...'

He hunkered down in front of me. There was a two-centimetre scratch beneath his eye. 'Believe me, if I could undo last night I would. I am sorry that your first time was like that.'

Yet there was no remorse in his eyes; he seemed pleased. Hadn't he been sure I was a virgin?

'It will never be like that again.' He lifted my chin so I had to look at him. 'Never, you understand?'

I pulled away from him.

'We are joined now and it will only get better.' He smiled slyly. 'We could do it again and I'll show you what it's meant to be like.'

I pulled my knees up to my chin, then thought better of it; I ached inside. 'What happened?' I asked, choosing to ignore his last comment.

He didn't meet my gaze. 'That damn Amin must have put something in the hookah. I've told him before not to, but he thinks it's a joke.'

I wondered how much of it was true. 'So you had no idea what you were doing last night?'

'I wish I did.' Then he saw the look on my face. 'I'm sorry, I can't remember details but I can see the evidence.' He put a finger to the scratch on his cheek. 'Can you forgive me?'

I couldn't answer him, just stared into space. I'd spent seventeen years keeping my virginity intact. Papa talked about honour but all I felt was shame.

Shaukat sighed. He stripped the bed, then went out. I crawled into the single bed and eventually slept.

In the evening Shaukat came bearing soup. He sat on a chair by the bed, lifted me up against the pillows and fed me. 'I'm afraid you're suffering from shock.'

Natasha would have said, 'Der.'

'I only hope you understand that in my right mind I never would have acted like that.'

But he had. And how often would he not be in his right mind? Was this something else Papa didn't know? Shaukat is a good man, they all said. But they didn't know he smoked hashish and that it changed him.

I stayed upstairs for days; I lost count. It didn't matter about Frank coming any more. Mrs Rahmet must have thought I was ill for she brought a tray of food when Shaukat was at the clinic fixing up other people's problems. He wouldn't be able to fix his own: the respect I'd had for him had flown like a bird from an open cage.

33

We had been in Oghi two weeks before I began to recover. Shaukat was solicitous, trying to win back the ground he'd lost. Were men in Pakistan told how to handle a bride they'd never met before? I hoped girls in normal arranged marriages were better prepared than I was. Maybe Aunt Bibi would have helped if we were living with her. My period had come, late, but I was amazed my body could manage it at all after a beating and a rape.

I rolled over in the bed to stare out the window at the fort. There was a Pakistani flag flying, and a black one at half-mast. It could have been flying for me, but I knew it was a tribute to Benazir. Whether people agreed with her or not, no one could deny she had been brave. She knew she had enemies, but she stood up for what she thought was right.

Although I'd known I'd have an arranged marriage, I'd always hoped for love as well. Dadi jan had said to remember Hir and Ranjha, but their story was tragic. In the stories, lovers were never united until they were dead. How romantic I had thought those tales but they had turned out to be closer to real life than I'd dreamt. Was a loveless marriage my destiny now? Or didn't I have another option? My choices were to go home to Mum, attend uni and become a teacher; or to stay here with Shaukat. Although I'd never love him, maybe I could still be a teacher and have children; though, like Mum, I would have no say in how they were brought up. If I went back to Mum, I couldn't marry for I wouldn't be able to forget Tariq. I weighed it up. Jane Eyre didn't mind Mr Rochester being so old, but she loved him. Aunty Khushida seemed to cope with being a lot younger than Uncle Rasheed. Did she love him, I wondered. Many women had a lot worse to live with than I did. I thought of Nargis at the tent school in Muzaffarabad; she was probably raped every night. I moaned. Just the thought of being intimate with Shaukat again made me feel ill. Would I ever see Mum again if I stayed? Shaukat had shown no eagerness to go to Australia; I suspected he'd prefer to visit England. Would he go to Australia for me? There was only one way to find out.

I showered and dressed in one of my wedding week outfits and went down for dinner.

Mrs Rahmet bustled around me. 'Memsahib, accha hai, how good you are well again.'

When Shaukat came in from the clinic and saw me I almost smiled at the relief on his face.

'Are you feeling better?' he asked. I knew what he meant: did I feel better about him too?

'Somewhat,' I lied.

After changing his clothes, he sat with me at the table and I asked him about his day. He told me about setting broken arms and tending a bullet wound. After we'd eaten, I asked, 'Would you allow my mother to come and visit?'

He sat back on his chair so that it swung with his weight. This would be the test. Papa obviously thought him a good Muslim or he wouldn't have chosen him for a son-in-law. I had never seen Shaukat say his prayers, but that didn't mean he didn't pray.

'Your father said she wasn't a good influence on you. He was very worried about you.' He paused. 'Actually I didn't expect you to be so Western.' I detected disapproval in his tone, as if that meant I was deficient in other ways too. 'He gave that as his reason for marrying you earlier,' he added.

I tried to calm my breathing. 'It's not true about Mum. Everybody thinks that because she's Christian and Australian, but she's never gone against Papa's wishes.'

He was frowning slightly, no doubt weighing up how to put his next comment. 'Yes, but Western society is decadent. I've seen it first-hand. They think you need love to make a marriage work, and they even try it out beforehand. It's so hedonistic, so self-seeking.' He sounded just like Papa.

'Mum isn't like that.'

He nodded, possibly not wanting to disagree on my first day up. I wondered if Papa had asked him not to have anything to do with Mum, for my benefit, of course.

Then Shaukat said, 'We could visit, if you like. But, Ameera, it is the wife's duty to live where her husband's work is. I thought your father would have taught you that.'

I chose not to argue, and that also was what Papa had taught me. I could see how it was going to be with Shaukat: everything would go smoothly as long as I acted in a way he approved. I thought for a while as Mrs Rahmet brought the chai in. I had been forced to marry; that was wrong. If I accepted this situation, I would be reinforcing that wrong. If I did nothing, no one would ever know it was a forced marriage. How many girls did this happen to, I wondered, girls who couldn't do anything about it? If it weren't for Frank and Mum I would be helpless too. Try to look happy, Frank had said, play along. *Do what Frank says*, I told myself.

I smiled at Shaukat. 'I'd like to go shopping with Rebekah. I met her at the party.'

He winced when I mentioned the party and I pressed my advantage. 'Ibrahim could take me to Mansehra while you're at the clinic. She said it's the closest bazaar.'

'Very well, but you'll need to wear a burqa if you leave the garden. I don't want men seeing my wife's face. The tribal men don't understand Western ways.'

I couldn't hide my dismay. 'I don't have a burqa.'

'Mrs Rahmet will lend you one until you can buy your own.' He glanced at me. 'I know you are not used to it but many women around here wear them of their own volition, like nuns used to wear habits. Here.' He took his wallet from his pocket and gave me two thousand rupees.

'That's too much, surely?'

He shrugged. 'You may see an outfit you like. Those

new shops are expensive, but they have the latest fashions from Karachi, I'm told.'

So I was to be bought off. 'Thank you.'

If he was worried about me going without him, he didn't show it. I used the phone in his office to call Rebekah. She could come with me the next afternoon. I would take the mobile with me and get in touch with Frank.

The next day I stood in front of the mirror, donned the black burqa and pulled the chiffon veil over my face. I watched myself vanish. A faded shadow peered out at me. I managed to resist the urge to pull it all off again. I had disappeared in so many ways since I'd left home; this was just one more.

Ibrahim was more at ease with me in a burqa. He even smiled at me and hummed as he drove to the aid agency office in Mansehra to pick up Rebekah. Then he took us to the bazaar.

The first thing Rebekah said when we were alone was, 'I'm surprised you wear a burqa.' Then she apologised.

'It's okay,' I said, 'I'm surprised too.'

'You seem down today. Are you all right?'

I looked at my hands. The faded henna shouted joyfully that I was newly married. *What should I tell her?* She worked with Shaukat; would she repeat what I said?

'I miss my mother,' I said. It was the truth.

'You're so brave to travel so far to marry. You must love Shaukat so much.'

I was silenced by her free use of his first name. So he had two standards: one for Westerners he met as part of his work and another for his wife. It was unfortunate for me that I was also Western.

Mansehra had a huge sprawling marketplace and a few emporiums — the special shops Shaukat had referred to. I said I needed to go to the post office. Rebekah waited for me outside, and Ibrahim wasn't far away either. I hesitated; everything I did would be reported back. *But I mightn't get another chance in a hurry.*

This time it took Frank four rings to answer. 'Frank here.'

'It's me, Ameera.'

'Where on earth have you been?'

'I'm sorry, there's no coverage at the house, and this is my first trip to the bazaar.'

'Mansehra?'

'How did you know?'

'I visited your family — incognito, of course — and you have an admirer there.'

'I do?'

'Young Asher. He told me exactly where your husband's clinic is at Oghi.'

'He won't tell his father?'

'Doubt it.' He chuckled shortly, then his voice became businesslike. 'Are you ready for us to get you out?'

I hardly hesitated. 'Yes.'

'Tomorrow evening it is then. Have a bag packed.'

'Be careful,' I said. 'There's a security guard.'

34

The next evening when we sat at the table to eat, my backpack was hidden behind the door. I wore the shalwar qameez that I had come to Pakistan in and was surprised to find it a size too big. I wore Tariq's necklace on my ankle. I'd left my wedding clothes and gold jewellery in the bedroom. I had to wear my wedding ring or Shaukat would notice, but I didn't want to take anything else that I hadn't brought with me.

Mrs Rahmet had made the chai and left for her own quarters when it began to rain. I had hardly touched a thing at dinner and now my nerves jumped at a flash of lightning.

'Aren't you feeling well?' Shaukat asked.

His smiles were becoming confident again. He'd been sleeping downstairs but I knew he was just biding his time.

'I'm fine. Shaukat ...'

I needed to say something to him, but what? I would never see him again. Yet surely he deserved something from me, this man Papa had chosen for me. He may have been a good man, as they all said, but Meena was wrong: if Papa had let me choose, I wouldn't have chosen Shaukat. I had wanted a different life: one where I could choose, which I could share with a man my own age, be myself. I had almost forgotten who that person was.

Shaukat raised his eyebrows. 'Hmm?'

'I … I just wanted to say that I appreciate what you've tried to do, to help me settle. It's been such a shock, coming here, getting married. You have tried to be kind.'

The memory of that awful night edged into my mind. It strengthened my resolve to leave.

'Thank you,' he said but his tone was wry. I guessed it wasn't what he wanted to hear.

It was then we heard the shout outside. A shot. The gates opening. A vehicle driving in, tyres squealing. The front door burst open and the security guard was marched in by two policemen. 'I'm sorry, Sahib, they say they have authority.'

Shaukat jumped to his feet; his chair clattered behind him on the tiles. 'What's going on?'

A Western man the same age as Shaukat was with them. He saw me. 'Ameera Hassan?'

'Frank.' I recognised his voice; he was shorter than I'd imagined, but muscled like an SAS soldier.

'You know this man, Ameera?' Shaukat couldn't suppress his rage; his eyes glittered.

Then I saw Riaz and Tariq. *They came for me?* I didn't trust myself to meet Tariq's gaze. How had the embassy let him come? But this was Pakistan, anything could happen. I stood and put my dupatta over my head.

Shaukat addressed Frank. 'Would you mind telling me why you have broken into my home? I'll be reporting this.'

He said the last part in Urdu and swept his gaze over the police. They lowered their eyes. He had influence; would they still go through with it?

The older policeman turned towards me and intoned, 'Ameera Hassan Zufar, do you testify that you were forced into a marriage with this man, Shaukat Iqbal Iman?'

Shaukat turned to me as if he expected me to deny it.

There was no joy in my answer. 'Yes.'

'You did not willingly give your permission?'

'No.'

'Ameera —' I couldn't bear to see the horror on Shaukat's face.

Frank turned to Shaukat. 'Did you take Ameera Hassan Zufar in marriage knowing she was being forced?'

The rage was gone; Shaukat was stunned.

I cut in. 'Excuse me, he didn't know. My father deceived him.'

Riaz made a noise and Frank held his hand out behind him. He would have discovered already how hot-headed Riaz was. I glanced at Tariq; he was watching me with such pain on his face that I looked away.

Realisation finally dawned on Shaukat's face: he had recognised Riaz. Did he guess who Tariq was? He stared at me and his shoulders slumped; his eyes were dark hollows. 'Ameera, don't do this. You don't understand. This will affect the whole family, not only you and me. And you are safe with me — you won't be if you leave.'

He came around the table towards me, but a policeman stepped in front of him.

'Your father won't bear this. Haider will find you before you leave the country. A runaway bride is a dishonour he'll have to avenge.' His voice had risen and I didn't like to see him like that; his cultured poise had slipped.

He appealed to Riaz. 'If you love your sister, don't do this. He'll kill her. She'll have a good life with me, I can give her anything. You know this, Riaz.'

But Riaz, with his Australian girlfriend, was in no mood to listen to Shaukat. He moved forward to stand near me. 'Sign the paper,' he said.

I sensed Frank's impatience but I needed to explain. 'I'm sorry, Shaukat, but it isn't right. I want to go home.' My voice squeaked to a stop; this was too hard.

'But why?' he said. 'We're married now. What life can you have if you leave, a runaway bride?'

I heard an exclamation behind me — was it Tariq?

Shaukat tried again. 'We can live in Australia if that's what you want.'

Frank gave a signal with his head and the older policeman stepped forward. 'Shaukat Iqbal Iman, knowingly or not you have participated in a forced marriage. This is an offence according to the government of Pakistan and we have the authority to remove Ameera Hassan from your home.' He waved a paper in front of Shaukat.

Riaz handed me a pen and guided my hand to the page in front of me. Yet again the form was in Urdu. There was a sticker with my name on it to show me where to sign. I signed more willingly than I had my marriage papers. Even if I had wanted to hug Shaukat to show I was sorry, I couldn't, for Riaz had taken hold of me. One thing I could do: I took off the ring Shaukat had put on my finger at the wedding and set it carefully on the paper.

'Ameera —'

I never saw how they got Shaukat to sign for Riaz guided me out of the room. I could hear Shaukat shouting as Riaz picked up my backpack. 'Riaz! Can you keep her safe now? Ameera! You're my wife! Ameera!'

I slumped against my brother, but it was Tariq who lifted me into his arms. His eyes were as dark and warm as I remembered. My own eyes filled with tears at the enormous thing I'd done and I hid my face in his coat as he carried me out into the rain. Now my life was ruined, but I chose to go back to Australia. I hoped Shaukat was bluffing and I could make a life for myself back home.

It wasn't until Tariq had put me in the back seat of an embassy car, next to a woman, that I began to shake. The woman was prepared with a blanket and a flask of sweet chai.

I must have slept, for I woke when we arrived at a gate that was opened by security guards. I had the impression of high fences and barbed wire. It looked like a prison. The woman reassured me when she felt me stiffen.

'This is a refuge for women like you,' she said. 'You are safe here. No one can come in.'

I was shown to a room; it had the essentials and its own toilet and sink. It was all I needed. They let Riaz in to say good night. When he hugged me I shook with sobs.

'It's okay, Ames. You're safe now.'

'Am I?' I pulled away. 'Will I ever be free from the guilt? I've been so selfish. Now I'm a bad girl, a runaway bride. That's all people will remember. They won't know it was a forced marriage. And Papa — he'll be so angry. He'll lose everything.'

'Are you talking about your dowry?'

I fumbled in my pocket for a tissue. 'Shaukat and Uncle Iqbal were giving Papa money for the business — that will all fall through now. He's put so much money into the wedding, Jamila's too. He'll be bankrupt.'

'Shit.'

'I hadn't thought properly about the whole family,' I sobbed. 'The dishonour. I've broken up the family.'

Would Meena understand? Asher may, but how could Zeba? Then there was Aunty Khushida and Aunt Bibi. After all they'd done for me, they would feel so betrayed.

'You've got me and Mum,' Riaz said.

'But Papa will be shamed. I love him — how could I do that to him? And Shaukat — I didn't know he'd get so upset.'

'Don't forget what Dad did was illegal.'

'Only governments think it's illegal, not fathers and families.'

'For what it's worth, I think it's illegal and I'm glad you're out of it. Someone has to stand up for what's right.'

'But at what cost?' I sniffed and stared up at him. 'Riaz, what makes us different? Raniya wouldn't have refused a marriage her parents had arranged.' Though to be fair, Raniya's parents would have chosen someone she wanted. 'How come you can see the marriage was illegal and Papa couldn't?'

'He had a lot to gain by the look of it.' Then Riaz stopped and looked at me, perhaps gauging how I'd take what he said next. 'Sometimes I think Dad's code of honour is overrated.'

I gaped at him.

'It's a permissible way to save face, to take the law into his own hands. Maybe they had to do that years ago in the mountains, but not now. It makes parents too responsible for everything their kids do, forces them to control rather than guide by faith. What honour is there in a forced marriage?'

I was too stunned to comment.

'Maybe being born in Australia changes the equation,' Riaz said. 'I'm not so tied to the old culture like he is.' He put his arm around me and we sank onto the bed. 'When you said you loved Tariq —'

'You understood.'

He nodded. 'I know what that feels like. I want to marry Cassie too.'

'Poor Papa. He thinks Mum's such a bad influence on us.'

'Poor Papa nothing. He needs to get over himself. We've got half Mum's genes. How could he not expect that by living in Australia we would want to have choices of our own? I understand where Dad's coming from and I'll stick by him, look after him when he's old, but it'll be because of my feelings for him, not a duty forced on me.'

I heard an echo of Jamila in my ear: 'You are so Western.' I also heard the sob in Riaz's voice. 'Dad will feel shame because of what we've done, but he has to understand us too. This is your choice. You have a right to live a life without abuse.'

'He didn't mean it to be abuse,' I said against Riaz's shoulder. 'He loves us.'

Riaz sighed and pulled away. 'Dad's love is conditional.'

I nodded. Lately I'd thought Papa's love depended more and more on how I behaved.

'But it's the only love he knows,' Riaz continued. 'He was scared of losing you, Ames.'

'How does he cope with you?' I half-grinned at him.

Riaz shrugged. 'He turns a blind eye to me at the moment. What he knows about, he thinks I'll grow out of.' Then he turned to face me properly. 'You are braver than me, Ames, and even if Dad disowns me because of this — it's worth it to see you rescued. I know I haven't been the best brother, but I couldn't have lived with myself if I left you here knowing I could have helped.'

I put my hand over his and thought how Bollywood movies always showed the bride being obedient and at the last moment her father relented and let her marry who she loved. But Papa wouldn't listen.

'It must be hard for Papa,' I said. 'He was brought up here and had to learn to live in Australia.' I had always thought I was both Australian and Pakistani but now all I could think of was returning home.

'You'll feel better when you're home,' Riaz said. 'Mum's buying a unit. You can go to uni.'

I shook my head. 'I've missed the first round — they'll have given my place to someone else.'

'That's where you're wrong. Dad opened your letter and I got your number. Tariq accepted your preference on the web. You're in at Adelaide uni, you start in March.'

I wanted to feel excitement but it was just words. Riaz lay me down and pulled the covers up.

'Everything will be okay, Ames, and I'll help all the way. There's Tariq too. I couldn't have done this without him. Mum and I made sure Frank let him come along.'

'He won't want me now,' I said.

Riaz paused. 'What do you mean?'

'I was married, Riaz.' I burst into fresh weeping.

Riaz bent his forehead down to the pillow and was quiet awhile. 'I know Tariq, give him a chance.' Then he sat up. 'Cassie slept with someone before she met me.'

I was shocked he'd tell me. 'Doesn't that bother you?'

He half-grinned. 'Sure, I was upset at first but I'm not going to break up with her over it. It's different in Australia. It doesn't mean a girl has to be bad to do that. Cassie's the greatest.'

He patted my hair while I tried not to cry again. He was being kind, but nothing was all right like he said. I hadn't realised I'd feel so bad, so ugly, so impure. I couldn't bear to think how Tariq's face would change when he found out. His parents wouldn't want a runaway bride for a daughter-in-law.

35

They said I slept for two days. The embassy lady who'd helped in the rescue was called Nazreen. She poked her head into my room and waved a phone. 'I have your mother on the line, would you like to speak with her?'

I sat up so quickly I felt dizzy, but I reached for the phone.

'Mum?'

'Oh, thank God, what a relief. Are you okay?'

'I'm fine. As fine as I can be.' What else could I say? She was so far away.

'When you disappeared for those weeks I thought we'd lost you. I thought the worst had happened.'

I wondered what could be worse than what had happened. Then I realised that for Mum, my death would be the worst.

'I nearly came over,' she said, 'but Frank said not to. So I sent Riaz and Tariq. Your grandfather paid their fares. They'll bring you home, sweetheart.'

Home. That was when I started to cry.

She paused. 'I'm so sorry.'

'I'm okay,' I said but I couldn't stop the sobs.

'You'll be with me soon.'

'I can't wait to see you, Mum.'

I had wanted to talk to her for so long but now I couldn't think of anything to say that wouldn't take hours. I guessed she understood because soon she ended the call.

Nazreen must have been waiting outside the door; she came in and asked how I felt. Almost without hesitation I told her about Shaukat.

'So he forced you?'

I nodded. 'Once. I'm not sure now why I left. If I stayed with Shaukat, Papa would be happy.'

'You wouldn't be though.'

'Papa says happiness for oneself is a selfish Western attribute. He tried to beat it out of me.' I met her quick glance. 'Metaphorically. He says happiness only comes when we know we are submissive to God and doing His will. To Papa, my marrying Shaukat was doing God's will.'

'Do *you* believe that?'

I stared at Nazreen. She was Pakistani, a Muslim and educated. She understood everything I was feeling.

'When I was with Shaukat, I could believe a forced marriage was wrong, that God didn't will it,' I said.

'But now?'

'Now I'm thinking about how I've made everyone else feel.'

Nazreen nodded. There was no glib answer for what I had thrown away. Then she said, 'What have you gained?'

I thought. 'My mother.' I smiled. 'My brother, my grandparents. A life in the place where I grew up. Study, friends, a career.'

'You are fortunate — we have rescued brides whose mothers and brothers have sided with the father.'

'To have no one — how brave were they?'

'Yes, they were brave.'

'Stupid, perhaps, selfish —'

Nazreen cut in. 'So far, only Western girls like you have the strength or resources to leave a forced marriage.'

I thought of Nargis. 'The girls living here may not realise they can leave.'

'We are raising awareness here and in the West that forced marriages are domestic abuse. But there is a long road ahead of us, and many don't like what we are doing. Our lives have been threatened.'

'Frank too?'

'Yes, though mainly it is we Pakistanis who should know better.' She half-laughed.

'Can you help someone else?' I asked. 'There's a girl called Nargis in Muzaffarabad, a teacher. She's too frightened to do anything — her husband beats her.'

'Normally a call for help has to come from her or a family member.'

'Can't you treat this as a call for help? One day he'll kill her.'

She nodded. 'We'll look into it.' She took my hand then. 'Ameera, the road ahead will not be easy. You may suffer some depression. It is possible your father will never see you again.'

I gasped. That possibility had never entered my mind. Would Papa be that cruel?

'But may I say this,' Nazreen continued. 'You have not compromised your faith by standing up for what is right. People need to acknowledge where there is abuse, even when those perpetuating it don't realise that's what it is. You have made a worthy stand for women's freedom in Pakistan.'

Her words only made me cry for I couldn't think on such a vast level. Two things filled my mind: the fear of never seeing Papa again, and the look on Shaukat's face when I was asked if I'd given my permission and I said 'no'. He couldn't have looked more stricken if I'd sunk a knife in his chest.

I wanted to thank Tariq for coming and being a support to Riaz, but he wasn't allowed in my room. I was confined and protected yet again, but this time I didn't mind.

Frank came to see me with Nazreen. 'The police need to know if you want to press charges. If what you said about your husband is true, he'll be free from suspicion, but your uncle faces three years in gaol here. In Australia, your father could get up to twenty-five years.'

I was horrified. 'No, I couldn't do that.'

'Look what they did to you.'

I shook my head.

'Okay. But your uncle will be told of his narrow escape. I don't think he'll give you any trouble.'

It wasn't Uncle Rasheed I was worried about. Haider, with his disproportionate sense of honour, was the problem.

'Will my father be told about it?' I asked.

'An official report will be sent to him, along with the length of sentence he could face.'

'But he won't be arrested?'

'No, but I don't think it hurts to warn him of what could happen if at any time you do decide to press charges.' Frank stared at his hands for a moment, then he leaned forward. 'If at any time you feel unsafe, go to the police. There will be a plainclothes policeman assigned to you for a time. But I doubt you'll have any trouble with the Pakistani Women's Bill protecting you.'

I glanced at Nazreen and she met my eyes. Was she thinking as I was that laws couldn't change centuries of customs? My family in Pakistan was Pushtun, an ancient culture based on a complicated code of honour. Modern education hadn't diluted that code in Haider.

'Your flight is fixed for tomorrow,' Frank went on. 'The airport run can be tricky. I'm afraid we'll have to put you in a burqa and you mustn't wear any clothes, shoes or jewellery anyone may recognise. Understand?'

I nodded.

'Nazreen has some clothes you can use.' Frank glanced at my backpack. 'Not that bag either, or your handbag. We'll give you a different one. Nazreen will be with you. She'll bring one of her children and you'll pretend the child is yours. A bodyguard will accompany you through the gates. He will appear to be your

270

husband. He and Nazreen have a special pass to go with you; he has a licence to carry a gun.'

I stiffened but Frank didn't notice.

'I will be behind you, but don't look for me. And, of course, you have an escort on the plane with your brother and Tariq.' He smiled at me and then looked away. When he looked back, his eyes glistened. 'For a while there, when we didn't hear from you, I thought you'd decided to go along with it.'

'It was difficult,' I said. 'My father will be inconsolable. And my ... my husband is not an evil man.' My chin wobbled. Tears were never far away lately.

'I understand some of it,' Frank said, 'but girls forced into marriages they didn't choose just isn't on in my book. No culture should condone that.'

'No.' But my voice was quiet. How could people like Frank affect centuries of culture? Only the moon can change the tide.

36

Frank was tense the next day as he put Nazreen and me into an unmarked car. We wore black burqas and Frank insisted that we lower the chiffon veils immediately. This time I welcomed the anonymity. The bodyguard, in a shalwar qameez, eased himself into the driver's seat. Saleem, Nazreen's little boy, was talking to me in English, but I was watching Tariq. He stood beside Riaz, both of them solemn. We would meet up on the plane. Any of my relatives would recognise Riaz; he looked so like Papa. In my borrowed purse was my emergency passport and ticket: my ticket to freedom. Yet I didn't feel elated. Not until I was on that plane would I be able to relax. What if Uncle Rasheed got all the relatives to stake out the airport? It sounded preposterous, but something was making Frank wound up.

He poked his head through the window. 'We'll be there, looking out for you. There shouldn't be a problem.' He smiled, but it did nothing to reassure me.

Saleem chattered all the way to the airport; I supposed it was helpful to keep me from fretting. Outside the airport, there were hundreds of people, mostly men. I kept my gaze on the footpath even though no one could see my eyes. We checked in — Gate 2 — so far so good. Security was tight: everywhere we went we had to go through X-ray machines. I couldn't see Tariq or Riaz. I half-turned and the bodyguard growled at me in Urdu, 'Look to the boy.' He must have had eyes in the back of his head. He glanced around a lot, but men often did that.

Then Saleem clutched the front of his shalwar. 'Ummie, I need to pee.'

'Hold his hand,' Nazreen said to me. 'We'll take him to the toilet.'

The bodyguard came with us and stood outside. It was when I opened the door to come out that I saw Haider. He swung out of the men's toilet in a security guard's uniform, carrying a gun. I backed up, breathing hard.

'What's wrong?' Nazreen's eyes screwed up in concern.

'I saw my cousin, Haider. He's in a uniform and he has a gun.'

'The one from Muzaffarabad? Are you sure?'

I nodded.

Nazreen flipped open her mobile. 'Frank, the cousin, Haider, is in the airport. He's armed. He must have jumped a security guard ... No, we don't know who's with him.' She raised her eyebrows at me and I shook my head. 'Okay,' she said and shut the phone. 'Come.'

She went out the door first and told the bodyguard what was going on. I followed, but it was difficult to force myself not to look around, not to walk too fast.

Was Haider nearby, was he buying a newspaper, was he behind us, how would we know? He'd vowed to kill me if I dishonoured the family. Maybe Papa would agree I deserved it, but I didn't think it a good enough reason to die.

Nazreen had a hand under my arm. I held Saleem's hand with my other, but he wanted to walk next to his mother so I switched hands. As I brought him in front of me, my burqa caught under his arm and there was a moment when my shalwar and ankles were exposed. I quickly pulled the cloth down and brought Saleem in between us.

'Oh no,' I said.

Nazreen glanced at me. 'What is it?'

'I forgot to take off my ankle bracelet.'

I made a movement and Nazreen tightened her grip on me.

'Leave it — you'll only draw attention to yourself.'

I was thinking how Haider would recognise those wooden and ceramic beads. When had he heard that I'd left the marriage? It had been days now, almost a week. Had he been camping in the airport, waiting? Were he and Uncle Rasheed taking turns? Would Riaz know what Haider looked like? Haider would have seen photos of Riaz. Not Tariq though. Haider wouldn't know Tariq.

I forced myself to breathe slower. We were making for the gate, but all Haider would have to do was look for a flight to Australia. How many gates would he have to watch? Not many. There was still half an hour before the plane left. We would be boarding soon; I could hear a man's voice calling passengers on the intercom.

Then I felt something hard pressed into my back, and heard a voice, low, 'Did you think I would not remember the way you walk, my beautiful whore?'

Haider. Fear made my scream freeze in my throat.

The bodyguard was a step in front of me. He turned. 'Let her go,' he said in Urdu and produced a gun.

'So this is Tariq,' Haider sneered. 'You passed up our dignified cousin for this scum.'

Suddenly he pushed me away and the hard thing that had been pressed against me was firing at the bodyguard. Nazreen grabbed Saleem, pulled me towards her and ran with us towards the gate.

'Ameera, you can't escape,' Haider shouted.

I looked back to see the bodyguard on the floor in a dark, spreading pool, people scattering, and Haider raising the gun, aiming it at me. Then a man jumped him and the gun skittered across the floor. I saw Frank and Riaz running towards the two men now wrestling together. Frank and Riaz — that meant it was Tariq fighting Haider.

'Tariq!' I screamed.

Nazreen yanked my arm. 'Come on.' Security guards were swarming from all directions. 'There is nothing we can do. You must get on that plane.'

As she pulled me again I saw Haider knock Tariq to the ground. How could I leave without knowing if he was all right? The intercom was calling a flight for boarding.

'That's you,' Nazreen said. She dragged me and Saleem along with her. 'Even if your cousin overpowers them, he can't get past the gate.'

At the gate stood two security guards with guns. One was speaking on a walkie-talkie. I stepped aside.

'What's wrong now?' Nazreen asked.

My breath came in gasps. 'I can't do it — can't go through. Not without knowing what happened — that's my brother and my —' I stopped. What was Tariq? Nothing to me now, and best no one knew how much I loved him.

Nazreen put an arm around me. 'We will go through the gate, but then we'll wait on the other side. If your cousin comes, you run onto the plane. But we can only wait a few minutes.'

A few minutes — the longest of my life. What if they didn't come? They could be arrested, hurt, anything. What would I say to Mum? That I'd left while Riaz was fighting a maniac? And Tariq — what if he was killed? Nazreen tightened her arm around me; I was trembling.

There was a commotion at the end of the line and a few people moved out of the way. I strained to see and let out a breath. It was them. Riaz had his arm around Tariq's shoulders. They were grinning, but Tariq had blood on his face and was holding his side.

When they reached the gate I heard Riaz say in his schoolboy Urdu, 'My cousin did not want us to go. He said he will miss us too much.'

The man on the gate wasn't impressed but the security guards motioned them through. They must have been warned. I lifted the veil and took a step forward. I didn't run; that just happens in Bollywood movies. Besides, I didn't know if Tariq would welcome me. When they reached me, I said thank you to both of them.

I wanted to touch Tariq's face but I had to let my eyes do the touching. He looked weary and I was in no doubt he had saved my life. Haider would have pulled that trigger.

'I'll hand her over to you now,' Nazreen said to Riaz. 'You both look like you had a battle.'

'He was clever to get past security, but he's a dirty fighter.' Riaz's voice was a growl. 'He tried to get Tariq with a steak knife.'

'Where?' My eyes flew to Tariq's side.

Tariq managed a grin. 'Don't worry, he only nicked me.' His eyes flowed over me, began to fill my empty spaces, but I looked away.

'And your cousin?' Nazreen asked.

Riaz answered her. 'Frank and the police have him. Stupid — he'd come by himself.'

There was a message on the intercom and Nazreen glanced behind her. 'Last call — you have to board now,' she said quickly.

I hugged her. 'Thank you for everything,' and I touched Saleem's head. 'Thank you, Saleem. You are very brave.'

He grinned. 'It was a good game.'

On the plane, Riaz and I made Tariq more comfortable. He had bruises on his face and chest. The 'nick' in his side bled more than a nick should have, but fortunately there was a steward on board with first-aid training and he bandaged it up. Tariq's nose looked broken but the steward knew what to do about that too: he straightened it in one movement while Tariq clenched hold of the armrests. 'Saw lots of those in soccer training,' the steward said. Now Tariq would have a nose like a Pushtun.

After that we all slept. My dreams were mottled black and grey. One moment I was in Tariq's arms; the next, Shaukat was dragging me back towards him. A man with an assault rifle stood in a corner, his shadow enveloping me wherever I went. I woke in the darkened cabin with Tariq watching me, his head against the seat.

'Are you okay?' he asked softly.

I nodded. 'Just a dream.'

'You're safe now.'

My eyes rested on him. The plaster on his nose looked almost funny, but there was nothing amusing about near death by Haider's hand.

'Thank you for coming, for helping Riaz ...' I paused. 'For saving my life.'

'It was worth it.'

'Sorry about your nose ...'

'It's a small price to pay.'

I wondered what he meant. A small price compared to what I'd been through, or a small price compared to having me back? Surely not the latter?

'For my freedom?' I asked.

'No — for your love.'

'You can't mean that.' I felt stricken. How could I tell him? 'I was married. You know what that means.'

He regarded me steadily. Those brown eyes never flickered. 'I know what it means,' he said gently.

Papa had taught me that virginity was everything. Without it I'd have no chance of marrying. 'But how can you overlook ... I feel like I've sinned. How can you forgive —'

Tariq laid a hand over mine. The shock of it stilled me. He leaned closer. 'Ameera, firstly, you did not sin.' His voice was firm. 'You were sinned against. And secondly, even if you had consented I would still want you. My faith commands me to forgive. Who is without anything to forgive? No one. Why do you think I said "whatever happens"? I said it so you wouldn't worry.'

'I thought you were releasing me.'

'Never; not unless you want it.'

He pulled a wallet from his jeans pocket and I saw a flash of gold, a filigree gold heart on a fine chain, before he fastened the clasp around my neck. He kissed the top of my head and I heard his words above me, whispered against my hair. 'When you've recovered from this, when you're older and happy again, my parents will come to your house and ask for you in the proper way. I bought this in the bazaar yesterday — it's to remind you to never,' his voice finally broke, 'to never doubt my love for you.'

Epilogue

May 2008

Dear Ameera,

I hope life in Australia is good to you. Here are the annulment papers. Your marriage has been annulled on the grounds that you didn't willingly give your permission.

Your Cousin Haider will serve only two years in prison as he testified that his action was an honour killing. That he killed the wrong man seems to have been overlooked. Please do not return to Pakistan to reconcile with your family, even if your father or uncle says it is safe to do so.

Your Cousin Shaukat gave a statement and seems to regret that he didn't terminate the marriage as soon as you told him of your circumstances.

I am sorry this has happened to you and I hope you will find the strength to live the rest of your life fully.

Please don't hesitate to contact us if you are concerned about anything. Nazreen sends her best wishes.

Kind regards,

Frank

It has taken me a long time to recover, as Nazreen warned. There were days at first when I stayed in bed and Mum read me stories. When I first saw her at the airport it was such a relief that I ran to her like a child and couldn't stop crying. She cried too. On the way to the car she kept thanking and hugging Riaz and Tariq. Even they cried. Riaz pretended it was the wind but Tariq was unashamed.

Mum and I live in a three-bedroom unit not far from Grandpa and Gran. When I first arrived I saw Haider in every crowd and refused to go outside. I have never spotted the plainclothes policeman who is supposed to be looking out for me. From the corner of my eye sometimes I see a man with an assault rifle standing watching me, but when I look again he is gone.

Maryam rings me and cheers me up. Soon we'll do those things we'd planned in December. Raniya hasn't rung but maybe she will one day.

All Mum's rellies have rallied around us. When Uncle Richard saw me, he lifted me off the ground in a huge hug and said how glad he was that I was back, that he'd been praying for me. 'You were never alone,' he said with tears in his eyes.

Riaz divides his time between Papa and us. I wondered whether Papa would forgive him for bringing me home, but Riaz says Papa blames Tariq. Mum allows Tariq to visit when Riaz is home. A few times Riaz has brought Cassie. She's blonde like Mum but her personality reminds me of Meena. Talking to her has helped and I'm slowly learning not to define myself by what happened to me. I'm lucky, I guess; some girls rescued from forced marriages are never accepted by any member of their family. Many have to say they were never touched by their husband so they can marry again. I'm glad I wasn't forced to lie. From now on I don't want to be forced to do anything.

I still love Papa, even after what he did. I understand enough to know he was acting out of his fear and insecurity within a Western environment and that he loved me in the only way he knew. He will not see me. Once I left a message on his answering machine, but I don't know if he received it. He has never contacted me. Mum says he is divorcing her and has washed his hands of me. I have shamed him too much. The lack of reconciliation with him is a pain I shall always bear.

No doubt he thinks that leaving the marriage meant I gave up on him and on God as well. But that's not true. Now I am able to separate my love for Papa from my love for God. God has not cast me off as Papa warned. Even the imam at the mosque here blessed me when he saw the annulment papers. 'The Prophet, Peace Be Upon Him, has made the provision of annulment for people in forced marriages. This sort of marriage is not permissible in Islam,' he said. No, it is just Papa who has cast me aside. I realise now that Papa confused religion with culture. He loved me but he let cultural pressures distort that love.

Now that I am able to go outside again, I attend university most days and it gives me different things to think about. Tariq is busy finishing his Masters thesis.

We meet for coffee in the refectory on the days we're both there. When he looks at me I see myself safe inside his eyes. He has a warmth, like a light, that flows through his whole personality. It washes over me and fills all my yearning spaces. Those folk tales echoed reality more than I ever suspected but now I choose not to be bound by them. Tariq and I will write a new story — one in which our love lives.

Author's Note

In 2006 I was visiting Pakistan on an Asialink Fellowship for research on an idea I had for another novel. My host school in Murree, Northern Pakistan, became a base to travel from and in between I worked in classrooms and did research in the comprehensive library on Pakistani culture and history, the Pathans, Gujjar nomads, as well as on societal customs such as weddings, folktales, crafts and religion.

The school was tight on security due to a terrorist attack four years previously, but since I had my husband with me I was able to take many research trips — including up the Karakorum Highway, where we passed the tribal areas of Kala Dhaka (Black Mountain) and Kohistan (Land of Mountains), to Azad Kashmir and other earthquake affected areas.

It was on that trip to Azad Kashmir that we met an English couple who knew a man from the Forced Marriage Unit in the British Consulate. I immediately could see the idea for a new novel. The next day at the school I was able to do mind maps on the characters and write up an outline. This rarely happens so quickly but all that I had been seeing and hearing for the last five weeks suddenly erupted into this story and I began writing it at once. I also started collecting folk tales, cloth, patterns for outfits, news clippings and Pakistani literature.

Although I had spent seven years in Pakistan when I was younger I felt that this time I understood the richness of the culture so much more than I did before. I was able to visit in local homes, even overnight, and gained much insight into the Pakistani people and customs, including experiencing first-hand Pathan hospitality with its gun firing at parties, and honour, segregation and protection of women. I was taught how to make local foods and parathas and was there during Eid celebrations.

For me writing is a way of talking, a way of interacting with the world and making sense of what I hear and see. Sooner or later what I experience becomes assimilated into my work, and although that has happened with what I saw and experienced in Pakistan and *Marrying Ameera*, it is a work of fiction.

It is not based on anyone's life and I do not know of any Australian–Pakistani girls who have had a forced marriage. However, I do know that in 2005 a dozen Australian girls under the age of eighteen (one was only fourteen) sought help from the Australian consulate in Beirut, Lebanon, after being sent abroad and forced to marry.[1] In Britain, hundreds of girls are sent abroad for

---

1 Mercer, P., 'Australia acts on forced marriage', BBC News, Sydney, 3 August 2005 (http://news.bbc.co.uk/2/hi/asia-pacific/4740871. stm).

marriages they do not want and many of these take place in Pakistan.

An arranged marriage is an accepted part of many cultures. However, a forced marriage occurs when one or both of the people getting married do not give their consent and they are married under duress. In many areas of Pakistan there is a clan or cultural honour system whereby a family is shamed if a girl doesn't obey her parents or if she does anything they consider immoral. So there is much emotional, psychological and often physical pressure on the girl to marry according to the family's choice.

In 2005 in Australia tough laws were introduced to prevent young people being sent abroad to engage in forced marriages. Every year the Forced Marriage Unit in Britain has thousands of enquiries and saves three hundred people from forced marriages in Pakistan, India, Bangladesh and beyond.[2] About a third are under eighteen years of age, and fifteen per cent of cases involve young men.[3] In 2007 the British Forced Marriage Unit in Islamabad rescued one hundred and thirty-one British girls from forced marriages.[4]

Forced marriages are against the law in Pakistan; a bill was passed in 2007 to stop the practice. Many

2 Richings, E., 'Caught in the grip of a culture clash', *Telegraph*, 3 January 2006 (http://www.telegraph.co.uk/culture/tvandra-dio/3649113/Caught-in-the-grip-of-a-culture-clash.html).
3 Manchester City Council Report for Information, Forced Marriage, 16 October 2007 (http://www.manchester.gov.uk/egov_downloads/forced_marriage_final_v1.1.pdf).
4 Buchanan, E., 'Tough choice between freedom and honour', BBC News, 1 December 2008 (http://news.bbc.co.uk/2/hi/uk_news/7754280.stm).

families do not realise that a forced marriage is a form of domestic abuse. I hope *Marrying Ameera* will shed some light on a practice that is kept so quiet that many young people are unsuspecting of it. If you do suspect that you, or a friend, are being forced into a marriage, help is available. The Foreign and Commonwealth Office in the UK has information on its website: http://www.fco.gov.uk/en/travel-and-living-abroad/when-things-go-wrong/forced-marriage. Or if you are already abroad, you can contact your embassy.

A journal of my experiences in Pakistan can be found on my webite at www.rosannehawke.com.

Acknowledgements

I wish to thank Asialink for awarding me a Literature Fellowship to visit Pakistan and to carry out research. Thank you to Arts SA for funding the Asialink Fellowship and for providing a grant to finish the first draft of this novel; and the SA Festival Awards Carclew Fellowship, which enabled me to complete it.

Thank you to Anne and Colin Bloomfield who planted the seed of the idea that grew into this novel. Thank you to Murree Christian School which hosted me during the research period. Thanks to Frank Lyman, who took us to so many places and is always a source of inspiration, and to Rebecca Lyman for a preliminary edit. Thank you to Lenore Penner for reading the manuscript and giving helpful suggestions, Celia Manning for helping with the right word, and my agent, Jacinta di Mase, for her invaluable advice.

Thank you to Lisa Berryman, Lydia Papandrea and Nicola O'Shea and all at HarperCollins for their wonderful support and expertise.

I wish to acknowledge the excellent volume of Indus

folk tales by Samina Quraeshi, *Legends of the Indus*, Asia Ink, London, 2004, from which I retold Ameera's folk tales.

'The Girl Who Cried a Lake' is from Sally Pomme Clayton, *Tales Told in Tents: Stories from Central Asia*, Francis Lincoln, London, 2005.

The mehndi songs are from A.B. Rajput, *Social Customs and Practices in Pakistan*, RCD Cultural Institute, Islamabad, 1977, pp. 52–53.

Rumi's poem 'This Marriage' is found in full in *Love is a Stranger: Selected Lyrical Poetry of Jelaluddin Rumi*, translated by Kabir Helminski, Threshold Books, 1993.

The story 'The Ruby Prince' can be found in Flora Annie Steele, *Tales of the Punjab*, Bodley Head, London, 1973 (first published 1894).

Author photo: Dylan Coker

Rosanne Hawke is a multi-award winning Australian author. She has written over fifteen books to date, among them *Mustara*, which was shortlisted in the New South Wales Premier's Literary Awards in 2007, and *Soraya the Storyteller*, which was shortlisted in the Children's Book Council of Australia Awards in 2005 and in the South Australian Festival Awards in 2006. She was awarded an Asialink Fellowship to write in Pakistan in 2006 and the Carclew Fellowship in 2008. Rosanne was an aid worker in Pakistan and the United Arab Emirates for almost ten years and now teaches Creative Writing at Tabor Adelaide.